Hidden Secrets
at the
Little Village
Church

D1253156

TRACY REES

Hidden Secrets at the Little Village Church

Bookouture

Published by Bookouture in 2021

An imprint of Storyfire Ltd.
Carmelite House
50 Victoria Embankment
London EC4Y 0DZ

www.bookouture.com

ISBN: 978-1-80019-599-8
eBook ISBN: 978-1-80019-598-1

For Phil, always.

And for David Joshua, who would have been kind to Gwen and who would have called Jarvis a 'hell of a boy'.
You're missed, Dai Josh.

CHAPTER ONE

Gwen

Sunday morning. Gwen opens one eye then closes it. The prospect of the day ahead doesn't fill her with joy, but that's nothing specific to Sundays, or today in particular; Gwen never feels excited or enthusiastic anymore.

She can hear Aunt Mary clunking around downstairs. There's no tiptoeing for her aunt, no boiling the kettle with bated breath, hoping the noise won't disturb Gwen. If Mary's up, Gwen should be up.

And actually, Gwen realises, opening the other eye and seeing the time, she *should* be up. Church is at ten, and although she's not, strictly speaking, religious, it's a regular outing, one of the very few anchors in her week. It's not a commitment – no one would actually notice if she was there or not – but without it, Sunday would be just another grey, formless day.

It takes her a while to move. Bed is comfortable and warm and everything's such an effort these days: getting dressed, making food, conversation. Both eyes open now, her gaze rests on her bookcase. Amongst her many novels, old and new, are the others: *How to Find Your Happy*; *Coming Back from Calamity*; *Good Planning, Great Results*; *How Is This My Life?* Really, how *is* this her life?

She actually felt quite excited when she bought them (from the lovely little local bookstore that went out of business last year), and reading them was comforting but didn't actually change anything. She also went to two or three workshops run by a lady called Mahira Halo (Gwen suspects Halo is not her real surname) and they were comforting too. Lots of candles and angelic visualisations, lots of deep breathing and positive intentions, the sense that she wasn't alone, that other people struggled too. But Mahira, who ran a little esoteric shop just off the high street, also went out of business and moved away. It seems to be the way of things in Hopley. Anything quirky or cultural fails to thrive and quickly disappears. These days, the plethora of strictly functional, fluorescent-lit shops selling mundane things at knock-down prices has a dampening effect on Gwen's already low spirits.

Gwen doesn't shower because there isn't enough time to dry her hair, which is long, thick and unruly. It's not 'crowning glory' type hair. It's light brown and dull, an inconvenience more than anything. Aunt Mary says she looks like Cousin Itt from the Addams Family but Gwen can't bring herself to cut it because it's so good for hiding behind, and because her mother always thought it was pretty.

She throws on a long skirt with an elasticated waistband, ankle boots, a T-shirt, blouse, cardigan and scarf, forces a brush through her hair, tucks it behind her ears – from where it immediately escapes – and braces herself for breakfast. In the kitchen, she's greeted by the smell of burned toast.

'You're late. I made you something,' says Aunt Mary, holding out a plate bearing two thick slices of black toast smeared with margarine.

'Thank you,' says Gwen, even though she doesn't like white bread, especially white bread that is black. She prefers nice, soft granary bread, with seeds through it, but her aunt says it's not worth getting two different kinds just for the two of them. They wouldn't get through their respective loaves before they went hard or mouldy, and Aunt Mary won't throw anything out; she hates waste.

'I put the washing on the line and when I came back, it had caught,' says her aunt. 'But you'll have to eat it; I hate waste.'

Gwen has learned that there's no point suggesting they alternate – one week white, one week brown – so that each of them has what she likes half of the time. It's Aunt Mary's house, so there's no earthly reason why she shouldn't have what she likes *all* the time. Besides, white is cheaper than that posh grainy stuff.

'You can wipe that look off your face,' says her aunt. 'I know you like that posh grainy stuff, but it's shockingly dear. I don't know why you can't get up in time to fix your own breakfast. Basic timekeeping shouldn't be a problem for someone with a fancy "degree".' She makes quotation marks with her fingers, as if there's some doubt whether Gwen did actually get a degree.

Gwen chews slowly, hating every mouthful. This is classic Aunt Mary: she'll do something that on the face of it is kind, like making you breakfast when you're running late. And Gwen really does believe that her aunt's impulses *are* kind, deep down. But it'll be something you hate, delivered with such a litany of complaints and insults that you end up having to thank her for something you'd far rather she hadn't done. Left to her own devices, Gwen would have grabbed a banana on her way out and eaten it on the way. That and the emergency chocolate bar in her coat pocket would have made a much nicer breakfast. *In fact...*

Halfway through the first awful slice, Gwen looks at her watch and feigns shock. 'Look at the time,' she exclaims. 'I'd better go; I'll eat on the way. Thanks again, Aunt Mary. Have a lovely morning.' She bolts, clutching the toast, out through the kitchen door. Her aunt's peevish voice follows her.

'A lovely morning. Chance would be a fine thing. I don't know why you bother with church. Waste of an hour every bloody week.

You could help out with the housework a bit, but I suppose that's beneath you. Well, I know my place—'

Gwen hurries to the end of the housing estate and round the corner onto the lane before resuming her normal ambling pace with a huge sigh of relief. The lane is quiet and she tosses the toast into the hedge, then fumbles for the Snickers in her pocket. This is why elasticated waistbands are becoming increasingly necessary. With very few edible meals coming her way, she's existing more and more on chocolate. It's a twenty-minute walk to St Dom's, a long walk by Gwen's standards, but it's a quiet route, and it's always good to be out of that house.

It's early April. The hedges are full of hawthorn, and birdsong fills the air. The way underfoot is dappled with sunlight and shade. It's a day for singing hearts, lifting spirits, bubbling gratitude. But all Gwen really feels is tired. She used to love this sort of thing. Occasionally she wonders if she's depressed, but she can't quite muster the curiosity to look into it.

When she arrives at the church, her heart lifts, just half a millimetre. It's a sluggish effort, but it's the only not-nothing she ever feels these days. And that's why she comes every week, despite Aunt Mary's disparaging comments.

St Domneva's is a beautiful old twelfth-century church built of soft grey stone, with a square turret and a trinity of lavish stained-glass windows along the front aspect. A path curves through the graveyard from a creaking lychgate beneath a pitched wooden roof. A giant yew tree sweeps a dark green fringe across the left side of the building. Gravestones and angels peep between the boughs. It's enchanting. This church embodies everything Gwen used to love: history, atmosphere, family, stories...

Back when Gwen was new to Hopley, she came here a lot, when it was empty and no one else was around. Inside the church is a visitors' book, a great tome with a navy, white and gold fleur-de-lys design, raspberry-red endpapers, a sighing spine and yellowing pages filled with hundreds of different handwritings. Not so much now, but once upon a time, St Domneva's really pulled in the visitors. En route south from London to the coast, or across Kent to the Downs, people would stop off to enjoy the few shops that Hopley had to offer, the pubs and cafés, the ancient church. But as the soul leached out of Hopley, all that changed. It's apparent from the entries in the visitors' book, entries that grow scarcer as you turn the pages.

Still, Gwen loves to leaf through, reading all the names and the comments. Real-life, here-and-now people are difficult to deal with, but names on pages can't disappoint. Gwen has spent hours weaving stories about the people within those pages, elusive as pressed flowers. What brought them here? What happened to them afterwards? What was it about St Dom's that touched them?

As the last chime of ten rings out from the bell tower and dies away, Gwen hurries up the path. The good thing about being late is that she doesn't get caught up in the crowds on the way in. The bad thing is that she has to squeeze in at the back, feeling desperately self-conscious.

But the congregation of St Dom's are not, on the whole, an observant bunch. Gwen manages to slide into a pew without a single head turning in her direction. The church is never full, and most of the regulars are very short-sighted and hard of hearing.

Today, Reverend Fairfield talks about hope, connection and fullness of spirit. Gwen listens carefully, because she's polite, but his words are like dust motes, dancing in a sunbeam some distance away. She feasts her eyes on the stained glass and abundant flower displays, and draws her usual comfort from an hour away from Aunt Mary's soulless two-bed semi on the estate, but she doesn't feel connected, and her spirit isn't very full. When it's time for the hymns, she stands and sits with everyone else, but she doesn't sing.

The time passes all too quickly. Where is there for Gwen to go after this but home, to the place that isn't a home at all?

Reverend Fairfield makes his concluding remarks, then starts talking about the roof appeal, the urgent need for funds. Gwen feels desperately sorry for the rector, whose appeals have been falling on deaf ears, literally and figuratively, for some time now. But what can Gwen do? She's never been one to get involved. She's given several small donations, but they've been a drop in the ocean. The thought that St Dom's might be broken beyond repair is dispiriting. But if this, the only gentle spot in her life, were to disappear along with everything else, it wouldn't surprise her.

But Reverend Fairfield looks surprisingly upbeat today. His eyes are sparkling and he's talking about a brilliant new idea he's had to find the money. He's pleading for volunteers with more determination than he's shown in ages. Usually Gwen slumps in her pew when he calls for help, like a shy child at a pantomime. But today, when she hears his brilliant new idea, she sits bolt upright. Has she got this right? Fortunately, Reverend David Fairfield is a great one for summarising things. He's probably figured out that people don't listen a lot and he has to say things two or three times to be heard. He explains his plan once again. Yes, she has understood.

Gwen is paralysed and electrified at the same time – as though she's been struck by lightning.

CHAPTER TWO

Jarvis

Sunday morning. Jarvis doesn't have an alarm clock – not that he needs one when his mum comes in at nine on the dot to wake him, every Sunday without fail.

'Wakey-wakey,' she coos, shaking his shoulder then opening his curtains. Sunshine floods in, and Jarvis ducks under the duvet, shrinking from the light like a maggot. 'Time to get up, darling. Church in an hour. It's Sunday.'

'Exactly!' he cries in muffled outrage. '*Sunday*. A day of rest.'

'Rest from what?' asks his mum rhetorically and starts shaking out his jeans and sweatshirts, which are strewn on the floor. 'Jarvis, these clothes reek. I'm taking them and putting them in the wash. I *wish* you'd stop smoking.'

'And why do I have to get up *now*?' asks Jarvis to avoid the smoking conversation. He emerges from the cocoon and squints at her. 'Church isn't for another *hour*. And it's only a five-minute walk away.' It was the one good thing to be said for it.

'Because you need every minute of that time to shower – you smell as bad as your clothes. Jarvis, I've told you before. I come in here and I can smell beer as soon as I walk through the door. Rising off your skin. And after your shower, you need to sit down and have a decent breakfast to soak up some of that Saturday night out.'

Jarvis growls and sinks back under the covers. His mother *has* often told him how the smell of alcohol wafts off him through his pores. But Jarvis isn't convinced. It's probably one of those things mums make up to make you do what they want, like, 'Don't bite your nails because it'll give you a bad gall bladder.' He fell for *that one* until he was seven.

The duvet is brutally ripped from him, exposing his body to the air. That can't be right, surely? He's only wearing his boxers. 'Muuuum,' he wails.

'Jarvis,' she retorts in a crisp voice. 'Shower.' He hears the door click as she leaves.

He lifts a head, a painful experience. The duvet is way across the room. He swings his legs over the edge of the bed and sits until the room stops spinning. Resignedly, he then plunges into the shower where the hot water pummels him to wakefulness. He leans, resentful, under the steaming stream until his father comes to bang on the door of his en suite. 'Jarvis. Get out of that shower. Breakfast is ready.'

Jarvis scowls, turns the water off. *Get in the shower. Get out of the shower.* Honestly. They treat him like a teenager. Surely a man should be able to come and go as he pleases. Although, perhaps a man shouldn't be living with his parents at the age of twenty-seven and working part-time in the supermarket when he has a perfectly good degree and is supposed to be quite intelligent really. That little gremlin thought does occasionally occur to him. He can do without *that* at 9.20 a.m. And after a night on the tiles with Andy and Royston and the prospect of church ahead of him, FFS.

His parents don't insist on much, to be fair. He doesn't pay rent, he lives in luxury, he works part-time and they don't hassle him about his friends or anything like that. Yes, lately, there've been an increasing number of comments about the amount he drinks. And the cigarettes have always been a bone of contention.

But for the most part, they're pretty good, his oldies. The only time his mum ever uses the phrase 'while you're under this roof' is in connection with church. Jarvis could rebel of course, and point-blank refuse to go, but it means so much to her that he drags himself along. He usually dozes when he gets there.

Back in his room, after the sharp-scented shower gel, he must admit there's a bit of a fug. Stale smoke, stale booze, stale sweat. He grimaces. But hey, it's Sunday. Sunday comes after Saturday night. Nothing wrong with letting off a bit of steam on a Saturday night.

While he was in the shower, his mum opened the window. She's also made the bed and laid out clothes for him. Jarvis looks at them as if they're a dead bird the cat brought in. They're *his brother George's* clothes. His parents always wish he was more like his older brother or sister. George is thirty-four and an accountant in Bristol. Eulalie – nicknamed Lalie – is thirty-two and a partner in a London law firm. They go running at 6 a.m. and drink smoothies for breakfast. The clothes on Jarvis's bed are some of George's 'weekend casuals', left behind 'for when I visit'. Not that he ever does. Beige chinos and a check shirt with some wanky logo on the breast pocket. Jarvis takes them out of his room and slings them over the bannister. He dresses instead in his usual slouchy black jeans, cool hand-printed (by his own fair hand) T-shirt and black hoodie.

After what his mum terms 'a sustaining breakfast' (scrambled eggs, smoked salmon, granary toast with butter, a pot of tea for all) they set off *en famille* to church.

At the lychgate, Jarvis pauses. It's a beautiful spot; he painted it once – another lifetime ago. He slouches after his parents, conspicuous in his black hoodie and shades among the neatly put-together elderlies who are creeping up the path even more slowly than Jarvis. A few nod gamely at him; a few frown disapproval. There's one comment about 'young people today' that might be an attempt at a mutter from someone too deaf to gauge their volume properly, or might just be rudeness. Like Jarvis cares.

He lopes down the grey flagged nave and slides into the pew his family always take, four from the front because his mum always wants to sit up front, but she never wants to come across like she thinks she's really important. She's a good woman, his mum, if a bit overzealous with the laundry. Jarvis slithers into a semi-supine position and closes his eyes. His mum bats his arm for him to take off his sunglasses. Vicar Dave starts up about something or other. He seems like a good bloke. But Jarvis can't be doing with well-meant advice and higher wisdom.

Once, a couple of years ago, his mum 'had a word' with Vicar Dave about him. Jarvis was cornered after the service one Sunday and Vicar Dave edged the subject round to drinking, managing to deliver a piece of philosophy that was advice in disguise, without a trace of judgement, all in two minutes. Jarvis admired the ingenuity of it, but that was as far as it went.

'You know,' Vicar Dave said, 'there's a school of psychotherapy that believes the use of mind-altering substances is actually a quest for transcendence. You know, God, enlightenment, higher self, whatever you want to call it?' He waved his hand airily as if it was all the same to *him*, as if he didn't have a vested interest in the God thing. 'That's why things like vodka, whiskey and so on are called *spirits*. A way of reaching something higher. Interesting really,' he concluded, as if they were just two mates musing.

Jarvis extricated himself sharpish. He quite liked the suggestion that there was more to his constant partying than simply being a bum. If you could legitimately be termed a bum when you lived in a nice big house and your mum did your laundry. That idea – spirits, a quest for transcendence – did make him think. That was the problem once Vicar Dave got hold of you – earworm. But in the end, he concluded that it was obvious really. *Of course* he parties to transcend. To transcend the boredom and mediocrity of daily life. To transcend the jittery, uncomfortable feelings that plague him when he *doesn't* – the suspicion that he isn't good enough, that he's a waste of space. That's why *everyone* drinks – because it's better than when you don't.

The sermon drags on *forever*, making him itch for a nice cold pint. He obviously nods off deeper than he meant to because he emits a gentle snore, earning a vicious poke in the ribs from his mum.

'*I have never been so mortified*,' she whispers, looking death rays at him. Well then, why drag him out after a Saturday night with the boys? He wishes his mum would just bow to the inevitable.

The poke in his ribs means he's wide awake when Vicar Dave starts on again about fundraising and the eternal quest to fix the roof and save St Dom's.

The problem is that he keeps appealing to their community spirit, but most of this lot don't have any and naturally Jarvis includes himself in this assessment. Plus, most of them are also half-dead, so not the likeliest bunch to bring about a miracle really. His mum is fidgeting at his side. 'Oh, I *wish* we could do something,' she mutters, as she does every week.

His parents have already given sizeable donations. They've organised summer fetes and Christmas fetes two years in a row. They are, in short, exactly the sort of people Vicar Dave relies on. But two people isn't enough. Jarvis feels bad for them really. They're all so earnest. Vicar Dave is looking surprisingly chirpy today though, as if he has real hope that this time will be different. His naivete is endearing. What's that thing they say in therapy? Jarvis tries to remember the substance abuse group his mum blackmailed him to go to a while back. *If you keep doing what you're doing, you'll keep getting what you're getting.* Someone should tell Vicar Dave that; he's getting precisely nowhere.

But then he announces his new fundraising plan. Like most things, it takes a while to filter down through the layers of fog in Jarvis's brain. He spends his time in a bit of a haze, which he rather likes. In fact, they're all down the nave and chatting to Vicar Dave before the cogs start turning. Vicar Dave asked for anyone willing to volunteer to help with his new plan to see him after the service, but so far no one has said any more than, 'Lovely service, Vicar; regards to your wife,' and the poor guy's looking really dejected. The family have said their goodbyes and are walking down the path before the penny finally drops.

Jarvis stops. 'I need to talk to Vicar Dave; I'll catch you up,' he announces, noticing his dad's jaw drop in astonishment. Then Jarvis turns and races back into the church.

CHAPTER THREE

Vicar Dave

Sunday morning. The interior view of St Domneva's from the pulpit is absolutely beautiful. As he preaches, Reverend David Fairfield looks down the ancient flagged nave and easily imagines its early days, when struggling serfs would have limped along it to find solace in God, and the lords and ladies would have swept to the front in their fine tunics and wimples, proud, landed and keen to be seen.

The columns rise to graceful arches in the (eternally problematical) roof, and the stained-glass windows glitter in the sun. The flowers are frothy cascades. The only thing that *isn't* pleasing to the eye is the dearth of people. The pews are boxlike and deep, made of old, old wood, with stories to tell, polished to a deep shine. But they aren't very full.

David can't help feeling that he's failed. It's a judgement of ego, not spirit. God hasn't set him the task of making this church popular and full to overflowing. The Parochial Church Council, or PCC, might have wanted that when they appointed him; the bishop might have wanted it; David himself might have wanted it. But God asks only that he is here, ministering to the slightly motley crew that is his parish and, if St Dom's can't flourish, to bear witness to its dying days.

David isn't stupid. He knows all the reasons why people don't go to church as much anymore. And Hopley is no longer a community where people come to be married, where they christen their babies, where they know they'll be buried. So many people have moved away, businesses closing, the allure of bigger towns too great to resist. As the town suffers and dies, so does St Dom's. It's happening all over the country, and one man can't stop it. But he finds it sad.

The pesky roof seems determined to hasten the church's demise. The last four years have been a wearying succession of leaks, patches, flying tiles and, this past winter, large holes. David's working life, outside of his usual ministerial duties, has been spent scrunched over his keyboard in his office, scrutinising grant applications, match-funding guidelines, heritage lottery forms, not things that he (or anyone, surely) enjoys. Backache and headaches from eye strain have become part of his life.

He's doggedly addressed every step in every procedure. It's been like walking through soft sand, but at last everything has been approved. English Heritage are willing to give them half of the £100,000 they need for a new roof. But *they* have to come up with the other £50,000 and so far, they've raised £12,000. After *four years*.

And now the clock is ticking. In February, a chunk of roof *fell in* during Sunday service. He still can't quite believe it. It was the one time David was glad that the church was so sparsely attended. If it had been full, someone would have been injured, or killed. As it was, the shard of rafter, several tiles and shreds of rotting pitch like giant bats plunged from above before his horrified eyes and crashed into an empty pew. Dirt and splinters flew into the air, and palpitations started in several of his congregants. It woke Mrs Dantry, who, blissfully unaware of what had roused her, smiled and nodded at him airily.

David asked everyone to leave and called on his sympathetic builder, who, since there was no footie match of interest that day, came straight out. He patched it, checked the rest of the roof and assured David that it was safe for now. 'But you won't get much past September without a new roof and that's a fact, Rev. Hate to be the bearer of bad news and all, but it just won't hold up to another winter.'

Fundraising is a creeping sort of an affair at St Domneva's. The stalwarts of the church are elderly, for the most part, eking out their pensions, scared of parting with their pennies. (Literally, in the case of Agnes Soames; last week she gave him three pence, bless her.) He doesn't expect them to rustle up £50,000; it's a lot of money. But he can't help feeling exasperated that most of the others have so little get up and go.

He's tried all the usual community fundraising activities: summer fetes, Christmas fetes, concerts. He and Annie, during many a dark night, have dreamed up some more *un*usual fundraising activities: a talent show, a sponsored walk, clockwork sheep racing… But the parish of St Dom's is – and David apologises to God for the judgement – *useless*. He's worked in inner-city environments far more challenging than this, but he's never known any bunch of people so lacklustre. So 'meh', as his daughter Wendy would say. He's not suggesting a riotous lifestyle, for heaven's sake. He's not suggesting raves and flash aerobics.

Last month he had a thought-provoking conversation with the archdeacon. 'But if *they* don't want the church,' William said, 'perhaps it's time to let go? You know we can't just keep going for the sake of it. If there's no community involvement, David, despite your best efforts, despite four years of trying…'

And David can see the logic. He really can. He's hanging on by his fingernails and the archdeacon can see it.

'Are you sure you're not letting… personal considerations cloud your judgement?' he asked gently. 'Dear Wendy, I mean…'

David's daughter Wendy is autistic. She's fifteen. It's been hard – from initial concerns, to diagnosis, to adaptation. Now she's at a really brilliant school that suits her, and happier than she's ever been. It's true that if they have to move, they'll be hard-pressed to find as good a place for her. And of course he doesn't want his beautiful girl to have to leave all her friends. But Wendy's not the only reason that he's fighting. He loves this church, its beauty and its great age. He loves its atmosphere, powerful echoes of former times of passion and bravery. St Dom's has a hold over him, as if it's telling him that it still has more to offer, that it's not done yet.

A week after this rather depressing conversation with the archdeacon, something totally unexpected happened. He was staring – rather obsessively – at the total in the roof fund spreadsheet: £8,500 then. At that rate, it would take twenty years to raise the money. Never mind Wendy's schooling, she'd have a degree and be married by then. Eighty per cent of his population would be dead, he'd be retired and St Dom's would be rubble. He was, for the first time, just on the verge of giving up, when there was a knock on the door. It was the imam of the nearest mosque, ten miles away.

'Imam Aayan Abdelnour. What a lovely surprise. Come in, come in.' David had met the imam several times at an interfaith group in Folkestone but hadn't seen any of the group for years now. Fundraising had kept him too busy. 'How are you, sir?' he asked when his guest was seated with a cup of peppermint tea.

They exchanged enquiries about each other's health and families and then Aayan got down to business. 'I have come to bring you a gift,' he said, leaning forward and holding out a cheque.

David frowned. 'For me?' Had he loaned money to the other man and forgotten?

'For your church. From our mosque. We held a fundraising event for you.'

David was so astonished, he took the cheque. £3,000. 'What kind of event?' he marvelled, realising that was hardly the salient point but too stunned to make an appropriate response. All he could think about was how long it had taken St Dom's to raise the same amount.

'Two of our congregants, a married couple, are award-winning chefs. They catered a charity dinner. Price was £50 per head and the food alone was worth it. We also held a raffle and a short concert at the event. A lovely function.'

'I don't know what to say. This is so unbelievably kind. *Why*, Imam, when there are so many deserving causes and we are of different faiths?'

Ayaan shrugged. 'Different faiths, one God. My name means Gift of God. That is quite a name to carry. Not all my fellow imams agree with me, and I'm sure it's the same amongst your clergy, but *I* don't think God wants me to be a gift for just a select few. I think His gift is to offer help where it is needed. You need it, my friend.'

David smiled, emotional. 'You can say that again.'

'Besides, I believe that all holy life nourishes everybody. If your church stays, it contributes to a richer world for us all. That's my humble opinion.'

It was a chastening occasion for David. To receive help from so unexpected a source when he'd been teetering on the brink of despair was a lesson in faith.

Shortly afterwards, he was sent the proceeds of a collection held by the Folkestone Baha'i group. It was only a small group, but they had mustered £500, bringing the St Dom's total to its current heady amount of £12,000. The two gestures got David thinking. He'd been beating his head against a brick wall trying to squeeze support from his own congregation, but recent events showed him that other people might care. The church's visitors' book popped into his head, a record of happy days spent exploring the church and its grounds. Over the years, St Dom's had meant a great deal to a lot of people. If there was only some way of reaching out to *them*…

Now, in the church, David clears his throat. He can tell that at the very mention of the roof fund, he's lost whatever attention people had been paying. Jarvis Millwood, in the fourth row, is actually napping. A couple of the elderlies in the mid-section are nodding off too. Even that awkward girl Gwen looks glassy-eyed, and she usually sits rigid as a schoolgirl, nodding along in places. But David is sure that this time it will be different, that his new idea will inspire and intrigue them.

'The visitors' book is a rich resource,' he explains. 'Countless names of people who've come through here just once, or often, for a long visit, or fleetingly. Everyone who has taken the time to compliment our beautiful church has had their life touched by it, in ways great or small. Of course, not everyone has left enough information for us to find them. But some have, and in others there are clues that we might investigate. It may be time-consuming, but we might think of it as a modern-day quest. There must be some amateur sleuths among you, or some keen puzzle-solvers at the very least. I need volunteers…'

At the mention of the V-word, those who are listening start nibbling at fingernails, checking the time, brushing specks from trousers… David could cry. Does no one see the potential for excitement in this idea? He thinks it's rather romantic, in the broader sense. He would do it himself in a heartbeat, except that Wendy needs so much time and attention and Annie works part-time. There just aren't enough hours in the day.

'Here is a way we might save St Dom's without reaching into our pockets again,' he concludes. 'All I'm asking for is your time. Whether you can work on the visitors' book regularly, or just give an hour or two on a one-off basis, I would be so grateful. Will anyone who's interested please see me after the church? Thank you, and God bless.'

The congregation trickles out slowly. Most of them don't even mention the project as they say goodbye. Others, like Justine and Bradley Millwood, tell him what a brilliant idea it is and look genuinely regretful that they're already overcommitted. They've already done so much; he can't ask any more of them. Meanwhile their son, Jarvis, lolls against the door frame resembling a half-baked James Dean. Without its support, he looks as if he might fall down.

By the time the church is empty, there's only one volunteer, Gwen Stanley. She's twenty-five, twenty-six, something like that. David has only spoken to her a handful of times; she seems painfully shy, determined to avoid human contact. Of course, her story is heartbreaking. Her parents were killed on a hiking holiday, of all things, and she came to live with her aunt, Mary Cresswell, two years ago. It's not charitable to think it, yet David firmly believes that living with that woman is enough to make anyone socially phobic.

Gwen is pretty much the last person in the world he would have imagined volunteering for a job involving contacting strangers. She can barely talk to *him*. The only person *less* likely to put themselves forward for an act of service is Jarvis Millwood.

'I'm very grateful to you, Gwen. I'm sorry there aren't more volunteers; it's a big job for one person. Perhaps some others will come forward when they've had a few days to think about it – it happens like that sometimes. It's a bit of a strange idea, after all, a bit "out there" as my daughter would say.'

'It… it's a good idea,' says Gwen, not looking him in the eye. She has a long curtain of thick mousey hair that falls over her face. She carries herself as if her own weight is too much to bear. A terrible wound, the loss of her parents. David can't imagine how she will ever heal from it, living with that woman, in that house, which he and Annie have privately nicknamed the House of No Hope. But that's uncharitable. Some people have the gift of delight; they know how to make life a rich and gracious experience. Mary has not been blessed with that gift.

'Thank you, Gwen. I'm delighted you think so and really grateful. When would you like to start?'

'I… I only work two days a week, so I have lots of time. I could start tomorrow.'

'That would be just wonderful. Shall I meet you here at, say, ten, and we can talk about an action plan?'

She nods, looking everywhere but at his face.

'Can I just ask you, Gwen, why? What made you decide to volunteer?'

She meets his eyes then and hers are a surprising purply-blue shade behind her thick glasses. 'I like the visitors' book. I've looked through it often. I like thinking about the people, their stories.'

So *someone* has heard the clarion call of intrigue. Well done, Gwen Stanley.

Footsteps come running up the path outside. Gwen visibly shrinks. In bursts none other than Jarvis Millwood, reeking of smoke and alcohol, panting heavily and hitching up jeans that have slithered dangerously low.

'I've come to help,' he says. 'With the visitors' book.'

'No,' says Gwen, then blushes scarlet and droops even lower behind her hair curtain. 'I mean, I just think… it should be me. It's my book. Well, it's not but…'

David recovers himself from his amazement just barely. 'That's heroic of you, Gwen, but honestly, it's not a one-person job. The more the merrier, as they say. And quicker too. Remember we need to fix St Dom's by the end of summer. But, Jarvis, I can't say I'm not surprised. I wouldn't have thought this would be at all your cup of tea.'

Jarvis grins. 'Not my swig of whiskey, you mean? Yeah, well, I've got some time on my hands and… er… the church means a lot to my mum, so… I can start tomorrow afternoon if you like. Say three?'

David frowns. That doesn't ring true at all. Justine Millwood is *always* begging Jarvis to help out, and he's never bothered before. But he doesn't want to accuse the lad of lying – or look a gift horse in the mouth. 'Gwen and I have just arranged to meet at ten. I'd rather see you both together, if we can make that work.' He looks at them both expectantly. If they're going to be a team, they can start working things out now. But Jarvis looks at Gwen as if she's a particularly outlandish type of bug, and her expression can't be seen at all since her gaze is fixed firmly on the floor. *Oh boy.*

'If you're both free all day, shall we compromise and say twelve?' he prompts. 'Gwen? Would midday work for you?' She nods. 'Jarvis? Can you make it by twelve?'

He sighs. 'Yeah, I guess.'

'Great.' Dave claps his hands with an enthusiasm he doesn't feel. 'Well done, both of you. I have a wonderful feeling about this project.'

He doesn't. He can't think of any two people in the world to whom he'd *less* rather entrust the fate of St Dom's. He's always thought the word 'gormless' a cruel one and never uses it. But faced with these two, he can't deny it springs to mind. Jarvis Millwood and Gwen Stanley. The church is doomed.

CHAPTER FOUR

Gwen

When Gwen tells Aunt Mary about the visitors' book project, the expected derision pours forth.

'That vicar's cracked in the head. Well, you've got to be, haven't you, to believe in God? But honestly, trawling through some mouldy old book, hunting for clues like some jumped-up Nancy Drew. Doesn't he know that most people just write their first name and the area they come from? It's ridiculous. And if someone *has* been stupid enough to leave a phone number, does he really think it's alright to ring them out of the blue, years after the fact, and ask them for money? That's downright rude, that is. Shocking. Honestly, they think they can get away with murder, these church men. Crooks, the lot of them. And how are *you* going to get in touch with complete strangers to ask them for money? You can hardly say boo to a goose. It'll all end in tears, you mark my words. Don't come crying to *me*.'

Aunt Mary is actually the last person anyone would go crying to under any circumstances. Gwen hangs her head. She does feel rather stupid, because when she volunteered, it somehow hadn't occurred to her that she would actually have to get in touch with people at some point. She'd been so excited about the thought of perusing the book in minute detail, finding the clues, weaving stories, daydreaming for hours… but of course there's a point to all this, and that's to connect with anyone she possibly can. Well, for once, Gwen isn't going to stress. She can cross that bridge when she comes to it. Reverend Fairfield said that more volunteers might come forward in a few days. Maybe Gwen can go through the book, then hand the phone calls over to them. She certainly can't imagine Jarvis what's-his-name persuading strangers to donate to a heritage project. Invite them to the pub, maybe.

At first Gwen's heart had sunk when he came looming through the door. She's seen him at church before and has always felt completely intimidated. Edgy, cool, darkly brooding men have always terrified her and she wants to *enjoy* this project. And what was all that about doing it for his mum? There's no way Gwen believes *that*. She feels deeply protective of the visitors' book and doesn't want him spilling beer on it, or setting fire to it. But on the walk home she realised that he won't last. He probably won't even turn up. She just can't imagine someone like that taking pleasure in patiently working his way through those old pages. She doubts she'll ever lay eyes on Jarvis what's-his-name again.

The next day, Gwen feels excited all morning. She hasn't felt like that in years. With Aunt Mary muttering about housework, she decides to do something helpful, head off the worst of the complaints. The difficulty is that absolutely nothing in the house needs cleaning. Her aunt is a fastidious housekeeper. She cleans, right through, every single day. Two bedrooms, bathroom, sitting room, kitchen-diner, landing and hall, all hoovered, dusted, bleached, washed and polished to within an inch of their lives. So Gwen starts cleaning the windows. It will save Aunt Mary clambering onto stools and furniture. All she says is: 'That window cleaner smells disgusting. I suppose it would have killed you to get the brand *I* prefer.'

At 11.30 a.m., Gwen leaves and walks slowly to St Dom's. When she goes in, Reverend Fairfield appears from the back of the church and Gwen does her best to smile. She's always been shy, though it's worse now of course.

'Hello, Gwen. Right on time. How are you?'

'OK.' Oh, how she wishes she had more social graces. She should ask him how *he* is, but it's hard, sometimes, to get the words out, even though he is incredibly nice. What's the matter with her? She never used to be this bad.

'I can't tell you how glad I am to see you so keen. I've set up the office for you and Jarvis – I thought you'd be more comfortable there than in the pews. Come and see. We'll hear if Jarvis comes in.'

Gwen notes the word 'if'. Reverend Fairfield has the same ideas about Jarvis as she does. She picks up the visitors' book and follows him to the back of the church. To the right, there's a door to a little extension that's been converted into an office-slash-kitchen. There's a table with four plastic chairs around it, an old laptop and paper and pens. An enormous, old-fashioned photocopier stands in the corner. There's a sink with a draining board, on which stands a kettle and two jars reading 'Coffee' and 'Tea'. Also, some chocolate bourbons. On the shelf above are some mugs and plates.

'It's not exactly state of the art,' says the vicar, looking around. 'But at least you've got the basics. You're welcome to bring things in if you prefer other drinks or snacks. You can use the laptop; astonishingly there is Wi-Fi here.'

Gwen so badly wants to tell him that it's all very thoughtful. She's already looking forward to boiling the kettle, settling down at the table with a mug and a bourbon. 'It's perfect,' she says, and he looks a little surprised but pleased.

'Can you think of anything else you need? No? Alright then. Well, I can't stay long, so shall we take a look at the book together? Come up with some sort of plan of action?'

Gwen already has hers – start at the beginning and work her way through, reading every last word and not missing a possibility. It's a long time since Gwen has looked for possibilities. But she sits down anyway and lays the large book on the table. The pages are divided into squares, and Gwen loves to see the different handwriting in every box.

'Now,' says Reverend Fairfield. 'I took a look last night and there are 190 pages filled in. Ten entries on each page, so that's 1,900 entries to look at. But as I'm sure you've seen, most are just a name and an area, so you'll be able to see at a glance that they're no use to us and skim through fairly quickly. If even one per cent of them are contactable, that would give us nineteen people to try. If even two of them would consider donating or holding a fundraising event… well, it's not likely to solve all our problems, but it's something to try.'

'I think they'll help,' murmurs Gwen. 'I'll find them.'

'Fantastic. It might be most useful to start at the end, do you think? Perhaps the most recent visitors will be our best bet, the church fresher in their memories, contact details more likely to be up to date. What do you think?'

Gwen's starting at the beginning – no one's going to change her mind. 'Maybe.'

'Well, thanks again. I'm not sure that Jarvis is going to make it – if he doesn't, will you be OK here alone?'

'Yes,' says Gwen. *Better than OK*, she wants to say. These days it's so much easier for her to be on her own than around other people.

'Good. And before I go, how are you, Gwen? I know you came to Hopley at a really difficult time, and I hope you're adjusting. It can take time, and I know the social life here isn't the best for young people. If you ever need to talk, or if Annie or myself can ever help you with anything, I hope you'll always remember where we are.'

'Thank you.' There's so much she wants to say, but she can't find her way into that conversation.

'Well then,' he says, looking concerned. 'OK if I leave you to it? I'll jot down my number in case you have any problems. And leave whenever you need to of course. I'm just grateful for whatever time you can give. Bye then.'

When he's gone, Gwen takes a deep breath. The little room is silent. The window's open a crack and a slight breeze trickles through, the sound of leaves rustling. A deep peace descends upon Gwen. The memories and sadness are always there of course, but now she has a project she can plunge into and she can push them aside, just for now.

So often she's leafed through this book, names, dates or comments jumping out at her, but now she's methodical. Gwen opens the book to the first page and pulls her own notebook from her bag. Sheets of A4 paper are useful, but she needs to give due respect to the visitors' book. She's chosen one of her favourite blank notebooks, with a pattern of swallows on the cover.

3rd July 2007. Susan, Worcs. A lovely day out.

Very expressive, Susan.

3rd July 2007. The Dayton Family, North Yorkshire. A beautiful little church. We enjoyed.

Gwen sighs. At this rate they're not going to get very far. More vague, uninspiring entries follow. It's not until the end of the page that Gwen finds something interesting.

5th July 2007. Greta Hargreaves. Winthrop-St-Stanhope, Devon. 'Life is but thought: so think I will/That Youth and I are housemates still.' Such a special place. Thank you for restoring my Nature, Hope and Poesy.

Greta, she jots down. *Page one. Likes Coleridge. Elderly. Small village.*

She carefully turns the page and starts reading page two. Twenty minutes pass in peaceful absorption. She gets up to fetch a bourbon. After another five minutes, she fetches another. She's reminded of study sessions in the college library in Oxford, snacking surreptitiously – a happier time. Gwen is in her element.

Some time later she hears the clunk and creak of the church door opening. Her heart beats faster. There's a pause, then she hears footsteps inside the church – soft-soled, slouchy footsteps. Gwen tiptoes to the office door. Jarvis is standing in the middle of the church, looking around aimlessly. Gwen says nothing. He's – she checks her watch – forty-five minutes late. Hopefully he'll give up in a minute and go away. Just as she thinks it, he sees her.

'Oh,' he says slowly. 'The office. Right.' He slopes over. 'How's it going? Have you started?'

He reeks of cigarette smoke and alcohol and makes an unusual clinking sound as he walks. Annoyance trumps her shyness. 'Of course I've started. I've been here since twelve. Like we agreed.'

'Cool, nice one. Vicar Dave around?'

Do you see him? Gwen wants to say. *Do you think he might be hiding behind the photocopier?*

'No, he was here at twelve. Like we agreed.'

'Right, right. Well, I'm here. What can I do?' He pulls out a chair, slides into it and reaches into the open-sided pocket on the front of his hoodie. To her horror, he draws forth a bottle of beer. Then he reaches into the back pocket of his jeans and whips out a bottle opener. Catching Gwen's expression, he sits up straighter. 'Oh I'm sorry,' he says amiably. 'Would you like one?' From his kangaroo's pouch he takes a second bottle and holds it out to Gwen.

'No!' she cries. 'You can't drink in here. We're in a *church.*'

Jarvis nods at the painted breeze-block walls, the utilitarian plywood door. 'We're in a 1960s extension. I don't think it's exactly sacred space.'

'But we're on church *business*. Looking at a church *book*. It's not even one o'clock.'

Jarvis raises his eyebrows and flicks the lid off one bottle. 'It's yours if you change your mind,' he says in a placatory tone, placing the other on the table in front of Gwen. He takes a long, happy swallow. 'Aaaah. A little brain stimulant to wake me up.'

'Alcohol's not a stimulant; it's a depressant.'

'Is it? It'll calm me down then. Right. Put me to work.'

If he gets any calmer, he'll fall asleep in Gwen's opinion. He's a strange mixture, this Jarvis. Once you get past the black clothes, the scowl, the unhealthy pallor and the falling-down trousers, he's actually not bad-looking. Not Gwen's type, but objectively speaking. High cheekbones, dark tousled hair, tall, slim and smouldering. He seems willing to be helpful, even if he is late, and his manner is quite gentle. 'It's not really a two-person job…'

'Really? I thought Vicar Dave said it would take ages.'

'Oh stop calling him that,' snaps Gwen, immediately feeling as if she's kicked a dog. But really, it's so disrespectful.

'Well, I don't think you should just call him *Dave*. I know some people do, but I don't think it's very respectful.'

'I *don't* call him Dave. I call him Reverend Fairfield.'

'That just sounds like we're in Victorian England. Anyway, we're on the clock. Save the church by September.'

'Yes, but it's only one book. Two people can't look at it at the same time.'

Jarvis pulls the book towards him and Gwen fights the urge to snatch it back. 'We can work on it together,' he says, his deep voice sounding sleepy. He pulls Gwen's chair close to his. 'Come on, I'll take the left-hand pages and you can take the right and we'll go through it twice as fast.'

'I've already started the left-hand page,' snips Gwen, aware that she's being very churlish. It isn't like her to be difficult, or contradictory, but Jarvis seems to irritate her into assertiveness.

He heaves a sigh and gives her a look. 'Then we'll swap sides. Or I'll have a head start on this one. Come on, let's try.'

Gwen sits reluctantly, reminded again of student study sessions. As well as the cloud of smoke and beer that surrounds him, she can smell shower gel and laundry powder. 'You do laundry?' she asks without thinking. He always looks so dishevelled and debauched that she assumed he'd be filthy too.

He winces. 'My mum does it, alright? But she *likes* doing it. She *enjoys* washing.'

Right, thinks Gwen, enjoying watching him colour up. Lucky Jarvis, to have a mum. She remembers her own mother neatly pressing everything for her, even those things that didn't need pressing, even those things Gwen explicitly stated she didn't *want* pressed because the wrinkled look was in. She feels a wave of emotion and hastily looks at the book. 'So what I'm doing is this…'

She begins to explain her investigations so far, and Jarvis grabs her notebook to see what she's written. She fights the urge to rescue it.

'So, explain it to me. Like, page one.' He turns back to Greta Hargreaves and reads her comment in a confused voice. '*Life is but thought: so think I will/That Youth and I are housemates still. Such a special place. Thank you for restoring my Nature, Hope and Poesy.* What does that even mean? Why have you written it down? How do you know she's old?' He reaches for his second beer.

'Oh, *don't*,' says Gwen. 'It's only lunchtime. Why not have a cup of tea instead?'

'If you're making it?' Jarvis winks cheekily at her.

'Well… alright,' she relents, getting up, and he puts the beer back on the table.

'Greta's comment is from a poem by Coleridge,' she explains as she puts the kettle on. 'It's called "Youth and Age" and it's written from the perspective of someone old, regretting the loss of all the things they loved about youth, like nature, hope and poetry.'

Jarvis squints at the book. 'She's spelled poetry wrong.'

'It's how Coleridge spells it. It's old English. Anyway, she's saying St Dom's restored all that for her. So I bet she'd help. I know we need people that are contactable, but we need people who are motivated too. Not like...' She leans over Jarvis's shoulder and stabs a finger at Stephen, Norwich. '"Nice place." I mean honestly. What kind of a comment is that? Nice place. *He's* not going to cough up, is he? I was thinking that Winthrop-St-Stanhope is a small village type of name, isn't it? And we know it's in Devon. It might be possible to find her.' She turns back to the tea and Jarvis falls quiet.

'That's really clever,' he says. 'I'd never have thought of it like that, but you're right.'

Gwen drops a teaspoon. 'What?' she demands grumpily, bending to pick it up. She had braced herself for Jarvis's too-cool-for-school act. She doesn't know what to make of Jarvis being friendly and enthusiastic. 'Are you serious?'

'Yeah, it's kind of cool. And really creative. Only... all we *really* need to do is go through and see who's left phone numbers or emails or whatever and write them down. Right?'

'Well...' says Gwen. She can't deny that he *is* right, but she's enjoying doing it her way. And she doesn't want to finish too soon, even though Reverend Fairfield needs the money in a hurry.

'And shouldn't we start from the end?' says Jarvis thoughtfully. 'Aren't the more recent visitors likely to be more useful? Say... the last three years?'

Gwen stares. He's almost horizontal in the chair, his long legs stretched out under the table, but he's not stupid. 'Reverend Fairfield said the same thing. But I want to start at the beginning.

I know it sounds stupid. I want to… get to know the visitors a little bit.'

'OK,' says Jarvis. 'Let's do it your way. It'll be slower but way more interesting.'

'*Really?*'

'Sure, why not? From the point of view of being willing to part with money, I reckon Greta's a good bet. The only problem is that she came here' – he checks the date – 'ten years ago. If she was old then, she might be dead by now.'

'Oh don't,' shrieks Gwen, covering her ears. 'That's a horrible thing to say. She loves good poetry and beautiful old churches and she's a really nice lady.'

'She still might be dead.'

CHAPTER FIVE

Jarvis

She is the weirdest girl he's ever met. She's like, really uptight, and really bossy, and she looks a mess. Long, long hair, but it's not all slinky and shiny – it's bushy and dull. Thickest glasses he's ever seen. Terrible posture, almost as bad as his own, but he's a six-foot-two beanpole. What's her excuse? And her clothes. Layers of blouses and cardigans and God knows what. No look at all. Not grunge, not hippy-chick, not Victoriana, not peasant-chic… Jarvis knows his fashion. His own look is anti-fashion, obviously, because he's too cool for all that. She does *not* have a look. She seemed really shy yesterday when they were talking to the vicar, but *now* she's really critical and fussy and acts like she's the only one who can look at the book. At least she and Vicar Dave seem to buy his 'I'm doing it for Mum' excuse. That's something. And she's got an unusual way of seeing things, he'll give her that.

'What's your name anyway?'

'Gwen. Short for Gwendoline. Gwen Stanley.'

'You don't look like a Gwen. Hey, Gwennie, do you want your beer now?'

'No thanks. And please don't call me Gwennie. It sounds like an old-lady name.'

Whereas Gwen…? He grins. 'Got a middle name?'

'Actually yes – it's Poppy.'

'Gwendoline Poppy. I like that. I'll call you that.'

She furrows her brow at him and looks frustrated. 'You're weird.'

He doesn't want to be mean but look who's talking. He gives her a meaningful look. Point well made.

She flushes. 'Shall we get started?' she mumbles and starts peering at the book. After a moment she seems completely engrossed, leaning her chin in her hand, a dreamy expression on her face. *Weird.* Occasionally she jots something in her fancy notebook. Jarvis hasn't thought to bring one, so he avails himself of the paper and biros on the table. Not that he needs them – there's nothing here that's remotely useful.

15 July 2007. Jean Foster, Gloucester. A gem of perfect repose.

He sniggers at the rhyme and moves on.

15 July 2007. Katy, aged 6. I came here with my mummy and daddy and we had a nice time.

Sweet. But useless. And she's taken up two boxes with her kiddie scrawl.

In two minutes he's finished the page and waits for Gwen to finish hers. And waits. What the hell? It's like she's memorising the *Odyssey.* He tilts his chin a bit to see her side. There is *nothing* useful there. But already he knows better than to interrupt. He finishes his tea and considers the beer, but he doesn't want to be contentious. He's a lover, not a fighter. He gets up to fetch the bourbons and brings the packet to the table.

'Get a plate. We don't want to get crumbs in the book,' orders Gwen.

Jarvis does a pretend double take. 'Mum?'

'Shut up. I'm concentrating.'

Soon, Jarvis is bored senseless. His attention span is not one of his most impressive qualities. 'Gwen, love, hurry up,' he pleads. 'What can you possibly glean from that lot? Let's turn over.'

Gwen sighs. 'Alright. That wasn't a very fruitful batch.' She turns the page reverently, as though it's a Bible. Smooths the pages open and gives them a little pat. Sinks deep into her perusal again. This really is going to take forever. Vicar Dave can kiss goodbye to his new roof this summer. And Jarvis will be stuck here much, much longer than he needs to be.

Jarvis turns his attention back to the visitors' book. Reads another whole page of mundane comments and no clues whatsoever. Fair enough, they came to see a church, not write an essay. But again, he's finished his page while Gwen's still frowning and tapping her teeth with her pen as if she's doing a cryptic crossword.

'Hey, is that photocopier working?' asks Jarvis.

'What? I don't know. Why?'

Jarvis gets up to see. He presses a few buttons but nothing happens. He reaches his arms to grasp the sides and gives it a little shake, then turns to see Gwen smirking at him. 'What?'

'I'm no technician, but might it help to plug it in?' she wonders. *Smart-arse.*

Jarvis bends over to fish behind the copier for the plug. He feels his trousers sliding down but it's OK; he's wearing his special red briefs.

'Woah, woah, woah,' cries Gwen behind him. 'I don't need to see your entire backside, Jarvis.'

'Don't look then,' he retorts, his voice muffled. Wouldn't you know, the socket is slap in the middle behind the stupid thing – it's a stretch to plug it in. He stands up red-faced with effort and tries the copier again but still no joy. They probably would've left it plugged in if it worked. 'Bollocks.'

'What do you need it for?'

'I'm working much faster than you. If I copied the last pages, I could work back while you're working forward and we'd meet in the middle.'

'Not a bad idea,' admits Gwen. 'Shall we carry on like this for today and then I'll take the book home tonight and take it to the copy shop on the way over tomorrow?'

Jarvis looks at her in disbelief. 'How long are you planning on staying? It's two already.'

Gwen snorts. 'You only got here at one.'

'Well yes, but I'm hungry. It's lunchtime.'

'Don't let me keep you then. I'm planning to stay all afternoon.'

'Don't you *have* a life?'

Gwen says nothing and Jarvis hovers. 'Oh alright, I'll do a bit more I suppose. But I'm out of here at half past. Mum's making stew.'

CHAPTER SIX

Gwen

Jarvis lasts until 2.15 p.m. then bolts. Will he come back tomorrow? Who can tell? She's relieved to be alone again, but all things considered, his company wasn't as bad as she'd expected. He's more intelligent than she'd thought and surprisingly amenable to her ideas, which she recognises might sometimes seem rather odd to anyone outside her head. That comment about her not having a life hurt though. Because she doesn't, basically. This project is all she has, and she knows she's making a meal of it but she really, really doesn't want it to end.

By 3 p.m., her stomach is gnawing and she knows she has to go. She'll take the book, get something to eat in Hopley, do the photocopying... It strikes her that she should let Reverend Fairfield know what she's doing in case he comes back later and finds the book missing. Despite having been unusually vocal with Jarvis, she finds phone calls difficult, so she keys the number into her phone and types out a text.

It's a typical spring day – cloud and bright light scudding overhead like disco lights, occasional showers rattling down but enough sunshine to lift the spirits. There's a brisk breeze, and by the time Gwen gets into Hopley, her long hair is wrapped around her face, and her scarf has escaped and been recaptured twice.

When Gwen moved to Hopley, she caught the end of its heyday. There used to be a lovely little café on the high street, the Miller's Store. It did delicious, healthy food, had paintings by Kentish artists on the walls and was the sort of place where the staff never made you feel bad for lingering over a bowl of soup for ages. Maybe that's why they went out of business. Now the only two cafés are uninviting, so Gwen buys a pasty and a bottle of water to take away. She eats on a bench in the tiny 'park', which is more like a village green that got left behind. On the bench opposite her, a man with a shaven head is talking angrily into his mobile phone.

She lingers as long as she can tolerate the expletives and the ball-scratching of the angry man then goes to the print shop. She copies the last two years of entries; that should keep Jarvis going a while. And then there is literally nothing for her to do but go home. She has no friends here, there are no galleries or cute shops to while away some time and her part-time job isn't the sort you pop into on your days off. She does admin at a local surveyor's office with only one other member of admin staff, Jeannie, who's not a youthful sixty-something. Between Jeannie's deafness and obsession with her grandchildren, and Gwen's chronic shyness, conversation doesn't flow.

When she came to Hopley in the wake of her parents' death, she grabbed at the first job she could find. The company were only able to offer her two days a week and that was perfect then; raw with grief, she couldn't have coped with any more. She always planned to get a more substantial job in time but now finds herself stuck in a horrible rut. Acute grief has dulled to numbing depression, and the confidence and motivation to look for something more rewarding have eluded her so far. Reluctantly, Gwen drags her way back to the house and arrives at 4.15 p.m. The sinking of her heart is remarkable.

'Oh you're back, are you?' says Aunt Mary as if she'd been in some doubt. She stands in the hall wearing an apron.

'Yes,' says Gwen, feeling like a fool for stating the obvious. 'How was your day? Can I help you with anything?'

'My day? Same as every other day. Prince Harry and his girlfriend dropped round for tea. Michael Bublé called to ask if I'd sing in his next concert.' Gwen would have laughed, except Aunt Mary's tone wasn't humorous, it was bitter, as if Prince Harry and Michael were personal acquaintances who'd badly let her down. All Gwen wants to do is go up to her room and look through her notebook, but she always feels rude if she doesn't spend some time with her aunt each day, even though Aunt Mary appears to derive no pleasure from Gwen's company.

Gwen trails into the kitchen where a chilli is bubbling on the stove. She thinks of Jarvis's lunchtime stew with envy. Chilli's fine, but Aunt Mary likes spicy food and Gwen doesn't – she always ends up with eyes and nose running profusely while Aunt Mary hands her kitchen paper and tells her she's disgusting. And she always makes the rice gloopy and tasteless. There was a period last year when Gwen tried to alternate the cooking, but after three meals Aunt Mary decreed that Gwen was useless and couldn't even manage edible food. She quickly took the reins back and makes a great hurrah about having to do all the cooking, but whenever Gwen offers, she says, 'No thank *you*. I haven't forgotten that strange Turkish thing you made me eat.' It was Moroccan, a tagine, but Gwen has given up reminding her.

'So how was the *fundraising project*?' Aunt Mary asks, wriggling her fingers in quotation marks. What can Gwen say that could possibly interest her?

'It's good. There's only one other volunteer so it'll take a while, but I find it interesting, and the reverend is very grateful.'

Aunt Mary tuts and shakes her head as if Gwen has spent the day shooting heroin. There are no further questions, to Gwen's relief. 'Shall I make us a cup of tea?'

'Oh yes. By all means let's fill ourselves up with tea when I've spent the past hour working to make us a decent evening meal.'

'I won't then,' says Gwen. 'I only thought you might like one. Let me know if I can do anything.' She sits on a kitchen stool, determined to be companionable.

Life here really is excruciating. The only person she can talk to about any of it is her best friend from university, Amma. But Amma lives in Bristol where she's doing her articles at a law firm. She keeps saying that when she's qualified she'll move to London and get a job there – *And then we'll be able to meet up every weekend. It's an easy train ride from Hopley.'* But although Gwen tells her friend a lot, even Amma doesn't know that nothing is easy for Gwen anymore.

It's been so long since she went anywhere that the thought of getting on a train and going to the big city actually makes her chest tighten, even though the two of them used to do it all the time from Oxford – carefree Saturdays when they'd forget all about their studies and just explore the markets, the shops, go to the cinema to watch a rom-com. Sometimes Gwen's mum would come up from Surrey to treat them to lunch. Once Amma's mum Akuba came over for a fortnight from Ghana and stayed half the time in a B&B, half the time in Amma's room while Amma happily slept in a sleeping bag on the floor. They showed Akuba all their favourite student haunts and took her to London for their traditional Saturday outing.

Gwen shakes her head, remembering. It's like it all happened to another girl. Life was so colourful back then. She never was the most confident person, never really felt able to reach out and grab life. But she had her parents to boost her from behind and

Amma to hold her hand and pull her along into new adventures. Now her parents are dead and Amma isn't nearby, and Gwen feels the gulf between herself and other people widening all the time.

'Move out,' Amma tells Gwen whenever they speak – she's the one person Gwen will brave the telephone for. 'The woman is pure evil. Move out.'

Well, she's not exactly *pure evil*, but living with her is singularly joyless. She's prickly, determined to be offended by whatever Gwen does or doesn't do and they have nothing in common. At seven most evenings, Gwen feels she can reasonably be released because Aunt Mary sits in front of the TV, watching whatever's on at some volume. Gwen steals away to her room where she either reads or watches DVDs on an ancient and tiny portable TV she's had since her student days. It's an awful way to live. But the thought of living alone now is daunting, and Aunt Mary's house offers a comfort zone of sorts. It's a vicious circle. Over the past two years, her sense of self has been eroded so much that now she can't even imagine what sort of independent life could possibly make her happy – and she has no faith in herself to make a go of anything anyway.

Amma understands to a point. 'You lost your darling parents. You were so close. Of course you can't feel happy or excited about anything,' she often says. 'But I don't think you'll heal while you're living there, Gwen. I think you'll go backward instead of forward, and you *know* your mum and dad wouldn't want that, girl.'

She's right. Amma's always right. Gwen should be pouring whatever energy she can muster into sorting out her life, instead of pondering the impenetrable mysteries of the visitors' book. It's almost certainly just a displacement activity, and the church's chances of getting a new roof aren't looking good so far. But just now the book is the only thing that makes her feel a little like her old self again, and she can't bear to let it go.

CHAPTER SEVEN

Jarvis

Jarvis arrives at St Dom's at 11.30 a.m. the following day. They didn't arrange a time to meet but he reckons that's not bad going. Naturally, Gwen is already there.

She looks up through her thick glasses, her curtain of hair. 'You came.'

'Well yeah.' Jarvis can't honestly add something like *I wouldn't miss it*, or *You can count on me*, because experience has taught him that no one can depend on him, least of all himself. But he does, for reasons of his own, want to be here. He's even excited, somewhere deep inside. Very deep. 'Saved the church yet?'

She actually smiles. 'Not quite. Here.' She pulls out a chair for him and takes a sheaf of paper from her bag. 'I went to the copy shop. Here you are – the last two years. Now you can start at the end.'

'Oh… thanks.' Jarvis takes the photocopied entries and sinks into the chair.

'What's wrong? I thought that's how you wanted to do it.'

'Yeah. I do. Only, two years isn't much. I thought you'd have done, like, *three*.' If Jarvis can't get to the bit he needs soon, he might die of frustration.

Gwen arches an eyebrow.

'I work faster than you, remember?'

'OK, but I can always go again. These should keep you going a couple of days at least.'

'Yeah, I guess. I just really wanted to start in 2014.'

'Why? What happened in 2014?'

Busted. Be cool, Jarvis. 'Nothing, I just feel like it'll be the good year, you know? The one with all the helpful people in it. Whatever, we'll get to it.'

Jarvis supposes another day or two won't hurt. He smiles at the thought that today he's actually helping the church instead of working on his own secret quest. He's so buoyed up by the thought of being the good guy that he even makes Gwen a cup of tea and puts their bourbons on plates. They don't talk much, but it's a peaceful silence, not an awkward one, and he finds himself going a whole hour without thinking about his beers, though he lays his hand on the bottles in his hoodie pocket once in a while. It's nice to know they're there.

At one o'clock the church door creaks open, and a minute later there's a little knock on the office door. Jarvis turns, expecting to see Vicar Dave, but it's his mum. He might have known she wouldn't be able to resist. She grilled him yesterday, and there was a certain light in her eyes when he told her about Gwen, even though he emphasised that she's not at all hot and isn't even remotely his type. She's always on at him to 'meet a nice girl'.

'*Mum,*' he groans, 'what are you doing here?'

'Lovely to see you too, darling.' Undaunted, she comes into the office and holds out her hand to Gwen. 'You must be Gwen. I'm Justine Millwood, Jarvis's mother.'

'Nice to meet you.' Gwen is back to her shy self, mumbling so badly the words barely come out. But they shake hands and his mum smiles.

'Jarvis has told me all about the project and your clever ideas. I think it's wonderful that you're helping the church like this.

Both of you. David must be so delighted. This roof fund is like the never-ending story.'

Jarvis notices Gwen's look of shock at the casual use of Vicar Dave's first name and smiles. She really is unbelievably uptight and old-fashioned. But his parents have done so much for the church over the years that they've become friends.

'Thanks,' mutters Gwen. She's tongue-tied again, like she was with Vicar Dave on Sunday. It's as though Jarvis is the only person who doesn't make her clam up. He's not sure that's a good thing.

'Oh, is this the book?' asks his mum, leaning over to look at it. 'It's funny, this must have been on the shelf at the back of the church for donkey's years. I looked through it once, ages ago, but I'd completely forgotten about it until David mentioned it on Sunday. It must be really fascinating reading all those comments and thinking about all the people who've come through here over the years.'

'Yes, exactly,' says Gwen. Two words. *Good going, Gwen.*

'Anyway, I don't want to disturb the pair of you, but I come with an invitation. Would you both like to come home for lunch? I've made sticky chicken and a heap of savoury rice.'

'I would,' cries Jarvis, jumping up. His mum is a great cook, and her sticky chicken is his absolute favourite.

At the door, he looks back to see that Gwen is still in her chair, frozen. 'Come on, Gwendoline Poppy,' he urges, feeling suddenly sorry for her. It's impossible to tell whether, underneath her reluctant exterior, she actually wants to come or not, but she always seems so alone, in a way that has nothing to do with actually *being* alone. He doesn't know her circumstances; he's not really into all that deep connecting stuff. He doesn't know where she lives, whether she works, what she likes (apart from the visitors' book) or anything about her. That she's lonely is just an assumption. But oddly, he wants her to come for lunch. She looks as if she needs feeding up. Not physically – definitely not that – but some other way.

Fortunately, his mum is not a hesitant sort of lady. 'Come on, Gwen. We're only five minutes away. It won't take up too much of your time. We'd love to have you.'

Gwen looks up at her with a look that's so... *wistful* that it almost makes Jarvis want to give her a hug. 'But I bought a pasty,' she whispers, producing a grease-stained paper bag from her tote, as if she needs to do full disclosure, so she's not getting the invitation under false pretences. What a weirdo. What's a stupid shop pasty got on his mum's sticky chicken?

'No, no.' Jarvis isn't the taking-charge type, but he needs to intervene. 'Never mind the pasty. Chuck it in the bin. It's only £1.90. Mum's cooking's the best, not that I want to make her vain. You need to come.'

Gwen looks surprised again. 'I suppose I could keep it for tea...' She trails off, as if there are implications and consequences of when she eats the stupid pasty that need her careful consideration.

'Great, come on.' Jarvis is getting hungry.

'Thank you,' Gwen says to his mum in a heartfelt way. And they are on their way.

Over lunch, undeterred by Gwen's reticence, his mum grills her determinedly. The woman could talk for Kent. Maybe he should warn her off a bit, give Gwen a break, but as a result, Jarvis learns many things about Gwen that he didn't know. No boyfriend (well, he could have guessed that), Oxford degree (not surprising; he could tell she was smart), parents both dead (total bummer), lives with an aunt on the new estate of little houses (that his parents say look like identikit matchboxes) out the other side of Hopley. She's been here two years, since the tragedy with her parents. Friends all elsewhere, not Kent. No wonder she looks so droopy.

'I came to… get my life back on track I suppose…' says Gwen in her diffident way. 'But it seems to be taking a while.'

'Well of *course* it is,' cries his mum. 'You couldn't recover from something like that overnight, you poor love. There's no right amount of time for something like that, Gwen – you remember that. But remember too that you do deserve to be happy.'

God, steady on, Mum. This is all a bit touchy-feely for Jarvis. 'How's the chicken?' he asks, to lighten the mood.

'Oh it's *wonderful*,' says Gwen fervently. 'Delicious. Thank you, Mrs Millwood.'

'Call me Justine, please. And I'm pleased you like it.'

Thankfully his mum subsides then, and the rest of lunch is a bit less intense. Over dessert (poached apricots with crème fraiche and a dash of rum) she asks Gwen about the visitors' book again, and this time Gwen's a bit more forthcoming about her favourite topic, explaining how she and Jarvis are starting at opposite ends of the book to cover more ground and giving Jarvis generous credit for coming up with this clever idea.

'Well done, darling.' His mum beams at him proudly, and he has to admit it's a nice feeling. Usually she looks at him with love, yes, but also confusion, frustration and, most depressing, concern. He doesn't like to feel that he's worrying her. But he's just not the career-path, buy-a-Nutribullet type. He's the arty type, a dreamer, sensitive, beneath his scowling and his partying. And he knows you can't make a living out of that – everyone knows that. So Jarvis has drifted into the middle way, the nothing-at-all way, living at home, spending his days in a sea of PS4 and pub banter, trying to escape from, or *transcend*, as Vicar Dave would have it, his constant uneasy sense that he's opting out, a coward – and that everyone else thinks so too.

Well, the visitors' book isn't a job but it's still making his mum proud, and it's something a bit different at least. The chances of his other, secret reason for doing it actually bearing fruit are small, he does realise. But you never know, right? You never know.

He and Gwen go back to the church for another couple of hours, then Jarvis gets bored again; level eight of *Uncharted 4* is calling to him.

'I'll copy 2014 for you on my way home,' says Gwen, by way of goodbye. He thinks it's her way of saying thank you for lunch.

Back at home, his mum takes him aside before he can slope off upstairs. 'Jarvis, about Gwen—' she says, looking serious.

'Oh Mum, please don't tell me to date her. She's nice enough and everything, but I *really* don't fancy her. Not one bit. And I don't need my mum to pimp me out.'

'That's not what I was going to say.'

'You weren't?'

'No. You're quite right, it's none of my business, and of course you shouldn't date anyone you're not drawn to. In fact, Gwen shouldn't be dating anyone – she's not ready. She's far too broken still, poor thing, and no wonder after that horrible accident.'

Jarvis looks at her suspiciously. His mum appears to be making total sense.

'All I was going to say is that I want you to be very, very kind to her. She needs a friend. Make a bit of an effort, would you, darling?'

And she's right. If anyone needs a friend, it's Gwen. He's not sure he's got much to offer, but he really is her only option around here.

CHAPTER EIGHT

Gwen

That evening, Gwen really, really cannot face another Gwen-and-Aunt-Mary special. After being in Justine Millwood's warming presence in a proper family home, even after spending time with Jarvis, who's odd and annoying but actually not horrible, the weird dynamics of her current living arrangements are all too pronounced. For the first time she feels that Amma is right and that despite her crippling fear of moving forward, she really must move out. But how? And where would she go? At the very least, she has to give herself one evening off from feeling like an unwelcome guest.

She's even worried about telling Aunt Mary that she doesn't want to eat with her that evening. She can just imagine all the sharp comments that will rain down, and whilst they're only words, Gwen has learned that words can diminish you, and she suddenly feels that pretty soon now she will break from them. It shouldn't be that way.

Jarvis is right – she could just throw the pasty away without breaking the bank. Or give it to a homeless person. How many other twenty-six-year-olds live with a relative and feel beholden to eat every single meal with them? Aunt Mary's not even her *mother*. It makes her boil inside a little bit.

After photocopying 2014 for Jarvis, she goes into Speedy-Spend and buys a slab of chocolate cake, a packet of mint chocolate Penguins and a bottle of Merlot – just one of those 187ml mini-bottles – she's not turning into Jarvis or anything. Gwen and Amma used to love sharing a bottle of red back in Oxford and she associates it with happiness. Today she's been to lunch at somebody's house and made progress with the visitors' book, and she wants to celebrate with a whole evening alone in her room – no snubs, sighs or bitter complaints to spoil her night. She pushes her purchases deep into her bag so they won't be seen. Then she heads home, preparing herself to tell a lie, something that does not come easily to her.

When Aunt Mary emerges into the hall, Gwen leans weakly against the wall. 'I'm not feeling well,' she says. 'I'm really sorry, Aunt Mary, I'll have to go straight up to bed. I'll put a film on and hope to drift off.'

'Oh. I'm sorry to hear that,' says her aunt. Sympathy is not her natural mode so it comes out a little rusty, but Gwen appreciates the sentiment. 'Nothing catching, I hope. I don't want germs in the house.'

'I hope not too. That's another reason I want to go up, so I don't pass it on to you.'

'Will you be wanting your tea? I've made it, you know. I don't want it to go to waste. I'll have to bring it up to you I suppose.'

'Oh no thanks, Aunt Mary. I'm really sorry but it's my stomach you see. It's all queasy. I couldn't eat.'

Aunt Mary tuts. 'I'll keep it for your lunch tomorrow.'

Gwen almost wants to laugh, but she nods gratefully. 'Yes, hopefully it's just a twenty-four-hour thing.'

She fetches herself a large glass of water and a big mug of tea. 'That'll save me having to come down again,' she says to her aunt in a weak voice. 'Night, Aunt Mary.' Then she goes up, dragging heavy footsteps up the stairs, fighting the urge to skip and run.

Alone in her room, she turns the key in the lock, glad that there is one. Not that she thinks Aunt Mary will come and check on her – she doesn't suspect her of having nurturing tendencies – but given that she's just lied through her teeth, she'd die if she were caught out. Despite everything, she doesn't want to hurt Aunt Mary's feelings.

Now, she dives on the bed in a state of perfect glee. It's only 5.30 p.m. *Hours* ahead of her, to do *whatever* she likes. Hours in which to be perfectly self-indulgent. What bliss.

She slides a DVD into her trusty old set: her absolute favourite ever film, *The Princess Bride*. This is going to be her best evening in quite a while.

Halfway through the film, she tucks into her pasty, then the cake, and swigs the wine from the dainty little bottle. It's not exactly healthy eating, but it's comfort food of the first order. Gwen feels light, free, giddy with indulgence. The film does what it always does and makes her feel happy, as though there's a realm somewhere – somewhere you can only reach through a story – where everything is beautiful and everything is fine and everything always turns out alright, even death.

Gwen's was never a big family, but she and her parents were always close. After graduating, she'd stayed on in Oxford, working in a library and living in a lovely little flat for a couple of years, but when she decided to start a PhD, she moved home to keep her living costs down. It's not every daughter who'd be happy with her parents after tasting freedom – and not all parents would rejoice to have a twenty-something daughter back in the fold after they thought she was settled. But the three of them were content, and it was only to be for a year or two. That was the plan anyway. She never finished that PhD.

Her mother had one brother, who was in Australia, and her father had one sister – Aunt Mary. At the funeral, both offered her a home. Whether they genuinely wanted a shy, bookish, bereaved niece in their home, or whether it was a sense of duty, Gwen couldn't judge. In hindsight, she might have been better off with Uncle Floyd, but at the time Australia had felt like a stretch too far. It was a place she associated with bikini-ready bodies, sports and barbeques on the beach, not a mould Gwen had ever fitted. And it was the other side of the world from her Surrey home, where all her memories of her parents lingered. Kent felt more relatable, so she chose Aunt Mary.

It took her a while to realise that life at Aunt Mary's was not all that could be desired. There was none of the affection or warmth of her parents' house, none of the interesting conversations or delicious meals, none of the music, films or books. There were no outings to museums or parks. But Gwen was so unhappy she didn't notice. It was only months later, when she recounted two or three of Aunt Mary's barbs to Amma, that Amma said she sounded quite cruel.

Aunt Mary doesn't *mean* to be cruel, Gwen is convinced. She's just become what disappointment and tragedy have made her. But it still makes it hard to be on the receiving end. Her aunt was widowed twenty years ago at the age of forty-five. Uncle Benjamin was her second husband. Her first, Neil, had been acidic and unkind. Gwen only knows what her parents told her, but apparently Neil had given Aunt Mary a life of hell. They divorced and she became quite reclusive, declining invitations, taking a gloomy world view and nursing her wounds. But then, in a meeting as unlikely as it was marvellous, she met Uncle Benjamin in the supermarket. He tripped over a crate of cornflour left on the floor and cannoned into Aunt Mary. The manager yelled at the shelf stacker. Benjamin intervened, and her aunt was struck by his kindness and clumsiness in equal measure. He was the opposite of Neil in every regard. She had a short period of happiness – of another way of living – before Benjamin died and then she gave up on joy for good, it seemed.

She downsized immediately, to this poky little modern house which she said was easy – easy to maintain, easy reach of town, easy to clean. There are no pictures of Benjamin, or her brother, Gwen's dad; no happy memories. Her shutters went up again and now there is only day-to-day existence. She retired from her job with the council at sixty and paid off her mortgage. Her tastes are minimal, her habits frugal. So she doesn't need Gwen to pay rent, only to contribute to the bills and food. Gwen is grateful for that: it means that her undemanding two-days-a-week job is ample to pay her way. She thought all the spare time would be a good thing. Instead she finds herself purposeless and numb.

It's not even as if she doesn't have any money. She has her parents' legacy. She's not rich – they were always a modest family – but it's not a bad position to be in at twenty-six, financially speaking. She could put a deposit on a small place of her own, or she could rent somewhere, knowing she has a cushion, or she could travel… she knows how fortunate she is to have such options. But they all scare the life out of her. She's never travelled alone – what if she hates it? Renting or buying both depend on her holding down a full-time job, and all this time with her aunt has made her doubt that she can.

Aunt Mary tells her constantly that her university degree is useless and she would've been better off doing something vocational or practical like nursing or business. Aunt Mary tells her that she's impractical and not very good at cooking or clean-ing. Aunt Mary sneers when Gwen tries to talk about history or literature, and worst of all, she once inadvertently hit on Gwen's secret dream: 'What do you think you can do with *literature*?' she demanded once. 'Be a writer? Well let me tell you, no one makes any money out of *that*. It's a fool's game. Self-indulgence taken to the nth degree.'

Gwen denied it of course, but it's true, it *is* her secret dream, though it's a long time since she's admitted it to herself or anyone else. She loves reading the acknowledgements pages at the back of her books. Every author seems to have two or more pages' worth of people to thank. They all seem to have 'the best agent I could have asked for'. (Gwen imagines agents as wise, Yoda-like figures.) They all praise their publishers to the skies (Gwen imagines publishers' offices as a sort of shimmering Emerald City), and they all list endless family and friends. 'My wonderful cheerleading squad' is a phrase Gwen sees often. She would give anything to have a cheerleading squad. Even a single cheerleader would be nice. But Gwen only has Aunt Mary.

Home always used to be her haven. When she got bullied at school, when a holiday with friends went wrong, when she had romantic troubles, home was where she always fled. She doesn't have that anymore. Aunt Mary has suffered – Gwen tells herself that over and over again. But Gwen has too, and she doesn't want to end up like her aunt – bitter and penny-pinching and sharp-tongued. Nor does she want to remain as nervous and directionless as she is now. Surely there must be some choice in the matter?

CHAPTER NINE

Gwen

The next day, Gwen sets off to the church at eleven, figuring she can't seem too eager after 'being unwell'. As she leaves, Aunt Mary hands her last night's dinner in orange Tupperware. Gwen can spot some cold lamb with congealed fat glistening on it and some cabbage and potatoes. Her aunt has a knack of making things that could be wholesome and delicious fatty and bland. If Gwen is asked to Jarvis's house, she will throw it in a bin without hesitation.

Jarvis isn't there, so she sets to work and soon finds an enthusiastic comment from a woman with the most wonderful name: Lavender Hamilton. That's a storybook name if ever there was one. And she's actually left a phone number. Gwen looks up the dial code on the internet and it's Ludlow. Lavender from Ludlow. Gwen feels sure that Lavender will give a massive donation and Gwen will be vindicated in trawling through the old first pages. There's nothing stopping her calling right away, except inhibition. Downright fear actually.

Jarvis turns up at twelve, reeking of beer again. 'Sorry, meant to come earlier,' he mumbles. 'Royston called last night and I went to his. Whiskey and poker until three. Bit rough now.'

Gwen has no idea who Royston is. Jarvis looks awful, eyes bloodshot and drooping, skin really white and porous, like china clay. She's on the verge of telling him he stinks but instead gets up to put the kettle on. 'Are you alright? I'll make tea.'

'I'll live. Why do I do it to myself?' he mutters.

'I was going to ask you the same thing.'

'I'm not an alcoholic, if that's what you're thinking. I've read about it a lot, because my mum keeps worrying. But alcoholics hide things. They keep secrets… I don't. *Everyone* knows I like to go out. I even boast about it because I'm a bit of an idiot. I'm not an alcoholic; I just like a good time.'

'Oh,' says Gwen. 'That's good, I suppose. Look, this'll make you feel better.' She puts her latest photocopying on the table before him.

He beams, delighted as a small boy. 'Is that 2014?'

'Yup. The magic year.'

'You think so too?'

'There certainly were a lot of visitors. So you could be right. Here you go.'

She passes him tea and biscuits. As Jarvis reaches for them, Gwen hears clinking coming from his hoodie again. '*More* beer?' she asks, a little exasperated.

'Hair of the dog.'

'Does that even work?'

Jarvis opens his mouth eagerly then stops and frowns. 'I don't know.'

They get to work. 'How's your mum?' asks Gwen casually after about ten minutes.

Jarvis shrugs. 'Haven't seen her.'

'Oh. What's she cooking for lunch today?'

'She's not. She works Wednesday to Friday. No more home-cooked lunches until the weekend.' Jarvis looks glum.

Gwen feels it. Gross cold lamb it is then. She carries on and finds Ann from Aylesford, which is here in Kent:

I am a teacher at Morehouse Primary School, soon to retire after a long career. I have found it hard to adjust to the changes ahead and the new role in society that awaits me. At St Domneva's I have found a sense of peace and acceptance that had eluded me prior. Thank you for preserving this beautiful sacred space.

'Ah *ha*.' Gwen scribbles in her notebook triumphantly. A clear motivation to give money and easy(ish) to find, surely? They'll be able to email the school, who will surely remember an Ann who worked there for a long time.

'Got a live one?' asks Jarvis sleepily.

'Well…' Gwen hesitates. He has a point about starting ten years ago. Ann would be long retired now; Gwen hopes Jarvis won't say again that she could be dead. 'Look.' She shows him.

'Nice one.' Jarvis nods thoughtfully. 'Could be a lead. Could be dead of course…'

'Jarvis.' Gwen covers her ears with her hands. 'I don't want you to say that about anyone else, OK?'

'OK.'

'How's 2014 going?'

'Rubbish.'

Gwen peers over his shoulder. 'But you've already found three possibles. That's great.'

'Oh, yeah, it's not bad. Hey, it's lunchtime. Pub?'

Gwen stares at him. Oh God, it's not… a date is it? Of course not. She's not his type – Jarvis's type is the sort of girl that could be in an eighties rock video, all eyeliner and cleavage and pouting.

'Well, what are *you* doing for lunch?' he demands.

Gwen sighs and shows him her Tupperware. He recoils so dramatically that she giggles.

'That's disgusting, Gwendoline Poppy. Bin it and come to the pub. They do a decent steak pie. Salads too if you're into that sort of thing.'

'The Wheatsheaf?' she asks tentatively. It's the only pub in Hopley that Gwen can think of, a nasty chain pub from which spill forth the flicker and bleep of fruit machines and crowds of bald, tattooed men wearing offensive T-shirts.

He scoffs. 'The Swan. Much nicer.'

'But that's way out of town.'

'We *are* way out of town. The church is out of town. My house is out of town. Look, let me put your mind at rest. I'm not an axe murderer. I think we can both safely assume that I don't fancy you and you don't fancy me. It's not a big deal, only lunch. A man's gotta eat. And you can't eat *that*.' He curls his lip at the lamb.

Gwen finds herself smiling. 'Alright,' she says.

In the Swan, Jarvis appears to know *everybody*. Both bartenders, the family lunching at the big table near the hearth, the old man in the corner. Gwen feels overwhelmed so she scuttles through to the beer garden without a word. She doesn't want Jarvis to start introducing her.

It's a pretty pub on the edge of a stream. She chooses a table at the far end of the garden, close to the water, which is slow and sluggish just here, but a couple of ducks are paddling about, and there's a willow tree on the opposite bank. Jarvis comes out to join her, carrying two brimming pints of pale ale, a couple of menus tucked into his armpit.

'You didn't tell me what you wanted,' he points out, sliding onto the bench opposite her and lighting a cigarette, 'so I took the liberty.'

'Oh God, sorry. I didn't think. Thank you.' Gwen eyes the pint doubtfully. She's never been much of a beer drinker. 'What is it?'

'Kentish Galleon. Local brew. It's good.'

Gwen takes a tiny sip and can't help wrinkling her nose. Jarvis looks disappointed. She tries again, getting used to the complex, savoury flavour. After a third sip she raises her eyebrows. 'That's quite nice,' she says.

'And the more you drink, the nicer it gets,' quips Jarvis. 'You can order something else if you like – I won't be offended.'

'No, I like it. It's different, but I like it.'

'Why did you come rushing out here like that? Don't tell me you've never been to a pub before.'

'Of course I have. Just not for *ages*. I sort of forgot the drill. And I… I'm…'

'Shy?'

'Yes.'

'Me too.'

Gwen laughs heartily.

'No, I am. I just sort of party my way through it. Why do you think I take a couple of beers everywhere I go? Turns every new situation into a good time. But here, well, it's my local, so no one's a stranger.'

Gwen stares at him. Jarvis, *shy*? Jarvis, with his chiselled cheekbones, hooded eyes and all-black wardrobe? Life never gets any less surprising, that's for sure.

'Why did you volunteer to work on the visitors' book?' she asks when they've ordered – salmon risotto for Gwen, chicken and cider pie for Jarvis.

'I told you. My mum loves that church. Usually the fundraising stuff is all bake sales and sponsored hula hoops.' He shudders. 'This seems like a pretty harmless way to help out.'

Gwen narrows her eyes. She agrees with him about the hula-hooping, but she's not sure that's the whole story; he looks shifty. Before she can persist, he turns the tables on her.

'What about you? You've got some sort of weird relationship with that book, like it's your baby or something. I've never seen you join in with anything before so why did *you* suddenly volunteer?'

Gwen rotates her drink slowly in front of her, then picks it up and places it on a cardboard beer mat, centring it exactly. Condensation has trickled into a little puddle on the wooden table. 'I just… I didn't want anyone else doing it.'

'Yeah, see, weird possessive vibe. What is that?'

'The book's always intrigued me. It's the idea of all the stories inside it. All those names, all those lives. We've only got the tiniest bit of information about them, but they've got whole lives going on. They had reasons for coming to St Dom's, reasons for why it affected them however it did, reasons for going on to do the things they did afterwards. It just… fascinates me.'

Jarvis looks at her intently. He stubs out his cigarette in a heavy glass ashtray and lights another, then blows out a long stream of smoke off to his right and narrows his eyes at her through the cloud. Gwen braces herself. He's bound to think she's a loser.

'I don't know why you're so shy when you're so articulate,' he says instead. 'But anyway, yeah, I get why you're working through it the way you are, imagining all that stuff about them. Have you ever thought of… do you ever try writing? Like books and stuff?'

Gwen stares at him in disbelief. The astonishment is so great that she takes a long swallow of her beer and feels the start of a slow, excited fizz inside her. 'Why do you say that?'

'Because you're good with words and you clearly love stories. You've got an imagination, and you don't really look like the real world holds much interest for you, no offence. Seems like you fit the profile.'

'Really?' asks Gwen, breathless. 'You think I fit the profile?'

Jarvis smiles. 'Have I just accidentally hit a nail on the head?'

Gwen bites her lip. She hasn't spoken of this for so long. Aunt Mary's remarks are still ringing somewhere inside her. But Jarvis isn't a harsh person. He's so laid-back he's horizontal, as the saying goes. She'd *like* to tell him. No need to make a big song and dance out of it.

'I love books more than anything. When I was in school, I was one of those kids, you know? While the others were running around playing kiss chase and screaming, I was in the corner of the yard reading. I could never imagine myself being a go-getter, you know, making money or selling houses or whatever normal people do...'

Jarvis nods. 'Same,' he says briefly. 'Carry on.'

'Since I spent half my life with my head in a book, it was no surprise that all I could really imagine doing was writing them. But in school my careers advisor told me you can't make any money that way and you have to make a living...'

'Ever written anything?'

'A few short stories.' Gwen feels her face heating up. 'Some poems.'

'Cool. Any good?'

'I, uh, I don't know really. I don't know. How would you know?' She's flustered. She's never had anything she's done be called cool before.

'Good point. It's the same with art. How did you feel when you were writing them?'

'Oh, amazing. Like floating away. Like floating on the sea with the sun shining on you.'

Jarvis shakes his head and takes a long pull on his cigarette. 'Then I've got bad news for you, Gwendoline Poppy.'

Gwen's stomach lurches. 'What?'

'That's what you're meant to do. And if it's hard and impossible and you don't make any money, well... that sucks. But you'll make it. You'll probably be completely crazy by then. But you'll make it.'

She laughs, excited and uncertain. 'You really think I could?'

'Well look, you went to Oxford so I guess you're pretty smart. You never had any other ideas of what you wanted to do. You've found something you love. You're not exactly blazing trails in any other career.' He looks at her appraisingly. 'Seems to me like there's only one way forward.'

Gwen looks down and draws shapes in the condensation on the table. 'My aunt thinks it's a rubbish idea. She said… writing is self-indulgent and childish and I'm a dreaming fool. She said I need to wake up and get a proper job.'

'You need *her* approval?'

'No. But…' She hesitates. Jarvis is such a maverick. He'll never understand.

'But it would be nice,' he says. 'I get it.'

'You *do*?'

'Yeah, course. We're only human, aren't we? My parents supported my art all the way, so I had that. Even so, when I went to art school, not everyone was so impressed. Not the tutors, not the students. I folded pretty quickly. It's tough. But you might be stronger than me.'

A waiter brings their food out and Jarvis orders another pint. Gwen leans forward, fascinated. 'You're an *artist*?'

He shakes his head and waves his hand as though the question is a wasp. 'No, no. Not anymore. Dig in.'

CHAPTER TEN

Jarvis

Jarvis wanders the short distance home and lets himself in. The house is quiet, both parents at work. Normally he hates it like this, unable to understand why people like silence. Usually he fills the void with a beer and PlayStation at high volume, but today it suits his pensive mood. His own words are ringing in his ears; the words he spoke to Gwen in the Swan.

At the time, they were all meant for her. But now that he's alone he can't help noticing that they are – maybe – applicable to him too. To be fair, plenty of people have said similar encouraging things to him along the way, just not for a long time now. They've all given up on him, though not until it was obvious that he'd given up on himself first. Maybe tomorrow he'll tell Gwen about his own long-buried aspirations and see if they can encourage each other a bit. Although, does he really want to start all that up again? It's hard work, hoping for things.

And hasn't he got it pretty sweet, living at home, working part-time, plenty of time for pints with the boys and gaming? He remembers how it goes with art. There might be all these clichés about outrageous artists, debauched bohemians, but the truth is, anyone who actually gets anywhere does it by damn hard work. And by having, or developing, a skin thicker than rhinoceros hide. Jarvis doubts he will ever have that strength of character. Much, much easier to carry on as he is and enjoy it.

Except... *is* he enjoying it? Is being drunk six nights out of seven enjoyment? Is constantly opting out of the world enjoyable? Is ignoring everything you ever dreamed of as a child because you don't want to work for it conducive to a happy state of mind?

His phone jingles. He pulls it out of his pocket – message from Roy Jackson, otherwise known as Royston, for reasons no one can remember.

Jar-man. Swan at seven?

He vaguely remembers making plans during last night's revelry for tonight's revelry. Last night was brilliant, wasn't it? He remembers howling with laughter because Royston fell off the couch and made a joke about... what was it? Pockets. Pockets and potatoes... there was something funny about it. But Jarvis somehow doesn't feel like a repeat performance so soon. It's strange – he's never not felt like the pub before.

Forgot – have to help old man in shed tonight. Rain check?

The reply pings back at once.

Sure, man.

He's done it. A whole unsociable evening stretching ahead. Jarvis's worst nightmare on your average night. But tonight he already knows what he wants to do with it. He has 2014 with him. He slipped it into his hoodie pocket when he left the church. It's time to look for her.

He goes to the fridge and takes out a cold one, then he puts it back. He drank so much last night. It wouldn't hurt him to give it a miss for once. He pours a glass of orange juice instead – his mother's always on at him to get more vitamin C – and wanders upstairs. He throws himself on the bed and begins the tricky business of trawling the entries for two completely different sets of possibilities: 1. Finding people of any shape, size and description who might be up for forking out a bit of cash for the church, and 2. Finding people – women – who might fit a very specific description indeed.

Three years ago, a bit closer to summer than they were now, Jarvis went to the church to paint. His art course had a module on architecture and landscape. Painting your local church might not be cutting-edge, experimental or cool, but you couldn't deny it was a pretty spot and met all the requirements for the assignment.

He set up his easel outside the lychgate. It had that quaint roofy thing over it and the big, dark yew tree off to the left. The sweep of path; the square, grey tower – it was gorgeous really, if Jarvis looked at it with his inspired artist's eye, instead of his jaded art-student eye, which were two totally different things. Even now he can remember what he wanted to convey: all the things Gwen has talked about over the last few days. The history and continuity, the strength and staunchness of the place.

This was before Jarvis lost his nerve completely, before he started to get self-conscious about painting in public. Back then he was cocky, a bit of a poser really. He started painting, wishing the church was a bit more on the beaten track so more people could pass and admire this handsome *plein-air* artist-type with his prodigious talent. In fact, the only people who passed in two hours were Vicar Dave and Mrs Dantry, who was then eighty-nine and a bit confused, and who passed by and said, 'Hello, Colin, dear, that's a lovely castle.'

He scarcely heard the footsteps coming along the path at 3.30 in the afternoon. He would remember that time forever afterwards. The footsteps stopped directly behind him but Jarvis hardly noticed. He kept painting.

'Wow, that's beyond gorgeous,' said a voice almost in his ear. 'What a fab picture. It makes me feel… radiant.'

Then he looked up – into the face of an angel.

Everyone always assumes that Jarvis has an obvious type. When his friends set him up, it's always with someone who's attractive in a flashy way: sexy, bold. But, as stupid as he is perfectly aware it sounds, Jarvis lost his heart then and there that day and has never got it back. She was none of the things people assume Jarvis will like. Beautiful, yes, but in a totally different way. Long, wavy blond hair loose down her back. Conservative clothes, really – a long, billowy floral skirt, with a light sweater in lilac. Flat shoes. No make-up. Smooth skin and a lovely, considering smile. Blue eyes, bright and soft. *Wholesome*. Jarvis was completely tongue-tied.

They looked at each other for a long moment. Jarvis felt everything inside him line up and take position ready for his life to begin. At last he was able to thank her and smile. Her answering smile took his breath away all over again. 'You're really talented,' she said. Then she carried on her way, into the church.

To this day Jarvis berates himself for not going after her, but at the time it simply didn't occur to him that she wouldn't come back out again. He didn't want to leave his almost-finished masterpiece alone, and he knew that she'd felt at least a flicker of what he had. She would come back, and this time he would have more self-possession. He would tell her that he was finding art school a lot harder than he'd expected so her compliment meant a great deal to him. He'd ask her name and invite her for a drink at the Swan. He even started wiping down his brushes. There were some finishing touches to do but he could add those at home, tomorrow.

It wasn't until he'd cleaned all his brushes that he realised she was taking a *really* long time in the church. Maybe she was praying. He'd never really seen himself with a religious woman but whatever, he was spellbound by the girl in lilac. It wasn't just her beauty; it was her aura. There was a sort of gentle, rippling light about her, like sunshine playing on a stream. He didn't worry that she'd turn him down. He was handsome enough that women always gave him a second look, and she'd be able to tell he was sincere, not a player. So he waited, everything packed away, in the warm sunshine. And waited.

After a while he started to feel anxious. Most people had a walk around the churchyard, went inside to look around, sometimes lit a candle and said a prayer. Thirty minutes max. By now nearly an hour had passed.

Jarvis picked up all his stuff, even the painting, holding it awkwardly away from his body by the frame. He left it all just inside the church door and went to look for her. But she was nowhere.

He checked everywhere: the office where he and Gwen were now working, the bits around the back that laypeople aren't supposed to go in, even the ladies' toilet. It was only then that it occurred to Jarvis that the churchyard might have another exit. Call him stupid – well alright, anyone would call him stupid – but he'd never really noticed. For an artist, he wasn't terribly observant, always lost in his own world, his own dreams. Church was a place he came to with his mum, for his mum; because it was so close to home, they always came the same way. Jarvis didn't know the ins and outs of the building like some people.

Sure enough, there was another little gate behind the church, a soulless, modern affair in grey brushed metal. Jarvis stood in the sunlight again staring at it. But why hadn't she come back the same way? Why hadn't she wanted to walk past him? She *must* have wanted to see him again, she *must*.

He went out through the gate and stared up and down the road in case he could see her slender figure disappearing into the distance, but the road was empty, except for cars whooshing past, noisy and unsympathetic.

Jarvis hung around a long time, unable to accept that she'd slipped through his fingers. He'd said almost *nothing* to her. Perhaps she thought he was a numpty. Maybe, instead of artistic and fascinating and romantic, he'd come across as a bit thick.

He never saw her again. But he's never forgotten her either. He never thought to look in the visitors' book to see if she'd written something there. To be fair, he isn't sure he even knew the church *had* a visitors' book. When Vicar Dave announced his plan on Sunday, it took Jarvis the rest of the closing announcements, all the goodbyes and half the length of the church path for light to go on inside him. What if *she* was in there? What if she'd written something that day? What if she was contactable and he could track her down? Jarvis had never moved so fast in his life. He ran back to see Vicar Dave and the rest is history.

That first day with Gwen scowling at him and looking daggers at his beers and practically cradling the book to her breast like a baby, there was no way he could just dive in where he wanted to without attracting suspicion. Gwen didn't seem very friendly then – there was no way he was going to tell her something that would make him sound like such a sap. And she didn't leave him alone with that book the entire time; the woman must have a cast-iron bladder. Jarvis returned in the early evening to look through April and May of that fateful year in private. But the visitors' book wasn't there. Bloody Gwen had taken it home.

He'd meant to go to the church again last night but then Royston called and he forgot all about it; another reason he's thinking of cutting back on the partying. It's no way to find the woman of your dreams – getting so drunk you forget you're even looking for her.

Today he only got halfway through February, but he'll skip the rest of that and March too and get stuck in on April and May tonight while he has the pages to himself. Stupid that he can remember the exact time of day that she walked into the church but not the date. It was definitely late spring, early summer. He can remember the soft quality of the air and the smell of hedgerow flowers. He can't name them – he's not a flower kind of guy – but he knows it was that sort of time. And that module had been due on June first. Jarvis forgets a lot of things, but his art-school deadlines are branded on his heart.

Tonight, he doesn't even have to pretend to care about the church; he can just look for his lost love. He can go through it again tomorrow or the next day on church business.

Wait. Tomorrow? If he finds someone who might be her tonight, his secret quest is fulfilled. He'll have no reason to carry on with the project. When he signed up, that was definitely his plan – get a lead on the girl in lilac and then abandon ship, just like he always does. But that doesn't feel quite right now. How can he leave Gwen on her own like that? At first, he could tell that she'd rather be alone than with him, but now? They had fun today, didn't they? She seems to like talking to him about her ideas, and she loved meeting his mum – girls always do; she's that sort of mum. But is he seriously going to spend his days in Nerdsville with absolutely nothing in it for him? Unlikely.

It doesn't take Jarvis long to go through those two months. Obviously, he can immediately discount all the Alans and Peters and Edwards, all the jaunty *Family* entries – *We loved it. The Markham Family* – and so on. Scanning through the pages for solitary female names, he finds nine.

Imogen from Walthamstow
Mrs B. Bryce, Wilts
Hattie N. Price, Citizen of the World
Pavani Bansal, Potters Bar
Alice Griffiths, the Red Lion, Chepstow
Karla Freja Silburg, Copenhagen

Chandice Williams, Kingston, Jamaica
Nancy Tully, Ohio
Patricia Lansdowne, Chorleywood

Jarvis sits back and takes a deep breath. His lost beauty is either one of these or she didn't write in the book. He copied the names into a list as he went along. Considering it now, he crosses out Pavani and Chandice. Neither is likely to have long blond hair and blue eyes. After a moment's thought, he crosses out Mrs B. Bryce. Not only because he can't deal with the possibility that she's married but because to write Mrs and an initial is an older-person thing to do. She has older-lady handwriting too and her comment, *A very nice church*, is an older-lady thing to say.

That leaves six. Karla is the one who worries him the most. From her appearance, his mystery girl could easily have been Danish. And Scandinavians speak excellent English. If that's her, all hope is lost. There are no contact details bar her city of origin. He could, theoretically, search for a Karla Freja Silburg in Copenhagen, but what would be the point? How could he ask her on a date from 500 miles away?

He reads her comment, scanning for clues: *A beautiful church. I especially love the picture windows.* So she has artistic sensibilities. Beyond that, he doubts even Gwen could deduce anything. The feeling grows that Karla is the woman he's been longing for. It would even explain why she didn't leave the church the way she went in. Even if she had liked the look of him, what would have been the point if she was just travelling through? Jarvis gives a growl of frustration and doodles a broken heart and a question mark beside her name.

He considers the others. If it's Nancy, he's equally shafted. Ohio is even further away than bloody Copenhagen. And she's left just as little information to help him find her. So that leaves Imogen,

Hattie, Alice and Patricia. Imogen, surprisingly, has left a phone number, so she'll be easy to trace. His dream girl could be an Imogen, yes. He likes that name. And Walthamstow is definitely doable. They could meet at Victoria and do the London thing. He wants to feel hopeful, but it's a bit too convenient.

Hattie doesn't sound right either. He won't rule her out of course, but honestly, 'Citizen of the World'? She sounds like someone on a gap year, travelling and giddy with freedom. *She's* left an email address, so that's another very easy contact. But he just can't imagine the girl in lilac signing herself 'Citizen of the World'.

Alice will be findable if she's still connected with the Red Lion pub she listed, and a pub has always been a promising starting point for Jarvis. As for Patricia, well, that's always sounded like an older-person name to Jarvis, but that doesn't mean anything. A lot of these old-timey names are coming into fashion again; he was at college with a Minnie, a Hester and a Joan. Patricia is a posh name, and Chorleywood is where all the bankers live, and she *did* look classy. Chorleywood's quite small too and Lansdowne's not so common a name that it would be a pointless search.

He looks at his watch. Six o'clock. Not an unsocial time to call someone. He looks at Imogen's phone number. He could always leave it until tomorrow… put off the evil hour, defer disappointment… But Gwen will be at the church; he'll be embarrassed. He snatches up his phone and keys in Imogen's number, reminding himself that he's ostensibly calling on church business. He can't just call up a stranger and ask if she's beautiful and has long blond hair.

After three rings, a woman answers, a breathless hello, as if she's just been laughing. She sounds nice. Jarvis takes a deep breath; he's not known for his phone manner, but he has to do this right.

'Hello, am I speaking to Imogen please?'

'Yes.'

'Oh good. I'm sorry to interrupt your evening but I'm calling from St Dom's in Hopley?'

'Where?'

Crap.

'It's a church. In Kent. A place called Hopley. You visited it in 2014 and left your details in the visitors' book.'

A long pause while Jarvis scrambles to put her on speaker and switch to an internet search on his phone. He can't remember now the full name of the church – how *stupid*. He knows it's short for something, and he thought it was called St Dominic's until he was about eighteen. Google triumphs again. St Domneva's: that's it.

'St Domneva's church in Hopley, Kent,' he reiterates.

'In 2014,' she says slowly. 'I usually can't remember what I did last week. Oh wait, did you say Kent? I remember. Is it a pretty little Norman church with a square tower?'

'That's it.'

'OK, I'm with you. I'm sorry, what did you want?'

'I'm calling on behalf of the vicar, David Fairfield. We're raising money to fix the roof. It's been leaking for ages and it's pretty bad to be honest. We're wondering if anyone who's visited the church and liked it might want to help.'

'Oh, I see. I'm so sorry, I would like to, but I'm completely skint at the moment. I'm between jobs and rent in London is, like, crazy, and I'm really struggling. So I don't have any spare cash at all, not even a tenner.'

'I understand,' says Jarvis. 'Thank you for your time.' How can he know if it's her? Any minute now he'll have to hang up or he'll sound like a stalker and not only get done for harassment but discredit St Dom's too. If only he could *see* her.

'Um… one more thing,' he says desperately. 'We're going to hold a party to thank everyone who's talked to us, even if they couldn't make a donation. Would you like to come?'

'Really? That's pretty nice. When is it?'

'Oh. Ah, I don't know. I mean, the vicar hasn't fixed a final date yet, but it'll be in the summer sometime. I could let you know the date when he does. If you like.'

'Why not? Right now, I can't even afford the train fare to Kent, but who knows, my luck might have changed by then. Could I bring a friend?'

'Sure. So, are you an artist?' He slaps himself on the forehead. Not smoothly done.

'An artist? No, why?'

'Oh, I just wondered because, you know, struggling artist and all that.'

'Oh right. No. I'm an actor. Or trying to be.'

'Right. Just as bad. I mean, difficult. To break into. Well good luck, and thanks again.'

'Cheers. And what was your name, sorry?'

'It's Jarvis. Jarvis Millwood.'

'OK, well, let me know about that party, Jarvis. Bye.'

Jarvis hangs up and stares at his phone a long time, as if her face might somehow appear on the screen. Could it have been her? He remembers her clothes, her smile. She looked a bit conservative to be an actor, but then isn't it a cliché to assume that all actors are edgy and flamboyant? This girl sounded nice – and fun. Up for a party. Did she *sound* like her? He struggles to remember her voice. She said a handful of words to him, three years ago. It's really hard to tell. And he has absolutely zero reason to call her again until he can give her a date for a party that he's just made up. But if he *does* manage to persuade Vicar Dave to hold a shindig then he can invite her, and if she *does* make it, he will see her and he'll know. Oh well, after all this time what's another few months?

Quickly, before he loses his momentum, he does an internet search for the Red Lion pub in Chepstow, which he finds easily, and for Patricia Lansdowne in Chorleywood, which yields no results, though he does find an Adam Lansdowne and a Parker Lansdowne. She could be a wife or, preferably, a daughter, so he scribbles down the details, feeling like Jessica Fletcher in *Murder, She Wrote*.

First of all, he calls the pub. And what do you know: yes, there's an Alice, she's the owner and yes, she's there. He's on fire.

But when Alice comes to the phone, she has a strong Welsh accent and a voice deeper than Jarvis's own, broken by the smoke of unimaginable quantities of fags. Just hearing it makes Jarvis think about cutting back. There is absolutely no way this is the lady in lilac. His heart sinks, but he explains his official purpose anyway.

'Well I never,' growls Alice. 'St Dom-whatsit. I remember that place. I was in Kent visiting my granddaughter, I was. Five, she is, now and over the moon about the Easter bonnet parade. My girl Bronwen is making her a fab one: a chicken race track it's got on it.'

'Oh, er, right. Cool.' Jarvis can't imagine what she's talking about.

'She's learning to read already, loves those dragon films – she's half Welsh, see – and just when we thought our Bron would never conceive. Clever what they can do these days, isn't it?'

Jarvis is having trouble following her billowy train of thought. 'Yes, yes definitely. That's good news. So anyway, St Domneva's—'

'Oh yes. Sorry, lovely, I'm a terror for going off at a tangent, like. My boys are always telling me. Mam, they says, shut up and stick to the point, like.'

'Oh, that's alright, it's very nice talking to you…' says Jarvis a little desperately.

'Well, aren't you a lovely boy? Nice when the youngsters have five minutes, isn't it? Honest to God now, I work all the hours in the day and when Alun and Thomas come home, can you get them to sit down and *listen* for two seconds? No, you cannot, lovely boy. It's all, *Mam, shut up, I've got to send this email for work,* or *Mam, I need the girls babysitting,* or *Mam…*'

Jarvis has some sympathy with Alun and Thomas. He watches the hands on his watch creep round and wonders if she will keep him on the phone until it's too late to call the Lansdownes.

'Anyway, you were asking me about that church. Lovely place, it was, I remember. I took the baby out for a drive so Bronwen could get some sleep. Stopped in Hopley. I likes a new place, I does. Had a look around, saw the church and that nice shop with the crystals, run by a lovely Pakistani lady it was, Mahoni or something…'

'Mahira.'

'That's it. Pretty name. How is she?'

'How…? Oh, Mahira? I don't know – she left. The shop wasn't doing good business towards the end. It closed about a year ago.'

'Oh, that's sad. Always a risk, isn't it, a little shop like that? I'm sorry to hear that. Then I had a drink in the pub – always good to check out the competition, like, though honest to God it wasn't a patch on my place – and then I went home. That's all I can tell you, lovely boy.'

'Oh, good. That all sounds great, only what I really wanted to talk to you about was the roof. The church roof.' At last Jarvis seizes his chance to explain. And Alice comes up trumps.

'Oh never! Everywhere's struggling these days, isn't it? Especially the churches in this day and age – it's the same round by here. Of course I'll send you something, lovely boy. Always good to give back, isn't it? I did like that little church. I wouldn't like to think of anyone getting injured there. How can I pay then? Have you got a page set up? Or can you take payments over the phone, like?'

Shit. It had honestly never occurred to Jarvis that anyone would actually want to give them any money. He'd got a little bit ahead of himself. But he didn't want to waste Alice's good will. 'I don't suppose you could send a cheque? We're *very* old-fashioned here, I'm afraid.'

'I can do that. I like doing things the old way myself. Can't beat a nice cheque, I always say. I still send them to my grandkids. Alun and Thomas, they're always telling me, *Mam, why can't you do a nice bank transfer, like everyone else?* But how is that a present? I want something they can open in a card and see is from their nana. Who do I make it out to then? You?'

'No, no.' Jarvis is alarmed. It shouldn't be this easy for a strange caller to extract money from a grandmother not his own. 'To the church, please. St Domneva's Church.' At least, he hopes that'll work.

'Hang on, hang on, I'm doing it now. St… Domneva's… Church. What's today? The fourteenth? What year are we in – 2017? Sounds proper space age, isn't it? Five hundred pounds, is that alright?'

'Five…? *Yes.* That's amazing, Alice, thank you so much. We at the church couldn't be more grateful. Vicar Dave will be… well, he'll be so pleased.'

'Happy to help, lovely boy.'

'Oh, and Alice? I feel I have to say, you shouldn't have offered to send the cheque to me. I mean, I could be anyone – it could be a scam. Just so no one takes advantage of your generosity another time.'

Alice laughs, a sound like cracked pottery, which degenerates into a long fit of coughing, phlegmy and wheezy and barking all at once. Jarvis winces.

'I know *that*, lovely boy,' she says when she can speak again. 'That was a test, wasn't it? I didn't come down in the last shower.' She starts to cough again and Jarvis takes the opportunity to hang up.

Five hundred pounds. That's *half a thousand*. Jarvis doesn't know how much they need to raise, he wasn't listening on

Sunday, but that has to be a great start, doesn't it? And *he* did it. He, Jarvis Millwood, waste of space, has generated a substantial contribution to their cause. OK, so it was an incidental benefit to his own quest to find true love, but still. He feels a fizzing inside him – pride. The last time he felt proud was probably when he got accepted to art school. He can't wait to tell Vicar Dave, but more than anything, he wants to tell Gwen. But he doesn't have her phone number. He considers running across town to the estate, but he doesn't know the address, and that aunt of hers sounds like a vulture.

He runs downstairs but the house is still empty. He thinks about texting Royston, but immediately realises he would have zero interest. So back to his room he goes and phones Adam Lansdowne. A woman answers, but when he asks for Patricia, she only barks, 'No one of that name here,' and puts the phone down. Next he tries Parker Lansdowne and a woman answers again. It's Patricia. She has a cut-glass accent, and Jarvis launches into his now familiar spiel about the church roof, wondering how old she is – she has a neutral sort of a voice – and if she could be his mystery girl. They're interrupted by a man's voice in the background: 'Who is it?'

'*Quiet*, Parker!' screeches the woman, then adds in her honeyed telephone voice: 'Please carry on, Mr Millwood.'

'If it's one of your fancy men,' shouts the background voice, 'tell him to bugger off and stop calling the house.'

'Screw *you*. If you must know, it's one of my charitable concerns.'

Jarvis's eyes widen. He sincerely hopes this *isn't* his mystery girl.

A bitter laugh. 'Oh yes, you're all heart.'

Phone voice again. '*Do* excuse me, Mr Millwood. A little miscommunication with my husband. Do continue.'

Jarvis complies, struggling not to laugh. He gets to the end of his explanation without further interruption.

'Of *course* I remember that little church. The dearest little place. I'd be delighted to help. How can I donate?'

'If you want to keep giving money away, why don't you get a job, you lazy cow?'

'*Charming.* You're earning six figures and you begrudge a little church a new roof, you stingy bastard. It's that sweet little place in Kent with the pretty windows. Surely even your tiny brain can remember that?'

'No, I *don't.* You must have gone with one of your lovers.'

'Maybe I did,' murmurs Patricia, sotto voce. 'Again, Mr Millwood. Do you have a donation page?'

Jarvis trots out the 'we're terribly old-fashioned, I'm so sorry' bit again and Patricia coos that it's delightful and sweet and charming and promises to post a cheque the following day.

Jarvis gives her the address and Vicar Dave's proper name and hangs up, wondering how much she'll send and if she'll even send anything at all or if she and her husband will have strangled each other before she can do it. He's turned out to be better at this than he thought. No more phone calls until he knows the official way though. The only thing he *could* do tonight is email Hattie, but the phone calls have taught him a lesson. Better to wait until tomorrow and do it from the church account on the church laptop. She's his only remaining hope to be the girl in lilac – unless it's Imogen from Walthamstow.

He hears the front door and his mum's voice helloing. He leaps off the bed and lopes downstairs.

'Mum!' he shouts. 'Guess what?'

CHAPTER ELEVEN

Gwen

The following morning Gwen gets to the church for eleven. Jarvis is already there. 'What's going on?' demands Gwen. 'Is this some kind of alternate universe?'

'What time do you call this, Gwendoline Poppy? We need to see keen people on this project.'

'Ha ha. Seriously though?'

Jarvis shrugs. He looks less dissolute than usual: his eyes brighter, alcohol fumes not quite so strong. 'Suppose I'm getting into it a bit. And I've got some news.' Gwen raises a questioning eyebrow and goes to the kettle. 'Already boiled,' says Jarvis, uncurling from his chair. 'I'll make it. Sit down – settle in.'

'You're scaring me now.'

'Don't be like that. I'm just in a good mood. I took 2014 home last night and I got some great leads, a few really easy ones. So I made some calls and—'

'Wait. What? Jarvis. We should be doing that *together*. We need to agree what to say, check Reverend Fairfield's happy with it. What if someone had wanted to donate? What would you have done then?'

'That's just it, Gwendoline Poppy. Someone did.'

'But, Jarvis, you could have ruined everything! *How* will they donate? We need to get all the details before we start phoning up random strangers.'

'Stop being such a buzzkill. This is good news, woman. I realised that, didn't I, as soon as I made the first call. She's going to send a cheque, as a matter of fact. I won't do any more until we're properly set up, but we've got our first donation. You're supposed to be pleased.'

He sets a mug of tea and a plate of biscuits in front of Gwen. She takes one and munches absent-mindedly. She feels slightly miffed that Jarvis is forging ahead without her. But on the other hand… The corner of her mouth twitches slightly. 'We're supposed to do it together,' she says, not wanting to let him off too easily.

'Like you haven't been taking the book home every evening.'

'I haven't phoned anyone though.'

'Only because you're too scared. Ask me how much the donation's going to be.'

'How much?'

'Five hundred pounds.'

'Really? That's *amazing*, Jarvis. Well done.'

'That's more like it.'

'I mean it, I was just thrown for a minute. Five hundred pounds. You know what we should do? We should start making a wall chart, with the target at the top and markers along the way and we can colour it in as we get more and more…' Gwen feels all shiny; she loves a good chart.

'Steady, girl. I think we should wait until the cheque actually arrives. I mean, what if she forgets, or changed her mind as soon as she hung up the phone?'

'That's true. But when it arrives, Jarvis, can we make a chart?' Already she can picture it. She'll take a trip to WH Smith and treat herself to some stationery especially for it. They'll be able to see progress, actual progress. For the first time, it dawns on her that this isn't just about her spending time leafing through the visitors' book and daydreaming, that they might actually get some money for the roof fund. And it makes her feel excited.

He nods and sits down again. 'Knock yourself out. I also found an email address for some girl. But I waited,' he adds pointedly, 'until we were together and we could use the church account.'

'Wow, brilliant. Do you want to email her now or should we wait until we have more contacts?'

'Might as well do it as we go along. I guess.'

Gwen looks at him closely. He sounds casual but he's turned a little pink. A blush is easy to spot with his pasty indoors skin – not that she can talk. Is he really that excited about fundraising? 'OK,' she says, passing the laptop over to him. She glances down at his pages and sees that he's looking at May 2014. 'You're on *May* already? You did all those months yesterday?'

'Oh, no. I skipped ahead. I'm going back to February today.'

'Why?'

He shrugs. 'Just fancied having a look further on. Shut up now and let me write this email. Yes, I'll show it to you before I send it.'

'OK.' Gwen pretends to get back to her own work but squints at his notes. She can see a list of names, with lines through some of them. She squints more. Female names. She frowns. What's he up to? She thinks hard. He was super-keen to start work on 2014. He's suddenly all twinkly and motivated. He skipped ahead to early summer when he hasn't even finished the winter or spring. *That's* no way to work through the fundraising possibilities. Unless he's doing something else altogether. She glances at his list again. Is that a *heart* doodled by one of the names?

'Oh…' she says aloud.

'What?'

'You're looking for someone, aren't you?'

'What?'

'You're looking for someone. That's why you wanted to help with the project. I'm right, aren't I?'

He stops typing and looks at her, properly scarlet now. 'I'll tell you if you promise not to laugh and not to tell anyone.'

'OK.'

'And before you ask, yes I am doing it properly – the fundraising thing I mean. I'm doing that as well. But I just need to find this woman…'

As Gwen listens to his story, she finds herself beaming from ear to ear. Jarvis Millwood an incurable romantic. Who'd have thought it? By the time he finishes, she's filled with excitement. 'Oh, Jarvis. That's wonderful, it really is.'

'It is?'

'Well yes. It's so *romantic*. And imagine how you'll feel if you find her. No. *When* you find her. You have to. I'll help you. Show me properly.'

She pulls his notes towards her and listens while he talks her through his findings of last night. She learns that he didn't make just one call, but several, hears about Imogen and Alice, Patricia and her husband. Not only has Jarvis invited not one but two donations by cheque, he's also committed them to holding a party. It's all she can do not to grit her teeth in frustration, but just for now this is about finding his lost girl.

'It can't be Nancy from Ohio,' Gwen decrees. 'You'd have noticed if she had an American accent. It could be Karla, I agree, but equally it could be Imogen. Or someone who didn't write in the book. It doesn't mean she won't come back.'

'Well, I haven't seen her since.'

'How much time do you actually *spend* at the church?'

'Good point.'

'She could have been back two or three times. She might not have written in the book that day because she'd already written in it. She might still be coming, for all you know. Basically, Jarvis, she could be anywhere in this book.'

And Jarvis, whose colour had subsided, turns pink again.

CHAPTER TWELVE

Vicar Dave

It's time to check on Jarvis and Gwen. David wanders the path from the vicarage to the church, hardly daring to imagine how they're getting on. He's left them to it for a few days, to give them a chance to settle in together; they're such an unlikely pair. He can't imagine what they might have in common with each other – or, indeed, anyone. Gwen seemed less than pleased to have Jarvis on board and he can't say he blames her – Jarvis is a good lad at heart, but he can look a bit off-putting.

It's been a tough week, with the archdeacon on the phone again wanting an update – and there's nothing more dispiriting than an update when there's nothing to report.

'If we can't fix this by the first of September, David, we'll have to pull the plug,' William said at the end of the conversation. And David couldn't deny that it was looking very unlikely. But he hasn't lost hope altogether. He'd had a dream just a couple of nights before, surprisingly vivid – more of a vision really, he told the archdeacon. In it, he, his flock and a great number of other people, people of all ages, colours and creeds, were mingling at a party. They were celebrating the saving of St Dom's. It had been so real that he'd woken up truly joyful, thinking it had actually happened.

'So you're saying... God wants you to have a party?' The archdeacon's tone was scathing.

'I believe God is telling me there will *be* a party because there'll be cause to celebrate,' said David, a little nettled. The dream had meant something – David was sure of it.

The archdeacon sighed. 'The first of September, David – I mean it. I'll start looking into alternative placements for you.'

On top of all that, Wendy was upset at school when they tried to put her in a green costume for the school play. His fault and Annie's; they'd forgotten to tell the school that she hates green. There are so many odd things she hates, and they keep discovering new ones. It's hard to give a full picture, even though Annie had stayed up late writing a report when Wendy first went to the school, and when she'd showed it to David, he'd thought of quite a few more things to add. Anyway, poor Wendy had an absolute screaming fit about the costume and that always leaves her very jumpy. David yawns as he pushes the church door open. There've been some disturbed nights at the vicarage.

Inside the church, he pauses a moment to remind himself that miracles are possible in any moment, to say a quick prayer for the roof and the future of St Dom's, and goes to the office to look out his unlikely deliverers. A completely unexpected scene greets him. Jarvis and Gwen, working side by side, in silence, wholly absorbed. Jarvis is drinking tea and Gwen's plate of biscuits is pushed to one side. He gives a little tap on the door, and they both look pleased to see him.

'Oh hello,' says Gwen. 'I was going to text you today and ask you to call in. We need you.'

What's *happened* to her? It's as if she's forgotten to be frightened. 'Anything wrong?' asks David.

'No, we've got good news,' says Jarvis, lurching to his feet to give a clumsy handshake. 'Good timing, my man, good timing.'

'Jarvis, you can't call Reverend Fairfield *my man*,' scolds Gwen.

'I don't mind, Gwen, honestly. And I do wish you'd call me David, or Dave if you like, or Vicar… Reverend Fairfield sounds so formal. It makes me feel I'm in a meeting with the archdeacon and I've had enough of those lately. What's the good news?'

'You go,' says Jarvis to Gwen.

'No, it's your contact.'

'No, you…'

What are they, a team? *Friends?* He never would have predicted this in a hundred years. '*Someone* tell me,' David says, laughing.

'Well,' says Gwen, eyes sparkling, 'Jarvis has spoken to a lady who's going to send us a cheque for five hundred pounds.'

'So we need to get the details of all the proper ways to donate,' adds Jarvis. 'I didn't realise I didn't know them until I started calling. You need to get us all set up.'

'Oh yes, of course. It's all on the laptop – I'll show you. But, wait. You've started making phone calls *already?* Five hundred *pounds?*'

'Where will the cheque come to?' asks Gwen eagerly. 'Here or the vicarage? He gave her the church address. I want to start a chart so we can keep track of progress. But I won't do it until the cheque's actually arrived. Just in case, you know, it gets lost, or she changes her mind.'

David is lost for words. Gwen's like a different person. And *Jarvis* has just single-handedly raised more money than they've made from the last three bake sales. 'Er, to the vicarage,' he says, gathering himself. 'But I'll let you know as soon as it arrives, I promise. This is very exciting. I'm so impressed. Let me show you the donation page, and will you show me what you've been doing?'

'Take a pew,' quips Jarvis, 'or at least, a plastic chair.'

'I'll put the kettle on,' says Gwen.

CHAPTER THIRTEEN

Gwen

Gwen is so caught up in her new life that's suddenly flourishing and budding that she almost forgot about her job. She's supposed to work every Thursday and Friday, but she emailed at the last minute to take annual leave this week. Her boss was amenable; the office is hardly pressurised at the best of times. She's so glad she did it, otherwise she wouldn't have been there today to hear about Jarvis's unexpected success, or his secret love, or for Vicar Dave's visit. She's settled on 'Vicar' in conversation, but because Jarvis calls him Vicar Dave, that's how she thinks of him now. His *face*, when they told him about the donation. It's nice to please someone again.

Before she knows it, another day has passed and it's Friday evening. The equivalent of a whole working week has flown by. She's never had a job she enjoyed as much as this. It strikes her then that she'd far rather be at the church, or in Jarvis's house, than at home. That's not good. 'See you tomorrow?' she asks Jarvis, rather doubtfully, when they leave. He probably has revelling to do on the weekends.

'Nah, I work at Speedy-Spend on Fridays and Saturdays.'

'Oh right. Wait, *today's* Friday.'

'Yeah, I called in sick.' Jarvis looks sheepish. 'I wanted to do this instead. You're turning me into a nerd, Gwendoline Poppy.'

Gwen smiles. 'I work Thursdays and Fridays. I took annual leave this week so I could do this.'

'You know,' says Jarvis, 'for two people who have nothing in common, we have an amazing amount in common. We both live in Loserville, we both work two days a week in crap jobs. You live with your auntie, I live with my parents. I'm a failed artist, and you're a failed writer.'

'I'm not a failed writer. I'm not a writer at all.'

'Not trying is failure by definition,' says Jarvis sagely. 'That's what my father tells me. Anyway, will you come in tomorrow when I'm at work, or wait until Monday?'

Gwen's heart sinks. She can tell by his face that he wants her to wait. And she has to admit, it won't be the same without him. It's just that Monday suddenly seems an awfully long time away. 'I'll wait until Monday,' she tells him and is comforted slightly by his grin. 'Hey, do you fancy a quick pint at the Swan before we go home?'

'I can't,' he says glumly. 'My pain-in-the-ass sister is coming home for a night and I'm expected at a family dinner. Then after that I'm getting trashed with Andy. Not *too* trashed though because of work tomorrow…' He heaves a great sigh, as if balancing the different imperatives of his life is unbearably stressful.

Gwen heads home, listless, dreading the evening ahead. But what can she do? She has no friends in Hopley. She can't tell Aunt Mary she's sick again. Icky dinner and bile it is then.

On an impulse, Gwen stops at the Speedy-Spend to buy flowers for Aunt Mary. Some purple phlox and mini daffodils, pretty and Eastery. She can't go home in her current state of dread. Her mother always told her that doing something nice for someone you dislike can defuse the bad feelings. Even so, she enters the house with her stomach in knots. Immediately her aunt materialises in the hall, apron on. 'Oh good. I never know whether to expect you or not these days. I'm making bolognese. I could do with a hand.' She disappears back into the kitchen.

'I'm fine, thanks. Yes, my day was good,' whispers Gwen, taking her coat and shoes off.

'What was that?' calls Aunt Mary from the kitchen.

Dear God, the woman has the ears of a fox.

'I brought you some flowers,' says Gwen, going into the kitchen, which is steamed up and fuggy. She opens a window. Since her aunt makes no move to take the flowers, she lays them on the counter.

'Don't do that. Or that.' Aunt Mary snatches up the flowers, then dashes over to slam the window shut. 'You can't put flowers where food's being prepared, and I don't want flies getting in. Didn't your mother teach you anything?'

Gwen says nothing. She especially hates when Aunt Mary talks about her mum like that – so offhand and disrespectful, as if she's completely forgotten that she's dead and Gwen is still tender.

'What are these for then?' asks her aunt, about the flowers.

'Just a little present to say happy weekend.'

'Oh, weekend is it? Well, my work never stops. And now I've got to stop and put these in water I suppose, when everything's coming to the boil and dinner's at a crucial point. I never thought a present was something that created even *more* work, but I suppose some people don't think.'

'I can do them. Or I'm sure they'll last half an hour until after we've eaten.'

'No, no, I'll do them. You'll only mess them up. And I'll have to get them out of the kitchen before we eat. I won't be able to taste the food through the stink of those purple ones...'

And so it goes, another Friday evening, like so many others. At 8.30 p.m. Gwen excuses herself, saying she's tired and retreats to her room.

'I'm not surprised you're tired after all the time you've put in at that church. Shame you couldn't make the same effort with finding a real job. Well, you won't be going tomorrow at least. That man doesn't expect you to give up your weekends as well I hope?'

Because otherwise they're such a pleasure, thinks Gwen grimly. 'I will be going actually,' she says aloud. 'We're getting on quite well and I want to keep going.'

As she climbs the stairs, she's glad she thought to say it. Even though it's not true, at least it gets her out of the house for the day if she can think of anything she wants to do. If not, she can always say she's changed her mind. She feels a bit flat, wondering what's for dinner at Jarvis's house, what his sister's like, whether the cheque from Alice will arrive at the vicarage over the weekend. It's as though her real life is unfolding everywhere but here, the house where she lives.

The next morning, she wakes bright and early, with a daring idea. She's often dreamed of spending a day at the library, writing, but she's never been able to think of a credible excuse and she certainly wouldn't tell Aunt Mary the truth for fear of mockery. Now she has the opportunity. Her aunt will think she's at the church. Jarvis wants her to try writing again.

Although the thought of it sort of terrifies Gwen, anything's better than spending the day here. She jumps out of bed and showers with more energy than she's done in months. She puts a fresh notebook in her tote, together with the novel she's currently reading and two biros, and legs it. Saturday is the one day Aunt Mary has a lie-in. Gwen scribbles a note and leaves it on the kitchen table.

It's another pale, slightly sunny day. She's in a good mood as she saunters into town. She starts with breakfast at the café – scrambled eggs on granary and hot chocolate – then heads to the library. She finds a small table in the window and settles in. Bliss.

A whole day to herself, to do whatever she wants – her options being limited, admittedly.

Gwen opens her notebooks and realises she has absolutely no idea what she wants to write. She stares out at the shopfronts and pedestrians of Hopley's high street and the skidding spring clouds, feeling herself deflate. What was she thinking? She can't do this. It's all very well getting fired up when Jarvis is encouraging her and she's mellow from half a pint of Kentish Galleon, but this is real life. As Jarvis pointed out, she's not so good with real life. She sighs. She can't give up after five minutes, can she? She feels very self-conscious sitting there doing nothing, even though no one's actually giving her a second glance. The library is small and modern, encased in an unattractive concrete block, but inside it's airy and welcoming. She could always just sit and read her book. And then it strikes her how ridiculous her life has become.

Lying and making up excuses to get out for the day, in order to sit in a library. Working two days a week at a job that's so far from challenging her brain that it was in danger of turning into a cauliflower before the visitors' book came along. No one to spend a Saturday with.

And why does she stay? At first it was for the comfort of a family connection and because she was too devastated to do anything else. But Aunt Mary was never any comfort and now, well yes, she's still devastated of course, but not past the point of functioning. This week has shown her that she's capable of doing things, thinking constructively, even enjoying herself. Mum and Dad would be heartbroken if they could see her now. Gwen's never going to be a hard-nosed businesswoman, or a party girl. But that doesn't mean she should opt out of life altogether. All the lovely things she shared with her parents are gone. But there can be other lovely things. Everyone needs something to look forward to. Without that, you stagnate and shrivel – Gwen is living proof.

She's startled from the intense business of staring her life in the face by her phone tinkling a text notification. Mortified, she makes deeply apologetic faces at the disapproving librarian, scrambling in her bag and knocking her notebook off the table in the process. The librarian taps the *Mobile Phones on Silent Please* sign and Gwen feels like a disgrace to human beings. It just never occurred to her to put hers on silent because no one ever contacts her except for Amma.

But it's Vicar Dave.

Hello, Gwen, I hope you're well. The cheque is here. In fact, there are two. Do call in if you'd like to. David.

Two. Does that mean the philandering Patricia sent one too? What a shame that Jarvis is working. Gwen gathers all her things together and sidles out of the library, then hastens to the church. It's empty. He must be at home. Can she actually go and call at the vicarage?

Curiosity trumps shyness. Gwen sets off along the path and knocks on the door before she can lose her nerve. A sweet-faced woman answers, looking harassed. A teenage girl stands in the attractive flagged hallway wailing and hugging her arms around herself, swinging from side to side.

'Oh, is everything alright?' asks Gwen before she can stop herself.

The woman smiles and opens the door wider. 'Hello, you must be Gwen. David said you might call. Come on in. I'm Annie and this is Wendy, and yes, we're fine thanks, only Wendy's feeling a bit overwhelmed just now.'

'Oh God, I know the feeling,' says Gwen.

'Wendy, sweetheart, this is Gwen from the parish. Would you like to say hello?'

Wendy stops wailing and looks at Gwen. 'You're helping to do fundraising.'

'That's right,' says Gwen. She isn't sure quite what's wrong with Wendy, but the poor girl looks very much as Gwen feels most of the time, utterly distraught and wrung out.

'Would you like a cup of tea?' asks Wendy, pushing her hair out of her face and wiping her eyes.

Gwen hesitates and looks at Annie. 'Wendy makes a lovely cup of tea,' says Annie encouragingly.

'Then yes please, if you're sure it's no trouble.'

'It's OK,' says Wendy and disappears.

'I'm sorry if I've come at a bad time,' says Gwen to Annie.

'Your timing actually couldn't be better. I don't know if David mentioned it, but Wendy's autistic. She's normally pretty even and copes very well, but she's had a difficult week. You've distracted her. She's quite proud of her hostess skills – they haven't been easy for her to learn. Anyway, it's lovely to meet you, Gwen. Thanks for all you're doing to help David out. He's always so busy, and I've got my hands full with Wendy…'

'Oh, it's a pleasure. Wendy seems lovely. I know what it's like to feel rubbish so if I can help any time… Although I don't know anything about autism so I'd probably mess it up.'

'Oh no, you wouldn't. I'd be so grateful. Wendy could do with a bit of company outside school. Let's have a coffee sometime when things are a bit quieter.'

Gwen can't believe she's being so outgoing. It's not like her at all. She's starting to feel like she does have something to offer after all. It's only at home that she still feels useless.

Annie shows her into David's study and Wendy brings a cup of tea and a plate of biscuits, arranged on a pretty serviette. 'What a treat,' says Gwen. 'Thanks, Wendy.'

David shows her the cheques. First is the promised £500 from Alice. It's tucked inside a notelet with a picture of a bunny on the front. The note reads:

Happy Easter. It was a pleasure to talk to that nice young man. I wish you every success and prosperity. Alice Griffiths (Mrs).

The second is for £2,000. Gwen can hardly believe her eyes. It's accompanied by a business card, the name Patricia Lansdowne embossed in glossy black on cream with a mobile number, email address and Instagram account. On the back is simply scrawled *Best regards, P.*

'I can't believe it,' says Gwen.

'*You* can't? *I* can't. Gwen, you do realise that this is more money than we've added to the roof fund in two years? And to hear Jarvis described as a nice young man by a total stranger. I know he's got a heart of gold of course, but he doesn't always make the best first impression.'

'He's done really well. This is amazing. Can I take these to show him? He's at work today and I feel terrible knowing before he does.'

'Of course. You could bank them for me if you felt so inclined – it would save me a walk into town.'

'That's fine. Where do I go? What do I need?'

Suddenly Gwen's day is full of errands and purpose. First of all, she goes to Speedy-Spend where there's no sign of Jarvis. She asks a member of staff where he is, a hefty middle-aged man who says, 'You're his parole officer, are you?' Then, seeing Gwen's startled face, he guffaws. 'Only kidding. He's out the back on his break. Permanently on a break, that one. You're not supposed to go back there, but if you don't tell anyone I let you through…'

He swipes his staff card to open a grey door and Gwen finds herself in a concrete-floored storage room. The fire door is open and Jarvis is sitting in his usual, almost-horizontal position, his bum almost sliding off his chair, long legs stretched out in front. He's staring into space, smoking.

'Hey,' says Gwen. 'I've got something to show you.'

'I've told you before,' he says without turning. 'I don't want to see your bra.'

'What? No, it's me.'

He turns, laughing. 'I know. Just winding you up. I didn't expect to see you today. What brings you here? My animal magnetism?'

Gwen rolls her eyes. 'Undeniable though that is,' she says, entering into the spirit of things, 'I had a text from Vicar Dave earlier. I thought you'd want to see these.'

She hands him the cheques and the notes and watches his face turn that pale rosy pink. It's strange seeing him in the Speedy-Spend navy and white nylon tabard, with a little plastic name badge. Jarvis Millwood, working for the man.

'Alice came through,' he says fondly. 'And Patricia's scary but... *two thousand pounds*. How excited was Vicar Dave?'

'So excited. Oh, Jarvis, well done. You've really kicked things off in a big way. I think you should do all the phoning from now on.'

'No way. You ring your contacts, I'll ring mine. Unless one of us ends up with loads more than the other.'

'But you're *good* at this.'

'Yeah, but who knew, right? You might be good at it too if you try.'

Gwen sighs. They chat for a minute then the big man Gwen spoke to comes to tell Jarvis to get on the tills. 'Bummer,' says Jarvis equably. 'Sorry, woman.'

'It's fine. I have to go and bank these anyway.'

'You'd better get a rock on then. Bank closes at twelve.'

'Does it? Oh God. Bye, Jarvis.'

She races out of Speedy-Spend, down the street to the bank, only to find when she gets there that it closes at one. Puffing and panting, she takes her place in the queue. Her satisfaction at making such a sizeable deposit in the church account is immense.

Next, she treats herself to the promised spree in WH Smith. She buys several sheets of A3 card, large craft scissors, marker pens and some stickers. Then she walks out to the church to deposit it all, ready for Monday. There's no way she wants Aunt Mary seeing it and making fun of her. Then back into town for lunch… Gwen realises that she's done more walking this week – more walking today in fact – than she did in a month before. And she hasn't thought about chocolate all morning. Well, there's a lesson to be learned in that. She has lunch in the same café, then goes back to the library and forces herself to sit there until she's written something.

CHAPTER FOURTEEN

Jarvis

Jarvis gets coerced into working on Sunday too – he can't very well say no after calling in sick on Friday – which means he decides against going out on Saturday night. By Monday he's had two clear nights and is surprised to find himself arriving at the church at 10.30 a.m. Gwen is only just taking her coat off when he gets there.

'Hi. How are you?' She looks so pleased to see him that he can't help grinning. Sitting in a church office with a socially inept girl, unpaid, on a worthy quest, really shouldn't be so much fun. Well, maybe it won't be for much longer. Maybe he'll find his mystery girl soon. He may as well stay until then, he supposes...

'What's all that?' asks Jarvis, nodding at the huge carrier bag of stationery on the table.

'Oh, stuff to make a chart to see our progress. I can do that later. I thought maybe we should also keep a record of what ground we've covered. I've been chronological, as you know, but you've jumped around a bit, and we don't want to miss sections.'

'Let's do that first,' says Jarvis. 'Then we can see how many decent contacts we have from how much time. It'll give us an idea of how many we'll have when we're finished.'

Gwen beams. 'Good idea.'

It's so easy to make her happy that it's hard to believe she was quite so unhappy when he met her only a week ago. That aunt of hers must be a serious bummer.

'So, I've covered January 2007 to June 2008. And you've done…'

'January to November 2014. How have you done more than me? You work so slowly.'

'I'm not slow, I'm thorough. Probably just because I did longer days than you. So from a year and a half I've got… wow, only two definite contacts: one phone number and one email address. That's depressing. And about five I reckon we could definitely find with a bit of detective work. After that it gets a bit tenuous. How about you?'

'I've done nearly a year and I've contacted four already – the three I phoned, and I emailed Hattie on Thursday. Otherwise I've only got one more email we can try. Why don't we follow up those today? Maybe Monday could be our day to contact all the people we found the week before.'

'That's a good idea.' Gwen looks thoughtful. 'We may as well. It might take some people a while to get back to us and if anyone donates that'll make us feel really good. You know what else we should do? Make a spreadsheet. We can put in all the names we want to contact and mark whether we've contacted them yet, whether we need to find more information first and so on. Otherwise we'll get in a tangle about who's who and who said what. What? Why do you keep grinning at me?'

'Ooh! Ooh! Let's make a spreadsheet!' enthuses Jarvis, waving his hands about. 'You crack me up. You're right though. I'm getting confused already.'

'Easily done, I should imagine,' says Gwen, giving him a snippy look. 'OK, why don't I start the spreadsheet, seeing as you're too cool for Excel, and you keep going with the book so you can get to the end of 2014. That'll be nice and neat.'

'Lovely and neat. I do like neat things,' murmurs Jarvis innocently and dodges a whack on the arm. He is truly disconcerted by the feeling of well-being bubbling within him. What *is* it? He hadn't thought there was anything wrong before; he wasn't a walking misery, like Gwen was. *But*, he thinks, as he obediently pulls his copied pages towards him, *something was missing.* Several things. Purpose, self-respect, perhaps even friendship, which is a weird thing to think. Jarvis has loads of friends; he's an easygoing, fun guy. But all those friendships seem to revolve around the pub. He can't remember the last time someone asked him to watch a movie or invited him to a barbeque or suggested a road trip. He hasn't mentioned the visitors' book to any of them, not because he's ashamed of it, but because he instinctively knows they won't get it, and those aren't the sorts of conversations they have. Which is a little... boring, really. Does this mean he's more of a geek than he realised?

He sighs weightily and turns his attention to Derek Prosser, Edinburgh. *A very nice church.* Calm down, Derek – don't get too excited. Then the Mumford Family from Devon. *The highlight of our day out. Enchanting, tranquil and lovely windows.* That's more like it, Mumfords. The vast majority of the entries are like that though, pretty much impossible to trace. Jarvis knows he just struck lucky that first evening with all those people who were easy to find. It's almost as if the universe was teasing him: 'Look, Jarvis. All these people who *could* be your true love.'

Here's a really illegible one. Jarvis squints to make sense of the terrible handwriting and spelling.

November 30 2014. Jase Norris, Milton Keynes. I come to say thank you to the vicar but he wasnt here. I had a long-lost dorter what hated me. I was a rite bastud on the drink. Stopped all that now. Didn't see her for ~~ayteen ciht~~ 18 years but I come here and I preyed and she turned up. Never had much. Now she buys me a meal once a month and fixed me up with some nice curtins and 'emale'. I'm turning it around. Thanks to that preying.

The email address is squashed in at the bottom of the box. It's hard to see exactly what it is as the line of the box below is running through it. Is that an A or an E? An L or a number one? Jarvis will try all the permutations. He makes a note on his sheets of paper. There are a few of them now. Not to sound like Gwen or anything, but maybe he should get a notebook so he doesn't lose them. Jarvis has great experience of losing things. Sunglasses, sweaters, often a shoe, twice his wallet… What a lovely story Jase's is though. He feels a bit bad really, asking him for money when he'd never had much and gets excited about new curtains. But maybe the last three years have been kind to him. You never know. Next to him, Gwen exclaims before he can tell her.

'Oh!' she says in an excited tone of voice. 'Wait,' she adds, raising a hand. 'Wait… oh.' The second *oh* sounds disappointed. 'That's sweet though.'

'*What?*'

She turns the laptop so he can read the screen. Hattie has replied to his email.

Dear Jarvis,

Thanks for the note. I remember that place. I was on my third gap year when I passed through Kent – sixteen countries in twelve months. I thought I'd never settle down, but eventually I married a Londoner so I'm making a home there now. Jeez, it's expensive. London and the wedding both. Also, I now work as a fashion assistant on a magazine, which is my way of saying that I'm totally skint. However, I do have fond memories so I've made a small donation of £20 to your

JustGiving page. I'm sorry it's small. I hope you can raise the money you need.

Best, Hattie Walsh (Mrs…☺)

'Well,' says Jarvis, 'if she is the girl I saw, she's married now. Nice of her to send some money though.'

'I'm sorry, Jarvis. I know it's a cliché, but I really do believe that if it's meant to be, it'll be. And if not, then there's someone else out there for you who's even better.'

'Cheers, yeah. I mean, it's stupid really, isn't it? I only saw her once. What are the odds of finding her after three years, and of her being single, and being interested in me? It's just something I've got to do, I guess.'

'Fair enough,' Gwen says with a nod, turning back to her spreadsheet.

Jarvis likes the way she keeps things simple, doesn't make fun of him, doesn't make a drama out of it. He gets back to the book; she enters all the names, then pulls everything out of the carrier bag. Paper, pens… she's gone to town.

'I've been dying to do this,' she explains. 'Now that we've got three donations, it's definitely time to start. Well done, Jarvis, seriously. They're all people you contacted.'

'That's because you haven't contacted anyone yet. Why don't you phone that number you've got before you start your arts and crafts act?'

'Oh, no. I don't want to. I really don't. You do it, Jarvis. You're so good at it.'

'No. Give it a try. If you really, really hate it after you make a few calls, I'll do the rest. But you should have a go. You should be the voice of this project just as much as me.' He feels strongly about that. It seems to Jarvis that Gwen is smarter than him, more dedicated, and this whole thing is right up her alley. She shouldn't back away from it. Besides, look how she's... blossomed, his mum would call it, in just a week. Maybe the more she does, the more she'll blossom. And let's be honest, she needs to.

'Make the call, then do the chart. My parents always tell me to get the thing I'm dreading out of the way quickly, then reward myself with the thing I want to do.'

'And do you listen?'

'No, of course not. But I'm a dumbass. You're not. Shape up, Gwendoline Poppy.'

She smiles. 'Shape up. My gran used to say that. I don't know... give me a while to think about it.'

'No. It'll only feel worse then.' He tries to think of how he can persuade her. Then he hits on it. 'You're invited to lunch at mine, by the way. Mum said. But if you don't make the call, you can't come. How's that?'

He can't help noticing how she lights up at the invitation. His mother was right – as usual. She *really* needs some friends. Or even just some normal people in her life, though how many people would class him as normal is debatable, he knows.

'Alright, alright.' Grumbling, she consults her notebook, gets out her phone, then sits there silently for a long time. Jarvis gets on with his work and finds, at the very end of December, another good one. A Twitter handle. He makes a note. That'll be worth trying.

Gwen eventually keys in a number and lifts the phone to her ear. *Please let her get through*, thinks Jarvis. If the person doesn't pick up, it'll take her another couple of hours to try again.

'Er, hello? Hello? Oh. Hello. Hi. Um, is that, um, Lavender Hamilton please?' *Oh Gwen.* She sounds like a little girl, timid and squeaky. And trust Gwen to find someone called Lavender, for goodness' sake.

'Oh. Good. Well, my name is Gwen Stanley and I'm calling with a bit of a request... No, no, I'm not selling anything, honestly…' *Oh God, Gwen, don't start off warning them that you want something.* 'I'm phoning from St Domneva's Church in Kent. You visited, oh, nearly ten years ago, so I'm sure you probably don't remember…'

Jarvis fights the urge to groan and snatch the phone out of her hands. It's like listening to Gwen of a week ago. But gradually, falteringly, she gets into her stride. It's all a bit long-winded for Jarvis's taste, but obviously this Lavender person is the patient type, and Gwen's affection for the church and the project comes across loud and clear. Then comes a long gap, punctuated with 'mm hmm' and 'I see', and then Gwen thanks her and hangs up.

'Oh my God, that was horrible. Well, not at the end, but I felt so *uncomfortable.*' She's all flushed and hyperventilating.

'You did great. I take it she said no?'

'She's very elderly. She's a widow and really poor. But she was very nice and apologetic.'

'That's fair enough. See? You did it.'

'Yes. I wish she'd said yes though. I'll just email this address I've got, then that's both my contacts done.'

Soon, Gwen is sitting on the floor like a child in playgroup, her making-a-chart things spread out all around her. Jarvis watches her for a minute, smiling, then shakes his head in disbelief. He gets to the end of 2014 and reaches for the laptop to write to Jase Norris's various possible email addresses and look up @ purplemarcella on Twitter.

CHAPTER FIFTEEN

Gwen

A sudden high-pitched beeping makes Gwen jump. She's completely engrossed in making her chart. It isn't practical, like the spreadsheet. She wants this to be totally motivational, somewhere where they can see their progress at a glance. She's drawn a rocket pointing skywards, and marked off the numbers along its length, with the grand total they have to raise – £50,000 – at the top.

'What *is* that?' she asks as the beeping continues. Jarvis shrugs, busy doing something on the internet. 'It's coming from you,' she points out. 'It's your watch.'

'Oh. Yeah.' He presses a button on his watch and the beeping stops. 'My mum must've set an alarm. She does that because I tend to lose track of time. Yeah, look, it's lunchtime.'

'Great.' Gwen leaps to her feet, not disguising how excited she is about seeing Justine again and eating her gorgeous cooking. Jarvis shuts the laptop and slides to the vertical.

'Woah.' He turns and sees the chart she's made. 'Gwen, love, steady on.'

'What?'

'Why have you drawn a massive penis?'

'*What*? I haven't! It's a rocket, you fool. I thought it would be a bit more fun than just doing a graph or something. A bit more interesting.'

Jarvis squints. 'It's interesting alright. Gwendoline Poppy, maybe you should stick with words and leave the visuals to me. That's phallic. Must be your subconscious longings coming out.'

'Shut up. Look, those are the launchy bits, and that's the top of the rocket… Anyway, let's argue about it later – we don't want to keep your mum waiting.'

Jarvis chuckles all the way home, much to Gwen's annoyance.

After a warm welcome from Justine, a lovely meal and good conversation, Jarvis and Gwen head back to the church, ready to search out some more contacts. Jarvis has told her about Jase Norris's entry and Gwen is deeply moved. She can also feel herself glowing from Justine's motherly attentions. *I wish I could stay there forever*, she thinks and then realises something. She's been trying to recreate or replace what she had with her parents, first casting Aunt Mary in the role of senior family figure, guardian and guide. And now, in the face of her aunt's spectacular failure to be that person, she's pining after Justine. But it can't be done. The time to have that, for her, is over. The only option open to her now, much as she dislikes it, much as she doesn't feel ready, is to be her own person, standing on her own two feet. At some point, she knows, she will have to start moving forward.

When they enter the office, they find Vicar Dave. He's staring at Gwen's chart with a very perplexed expression and is slightly pink in the face.

'Hello,' says Gwen cheerily. 'We're getting on so well. We had another donation today, though only a small one – £20.'

'Oh good, marvellous. Well done, you two,' says Vicar Dave. 'And, er, this is…?'

'Oh, this is the chart I'm making to show our progress. See, here's zero, our starting point, at the bottom, and here's £50,000 at the top. We're here, just a little way up, on £14,520. She kneels down and marks it off with a little flourish.'

'That's great, Gwen. Only, can I ask, do you think that's entirely appropriate? I mean, why a… a…?'

'Vicar Dave thinks it looks like a penis too,' puts in Jarvis helpfully.

'He does *not*,' exclaims Gwen hotly. 'Do you?' she adds anxiously.

'Um… I'm afraid so.'

'It was meant to be a rocket.'

'*Oh*,' says Vicar Dave, light dawning on his face together with an expression of great relief. 'That makes more sense. I thought it didn't seem very you. It's not, um, *immediately* apparent it's a rocket – perhaps, if we're going to display it in the church, we should try something different. Even something simple, just a line chart.'

'Oh. OK.' Gwen feels sad. She wanted to do something fun. Not a stupid line chart. She even bought star stickers to dot around it, to suggest the rocket hurtling through space.

'Tell you what,' says Jarvis. 'Gwen, you show Vicar Dave the spreadsheet and I'll try something else, see if you like it.'

So Gwen gets up and Jarvis folds to the floor and starts wielding marker pens. Vicar Dave is very impressed with the spreadsheet, and they chat for a few minutes about the various people they hope to find ways to contact. Then Jarvis says, 'There,' and turns around with a flourish.

'Wow,' says Gwen at once.

'That's perfect,' says Vicar Dave. 'How clever you are, Jarvis.'

Jarvis has drawn the St Domneva church tower. Unlike Gwen's rocket, it doesn't look remotely phallic – it looks like a church tower. At the bottom, a little of the church roof can be seen, and on the left, a few yew branches sweep into the picture. He's marked off the amount in the same increments that Gwen did and coloured in their progress so far.

'Like it? Both happy with it? Good.' He picks up the packet of stickers. 'Do you want to put these on, Gwen? They can be stars in the night sky, or the stars smiling on our efforts or whatever.' He throws the packet at Gwen, who makes a great fumble in the air with her hands, then drops it.

'I'll leave you to it,' says Vicar Dave with a smile.

'Jarvis, this is seriously amazing,' says Gwen when he's gone, standing beside him, the pair of them looking down at his drawing.

'It's nothing,' scoffs Jarvis. 'Just a quick scribble. Nothing to get excited about.'

'No, it *is*. If this is what you can do in three minutes, if this is your idea of a scribble, I can only imagine what your real work is like.'

'There *is* no real work. Not anymore. Come on, Gwen, let's get back to it.'

Gwen backs off and sets to work sticking stars, liberally, over the A3 page on which Jarvis has drawn their chart. She likes how he bothered to draw something because he knows she didn't want just a boring old graph. And how he's leaving the stickers for her to do, so she's contributed a little bit to it even though she has – clearly – no artistic talent whatsoever. She goes pink thinking about her attempt. *How embarrassing.*

The rest of 2008 yields nothing. It's just a sea of people giving their first names and counties or countries of origin, for the most part. Easy enough to whisk through but not rewarding. Disappointed, Gwen glances at the time – 4.30 p.m. Beside her, Jarvis is working away quietly. She makes a start on 2009. It starts off much the same way, then in early March, something interesting, at last.

In the 'Name' box, the guy has just written 'Bry'. But his comment is wonderful:

Always look at the world with the eyes of a wanderer. Always greet people and places with the spirit of an adventurer. Always expect to find hidden treasures in unlikely places. This church has a little magic, I think, and not a few stories contained in its walls.

Oh, Gwen *loves* this guy. And under 'Contact', he's written a website address: www.bryanbolan.com.

Gwen reaches for the laptop and looks him up. He appears to be some sort of travel writer. His website is full of very amateur but still amazing photos. Some of them have thumbs in the corner and many are over or underexposed. But Gwen gets lost in them the way she gets lost in the visitors' book; they set her dreaming and imagining… Cherry blossoms in Japan – she's always wanted to see them – a Buddhist temple in Cambodia, surfers in Bali, a sunset beach in Australia… all places Gwen would never have the guts to go in a million years but oh, how beautiful.

She clicks on 'About Me' and sees, to her surprise, a photo of a middle-aged man with quite a few whiskers. She'd imagined 'Bry' to be someone young and intrepid. In the photo he's waiting at a bus stop somewhere remote, with a huge backpack. Unless bus stops are built differently wherever he is, he's not tall. He looks small and timid and rather unlikely. Yet the photos are captioned with thoughtful comments like the one he wrote in the visitors' book, and there are links to his blog. Gwen clicks on a couple and reads some really interesting posts. He writes in a very relatable way, not only describing what he's seen but sharing what they've meant to him personally. He's a widower, poor thing, and in all his travels, he imagines what his wife would have thought of them. Excited, Gwen clicks on 'Contact' and copies and pastes in the email that she and Jarvis have composed together. She hesitates then adds a paragraph at the end.

The above is all you really need to know. But I just wanted to thank you for leaving us your website address. I've just had a wonderful time looking through it. Your photos have transported me to beautiful places I will never see. Your blog posts have inspired me. I love writing myself and when I was younger always wanted to be an author – which clearly will never happen. I was also impressed by the way you share your personal experiences in your writing, so I just wanted to tell you that I'm twenty-six and terminally shy. My parents died two years ago and my world basically ended. I have not yet rebuilt it, but trying to raise funds for St Domneva's has made me a new friend and given me some happy days that I never expected to have. Thank you, and happy travels.

Gwen

She closes the laptop and looks at Jarvis. He's still quiet, jotting something on a piece of paper. She frowns. 'Wouldn't you like a notebook so you don't have all those loose sheets of paper?' she wonders. 'They must be a pain, and easy to lose.'

He looks up. 'Yeah, I thought that earlier. I'll get one.'

'I'll give you one – I've got loads. I love stationary.'

He grins. 'Why does that not surprise me. Thanks, Gwendoline Poppy.'

Gwen looks at his chart again. It's remarkably good. Just a few lines in black marker pen, and yet it's St Dom's. But something tells her she shouldn't bring up his art again. 'Guess what I did on Saturday?' she says instead.

'What?'

'I went to the library. Made myself sit there until I'd written something. I thought about what you said. In the pub.'

He sits up and looks at her. 'You did? That's great. So, did you get something done?'

'Not for ages. But then, yes. I started a short story.'

'That's cool. Will you finish it?'

'I think so. Maybe next Saturday, when we're not here. Or maybe one evening.'

'Can I read it?'

'No. God no. Or… maybe. Just not quite yet.'

'OK. That's cool. I never used to show anyone what I was working on until it was finished either.'

'I thought about how you said it's failing if you don't try, and how if it makes me happy then it's better than doing all the things I do that *don't* make me happy… I know I'll never get anywhere with it, but you were right – it did feel good.'

'That's cool. I think it's the first time anyone's ever taken advice from me that hasn't ended up with them flying down the high street in a shopping trolley, or climbing over park railings at 2 a.m. and slipping and ending up in hospital.'

Gwen raises her eyebrows. 'We live very different lives, Jarvis Millwood.'

'That we do, Gwendoline Poppy, that we do.'

'Do you really not paint or draw anymore? Nothing? At all?'

'Not really. Doodling, when I'm bored. And I do this.' He pulls his sweatshirt over his head and for a horrible moment Gwen thinks she's going to be treated to some lurid tattoo art. But he shows her his T-shirt. It's a soft, faded maroon and printed on it in black is a rearing cobra. Gwen never imagined she'd spend ages staring at Jarvis's torso, but she wants to take in every detail, from its flickering tongue to the pattern of its scales to the neat, deadly stacking of its coils. It's so brilliant that she shivers.

'And the back,' says Jarvis, turning round and pulling the T-shirt straight. On the back is a cartoon of some cheeky-chappie rodent, a chipmunk or a guinea pig, a wide grin on its fat face, a can of beer clutched in a paw. It's wearing a pair of boxers. Gwen laughs. 'You drew those?'

Jarvis turns back and pulls his sweatshirt back on. 'Drew them, printed them. I've got a screen-printing thing in the attic at home. I had this idea a while back to make a business, you know. Sell them at a shop in town. But then the shop closed. Of course. It wasn't really what I wanted to do anyway. I made one for my brother. He uses it for washing his Mercedes.'

'Will you make me one?'

'Really? It doesn't seem like your style. No one would ever see it under all your layers.'

'You can talk. You've always got that huge black sweatshirt on. Make me one. Any design you'd like. I'll pay you.'

'No way. You're not paying me. But yeah, I'll make you one. Give me a while to think of the right thing, OK?'

'OK. So, what was it you really wanted to do? If not a T-shirt business.'

Jarvis flushes, not his rose pink of mild embarrassment but a deep red wash across his face and neck. 'I wanted a gallery. Fine art. Not a big, flashy London one, but a small one by the coast somewhere. Not Cornwall – too many galleries there already. But maybe Wales or maybe here in Kent. But like that's ever going to happen. It's stupid.'

'Stupider than me writing a book?'

'Hey, look at this,' says Jarvis, showing her an entry from 2015. 'Harry Bramley and James Varden. Gushing with love about St Dom's. And they've written out their full postal address. I wouldn't do that, I tell you. But anyway. No phone number or email. We should write to them, right?'

Gwen recognises a change of subject when she hears it. 'Fantastic. I'll put them in the spreadsheet. And yes, I'll bring some writing paper in tomorrow. I've got some lovely notecards.'

Jarvis grins. 'I thought you might.'

CHAPTER SIXTEEN

Jarvis

Another week passes. Jarvis goes to work on Friday and Saturday as he's supposed to; Gwen goes to work Thursday and Friday as she's supposed to. Sunday to Wednesday becomes their working week in terms of the visitors' book project – Thursday to Saturday inclusive feel like annoying interruptions. And for what? To stack shelves and man the till at Speedy-Spend. And, in Gwen's case, to sit in a dusty office with a pensioner, moving files around.

Jarvis knows that Gwen's started using Saturdays to work on her stories at the library. He wishes he could find a similar purpose for his Thursdays. The last one turned into an all-day session with Matt and Whacko and he was glad Gwen wasn't around to see him the next day. He felt awful after it, even though, according to their texts, his mates have taken it in their stride. Maybe because he's eased off a bit recently, it's hitting him harder. Either way, he's not in a hurry to do it again, but if he's not kicking back with the boys, then what? There's no question of either of them working on the visitors' book when the other isn't around.

On Saturday night he turns down Royston's invitation to a party at his. His parents look completely flummoxed when he throws himself down on the sofa after dinner to watch TV with them. Halfway through some cheesy film they like, his mother reaches across and gives his hand a big squeeze without taking her eyes from the screen. The next morning, he wakes up early, feeling fine, for the first time on a Sunday in as long as he can remember. He has breakfast with his parents and Effie from next door then gets ready for church.

'Without me nagging,' marvels his mum.

Easter Sunday, a big day for Vicar Dave. When they get there, Gwen's sitting in her usual lonely seat at the back. Jarvis's mum leans over and tugs her arm. 'Don't sit there, silly. Come and join us.' So Jarvis finds himself sandwiched between Gwen and Effie.

He's slightly mortified that his church tower chart is on an easel at the front of the church, next to the pulpit, there in plain view. Unusually, he isn't tired and stays awake through the whole service. Effie, however, nods off on his shoulder. He spends the time wondering what on earth he can put on a T-shirt for Gwen. The one he showed her was one of his tamer designs. Most have naked women or drinking jokes on them. He doesn't imagine Gwen will appreciate either.

During the notices, Vicar Dave makes a big thing about him and Gwen and the wonderful work they're doing on the visitors' book. He tells everyone that they've already raised £2,520, showing them all the chart and explaining that Jarvis drew it. He tells them that Gwen and Jarvis have gone above and beyond the call of duty, putting in more hours than he ever expected, and reminds people that it's still not too late to volunteer. Gwen and Jarvis exchange an outraged look. *They* don't want anyone else muscling in.

They escape into the office as soon as the service is over. After a while, the church falls quiet again, with only the sounds of Vicar Dave moving around clearing up, sorting things out. No further donations have been made and Jarvis can't help feeling dispirited.

'I think you just had a really lucky start,' sighs Gwen. 'I mean, three out of eight, or nine, or whatever it was. I bet if you talked to a professional fundraiser they'd say that was unusual. We'll try another lot tomorrow and see what happens.'

'Yeah, but I've only got a handful of people we can try. Like four. If the return rate is one in ten or something, that's not looking good.'

'I know. And I've got two. What shall we do? Finish going through the easy ones, then go back and start investigating the ones that look like we might find them with a bit of work? Once we've contacted all the obvious ones, I guess we can spend as long as we like on the rest. I mean, what else are we going to do?'

It's a good question. Jarvis still hasn't admitted to himself that he's not just in it to find his mystery girl anymore, but increasingly it seems to be the case. Will he and Gwen still hang out when they no longer have this shared quest? He reckons he'd like to. But what will they *do*? He likes her company, yes, but he also likes having a project. Without that… well, he can't imagine going back to the way he was living two weeks ago. Partying and PlayStation and existing in a permanent fog? He shakes his head. No. The obvious thing is to grow up, move out, find gainful employment. He experiences a little internal shudder. As much as being the debauched, overgrown teenager doesn't appeal to him, neither does being the serious adult. The visitors' book has moved him into an in-between stage, and it's a very uncomfortable state to be in.

Vicar Dave comes in to say goodbye. He seems to be in a good mood, so Jarvis decides to raise the subject of a party to thank all the people they're speaking to. Initially it was a stupid thing he said because he wanted to meet Imogen and see what she looked like. But once Alice had so generously donated, once Gwen had spoken to the lonely Ludlow widow who couldn't afford to help, once Hattie, happily married, had spared what she could, he was starting to feel that these people really deserved a thank you, an acknowledgement. Maybe not Patricia. Those marital dynamics would kill any party vibe.

'Er, Vicar Dave. I sort of said something, to one of the people I spoke to…'

'Jarvis, am I going to get sued?'

'No, no, nothing like that. It's more a sort of promise I made. How would you feel about, y'know, when this is all over, and we've got all the money, holding a party?'

'A party?'

'Yes, to celebrate and thank the people who've spoken to us, or read our emails or whatever.' Jarvis suggests it with little hope. Vicar Dave's a… vicar. This isn't going to be his sort of thing.

'I think it's a brilliant idea. You must have read my mind.'

'*Really?*'

'Yes. Yes, you see, I had a vision…' Vicar Dave pulls up a chair and starts confiding in them about a dream he had, of a large group of people gathered together to celebrate the saving of St Dom's. 'The imam was there, Desiree from the Baha'i group, and lots and lots of strangers. That's when I knew the plan was going to work, however unlikely it seemed.'

'Oh,' says Jarvis. He's not sure about visions. 'Well, good then. So I can go on mentioning it to people?'

'Yes, I don't see why not. Well done, Jarvis; well done, Gwen. See you later.'

The words 'Well done, Jarvis' are becoming familiar. He hasn't heard them in forever and now they're falling on him like rain. He rather likes it. Gwen, however, wears a face of misery. 'What's up with you, Gwendoline Poppy?'

'I hate parties.'

'Don't be stupid.'

'No, I do. Too many people, I'm rubbish at small talk, everyone getting drunk… although maybe this won't be *that* sort of party,' she concedes. 'Whatever. I hate parties.'

'You'll like this one. Anyway, it's not for months – who knows what will have happened by then?'

CHAPTER SEVENTEEN

Gwen

Another whole week goes by with no donations. Gwen is starting to worry. What if their initial flurry of good fortune is all there's going to be? What if they can't save the church? She knows her life will have to change soon anyway, but whatever she does and wherever she goes, St Dom's has saved her, and she can't bear to think of it not being there, of Vicar Dave and his family not living up the path. *It's still early days*, she reminds herself. *We have plenty of things to try.*

She's also deeply disappointed that her enquiries have yielded nothing. One email address bounced back from the server as unrecognised. Another went through fine but there was no reply. And she hasn't heard a thing from 'Travelling Bry', as she and Jarvis refer to the guy with the travel blog and the great website. Of course, there's no obligation, but he looked like such a nice man; he seemed the kind of person who'd at least send a kindly one-liner. Maybe he's up a mountain in Tibet with no Wi-Fi. Or maybe, as Jarvis suggested, he's just a bit of an arse.

The following Sunday, she's invited back to Jarvis's after church for lunch. Justine had also invited Aunt Mary so that Gwen wouldn't have to feel guilty. Gwen delivered the invitation with a silent prayer that she would say no. She couldn't imagine relaxing at a Millwood family lunch with Aunt Mary at her side.

'Lunch with complete strangers? No thank *you*,' said Aunt Mary in outrage. 'You must do what you like of course, but in my day, we kept to our own.'

Well, good then. Gwen still feels guilty at leaving her alone, but as Jarvis (and Amma via email) have pointed out, how does it really help her aunt if Gwen spends a miserable day too? It doesn't. It isn't even as if Gwen's company cheers her up. Last Sunday, for Easter, she bought Aunt Mary a large chocolate egg from Thornton's, with her name iced on the front in white chocolate.

'Trying to give me diabetes, are you?' said her aunt, putting it on the counter with a sniff. They spent the whole afternoon in front of the TV, not talking. In the evening, Aunt Mary decided that the bathroom blinds needed taking down and bleaching.

So this Sunday, she's going to the Millwoods'. Jarvis's sister is visiting again with her boyfriend so it's a larger group around the table than Gwen is used to, but no one seems to mind her being quiet. The roast chicken tastes heavenly. Jarvis and his sister even suspend hostilities for the duration.

Gwen has brought the visitors' book and her notes, in case they find a couple of hours to work on it, but somehow the day slips away. Being around other people without the book as a focus is like cycling without stabilisers or swimming without armbands. It's a good thing, Gwen decides.

After dinner, Jarvis, his dad, his sister Lalie and the boyfriend, Mike, play football in the garden. Gwen stays in the kitchen with Justine, helping her clear away. Then they all collapse together in the den to watch a film. Mike falls asleep, Jarvis's dad ploughs through half a box of chocolate brazils. Just when Gwen starts mumbling that she really should be getting home, Mike wakes up and suggests a drink in the Swan.

'What do you think, Gwen? Just a quick one before you leave us?' says Justine.

'Well… OK,' says Gwen.

She gets home at eight, completely sated from a full day of enjoyment. When did she last have a day like that? Certainly not since her parents died. She misses them, so badly, all over again, a wave that knocks her sideways as she turns onto the estate. They would have liked the Millwoods very much. If she were going home to them now, they'd love hearing all about her day.

'How was it then?'

Gwen jumps as the voice floats out from the sitting room. She peers in and sees Aunt Mary sitting in the dark in front of the TV and feels terrible all over again that she's spent the day alone, so grim, while Gwen had a lovely time.

'It was wonderful, thanks.' She goes in and perches on the arm of a chair, unsure how much of a conversation her aunt really wants. 'Jarvis's sister and her boyfriend were there, and we all went for a drink just now. Dinner was lovely.'

Her aunt sniffs. 'No end to the gallivanting for some. Never mind me at home worrying.'

'You were worrying? It's eight.'

'On a *Sunday*.' She angles herself away from Gwen and ups the volume on the TV a little.

Gwen says goodnight and trudges upstairs. She feels deflated, uncertain. *Had* Aunt Mary been worrying about her? It doesn't seem likely, but you never know. She sighs, realising that feeling sad about her parents hadn't spoiled the warm feelings from the day, but talking to Aunt Mary did.

When her parents died, she struggled with acute emotions: grief, anger, pain, denial, all the things the books talk about. A year later, she was still in bits but she's pretty sure that's normal. If life had taken a different course, maybe she would have found a way out of her pain into a new and lovely existence by now, still sad of course, but beginning again. Instead she stayed in Hopley, in this greyness of days and crushing of spirit. Another year passed and she's *still* here, enduring the inexorable chip, chip away at her confidence.

OK, Gwendoline Poppy, she thinks, suddenly more clear-sighted than she's been in ages. *Enough's enough. You have to get yourself out of this. Saturdays, from now on, are for writing* and *job-hunting. By the time the visitors' book is finished, you need to have something good lined up. And you'll do the very best job you can of the project, and of life.*

She sounds very much like her mother.

She carries her resolve with her into Monday morning. So far, she hasn't raised a single penny – it's all been Jarvis. She trawls through her notes while the office is still quiet. She hovers over Greta Hargreaves. She still has some idea that they could go to Winthrop-St-Stanhope and ask about for Greta. She pictures a tiny village with a stream running through its heart and a hump-backed bridge, where everyone knows everyone else. They could find her in ten minutes flat. But a trip to Devon isn't really on the cards.

A more likely lead is Ann from Aylesford, the retired teacher. She looks up Morehouse Primary and emails the school. She should have done it sooner really, but she gets so caught up in working through the book. She scrolls slightly compulsively through the email account in case they've somehow missed a cheery email with a promise of a huge donation from Travelling Bry, but they haven't.

She turns back to the book. As if the universe has heard her promise to pull herself together, she straight away finds two brilliant leads. Willa from Tonbridge says:

This church may just have saved my life.

Well, that's motivation if ever Gwen saw it. And Willa has left a company name, T.P. Building and Contracting, which the internet reveals is still in business. Then a few entries later she finds an email address left by Danny from Dungeness: danny@ coastalbeauty.co.uk. Of St Domneva's, Danny has said:

> Inspired my first UK exhibition. A huge debt of gratitude owed.

Intriguing. Excited, Gwen looks up Coastal Beauty to discover that it's a boutique art gallery in Rye. Danny is Danny Martinez, a Cuban artist settled for twelve years now in England. His work is startling – shock waves of colour and feeling, abstract yet accessible. Gwen can't take her eyes off it, and for a while she gets lost in the website.

The gallery features other artists too of course, and she immediately thinks of Jarvis. In the archive she finds the pictures that St Dom's inspired. They're abstract too, but it would be obvious to Gwen even without the caption and date. He's used the colours and motifs of the stained-glass windows to render unexpected views and angles of the church: the ceiling from a mouse's viewpoint, the tower from an owl's, the nave with a great sweeping expanse of ocean either side. She can't wait to show Jarvis. She hastily emails the gallery, raving about Danny's art and explaining their mission.

Then she turns to Willa. The obvious choice for shy Gwen would be to email the building company too. But something tells her this won't work. The website shows they're a large company, and Willa's heartfelt comment was left eight years ago. If she's not there anymore, an email will get lost. There's a phone number, but Gwen hates phone calls. Then again, she's supposed to be doing life better, saying goodbye to the listless and lacklustre Gwen of the last two years. For goodness' sake, what's the worst that can happen?

Spurred on by the thought of telling Jarvis that she's made a phone call, she snatches up her phone before she can change her mind.

'Hello, T.P. Building and Contracting,' sings out a very young-sounding receptionist. 'Clarice speaking.'

'Oh, er, hello. Hello there,' stumbles Gwen, kicking herself. This is why she hates the phone; it seems to turn her into an instant pinhead. She's suddenly boiling hot.

'Can I help you?'

'Er yes, I hope so. Yes please. Please may I speak to, er, Willa? I'm afraid I don't have her surname but she's from Tonbridge and she certainly used to—'

'Willa's working from home today. Do you have her mobile number?'

'Oh. Er, no, I don't.'

'Would you like to take it down?'

'Yes. Yes, please. I have a pen. Wait just a second...' Gwen fumbles for the pen, drops it, bends over to pick it up and hits her head on the table. Fortunately her thick hair serves a useful protective function. 'Right. I'm ready.'

She jots down the number and the receptionist hangs up without waiting for thanks. Gwen can hardly blame her. She will *not* sound stupid on the next call. She *will not*.

When Willa answers, Gwen takes a deep breath and forces herself to explain her business calmly and clearly, without her usual panics and pre-empting, without imagining how annoyed the other person must be by the interruption.

'Of course I'll help you,' says Willa at once. 'That place has a special place in my heart. It saved my life, you know.'

'You did say, in your comment. I wondered... I mean, how did it...? If you don't mind me asking.'

'Oh, it was years ago now. I was newly arrived in England and the *weather*. Every single day it rained and it was so cold. I'd come for love, but being a newlywed far from home, without any familiar landscape, without the support of friends and family... it was lonely. You've no idea. I was terribly homesick. *Terminally* homesick, I used to feel. My husband tried his best, but he's a man, right? They're not exactly wired for sympathy. I wasn't going to sit around feeling sorry for myself, so I made myself explore. That's how I came across your pretty little church. I spent a whole afternoon sitting there, praying, and it was the first time I felt a little hope. Your vicar came to talk to me too, such a lovely man, said such wise and comforting words. I went back several times after that. Perhaps what I wrote was a little melodramatic, but it did feel that way at the time. It certainly saved my marriage.'

'I'm so glad. What a lovely story. You're very brave. There's nothing worse than being lonely and homesick and not being able to see your family.' Gwen hesitates. Willa has a very faint but discernible accent, one that is familiar and dear to Gwen. 'Um, can I just ask... do you come from Ghana by any chance?'

'Why good gracious. Yes I do. How on earth could you tell?'

'My best friend from university is from Ghana. Your accent is very slight, but it reminded me of Amma. It's lovely to hear – I miss her.'

'And where is Amma now? Has she gone home, lucky girl?'

'No. She's in Bristol, learning to be a hotshot lawyer.'

'Good for her. It's lovely to talk to you, Gwen. Thanks for the reminder of St Dom's – it's been a long time now since I was there. Maybe I'll come and pay you a visit. Is that lovely vicar still there?'

'Yes. Vicar Dave. I mean, Reverend Fairfield. He is. And we'd love to see you. Please do come.'

Willa takes the details of the JustGiving page and Gwen hangs up, feeling as if she's just finished talking to an old friend. A moment later, Jarvis arrives.

'Guess what? Guess what? Guess what?' shrieks Gwen the minute she sees him.

'Woah, steady on, woman,' protests Jarvis, raising a hand to his alabaster brow. 'Bit tender this morning.'

'Oh, Jarvis, you didn't?'

'After you went home, Whacko turned up. I stayed a bit later than I meant to. I'm OK though. Fire away, just at half volume please.'

'Alright, well listen.' Gwen tells him about emailing Ann and Danny and phoning Willa and shows him the art gallery website. He doesn't say much, but she can tell he's impressed. His sleepy eyes start to glow a bit, and there's an imperceptible tension to his languid posture as he looks at the St Dom's paintings.

'Wow,' he says at last. 'That guy's talented.'

'So are you.'

'*You* don't know. You've never seen my work.'

'And whose fault is that?' Gwen ripostes tartly. 'Anyway, I can tell, from the chart and your T-shirt. Still, I won't go on. Now look, I need to write to Harry Bramley and James Varden. Which stationery do you like?'

From her vast collection, Gwen has shortlisted her notelets with the geese, her letter cards with the vintage art and her smooth brown paper embossed with gold bees.

'You waited to ask me which stationery I liked best?'

'Well yes, the note will be from both of us. It reflects on both of us.'

A look she can't decipher passes over Jarvis's face, but by now she's pretty confident he won't laugh at her. 'The bees,' he says.

Gwen gets to work, writing with her best pen, and Jarvis checks the JustGiving page. Nothing showing from Willa yet, he tells her. A moment later he exclaims. 'Hey, Gwendoline Poppy? Reckon you can take the day off work on Thursday?'

'Um, yes, I imagine so. Why?'

'Because Danny from Dungeness has emailed back. He wants to meet us. He wants us to go down there on Thursday.'

Gwen's jaw drops. 'Let me see that.' She grabs the laptop and reads. 'Can we even *do* that? How would we get there?'

'Um, I can borrow my mum's car.'

'You can *drive?*'

'Yeah.'

'Are you *safe?*'

'As long as I haven't had more than seven beers. I'm *kidding*, Gwendoline Poppy. Yeah, I'm not a bad driver. You can ask my mum at lunchtime. What do you think? I mean, we'll go, right?'

Gwen imagines it. Jumping in a car, jaunting off to the coast, seeing new sights, maybe finding a nice place for lunch. The sort of day she hasn't had in forever. Meeting an artist, talking about St Dom's… maybe making some more money for the roof fund. Surely Danny must be thinking about donating – surely he wouldn't invite them down there for no reason?

'*Yes.* We'll go.'

Jarvis grins at her. 'Road trip, baby.'

CHAPTER EIGHTEEN

Jarvis

By Tuesday, Jarvis has recovered from drinking with Whacko on Sunday night. As the day wears on, he notices he's gone through three months of the visitors' book in one day, almost twice as much ground as he covered yesterday. He's never realised before what a difference it makes, not being hungover. No wonder he's achieved exactly nothing since he quit art school.

It's been a good day. Gwen's contact, Willa from Tonbridge, has donated £350. When Gwen saw it, she went bright red and Jarvis thought she was going to cry. She didn't, to his relief, but you could tell how chuffed she was. She hopped right out of her chair to colour in another little section on the chart. At lunchtime they went to his. His mum had made a hearty bacon and lentil soup with crusty bread and butter and a lemon tart to die for.

Jarvis has finally connected with @purplemarcella on Twitter – she appears to be some sort of journalist on a lifestyle magazine – and sent her a DM which he hopes will do the trick. He's found two more easy contacts and two more that might be possibilities, if you have Gwen's weird brain on the case. Gwen's found three more email addresses and written off to them. Between them, they're really making progress. Almost halfway through the book.

Yes, the day has been good. It's the evening that causes Jarvis the difficulty. By unspoken agreement, he and Gwen are working later than they did at first. They stay until about 6.30 p.m., when Gwen has to leave so as not to incur the wrath of her horrible aunt. Jarvis saunters home, as slowly as he can, and still arrives at 6.36 p.m. Not that his home is a bad place to be of course – he's glad he hasn't got Gwen's evening ahead of him – but still, when he's got free time now, he doesn't really know what to *do* with it. Before, he would have gone to the pub. But realising that that course of action reduces him to half capacity or less is a bit of a downer really. It's nice having dinner with the olds and everything, but then what? There's only so much TV he can take.

There are two obvious answers to his problem really, both of which he shrinks from. Find a job. Do some art. The very thought of either makes him shiver. Clearly the job-hunting has nothing to recommend it at all. And he hasn't done any proper art since he left college, nearly two years ago now. He slouches up to the attic and his eyes fall on his T-shirt printer. He needs to make one for Gwen, but he still has no idea what to put on it. Maybe on Thursday, when they go to the coast, he'll learn something new about her that will give him inspiration.

He looks around at his easel, his portfolio, the neat stack of boxes of charcoal and pastels and paints. When he came home, he was all set to throw it all out, but his mum rescued everything silently and organised it up here. He opens one of his portfolios at random. It's one of the last ones he did at art school, and honestly, it's terrible. He tosses it aside and grabs another, suddenly determined to convince himself that he's altogether rubbish at art so that he can crush the whole idea once and for all.

The second portfolio is the one he used as his application for art school and all the drawings were done, obviously, before he went. He looks at a pencil portrait of his mum. Lalie had just left home and Mum was so sad. But while she sat for Jarvis, he made her laugh with his usual Jarvis nonsense, and in the picture, the tears and the laughter are shining in her eyes.

Then comes an abstract in pastel; he remembers reading about sacred geometry at the time and being really captured by the idea. His abstract feels mystical and profound, if he's not flattering himself. He'd been so inspired by the whole concept that he did a series of charcoal sketches in the church, he remembers. That'll be in one of his sketchbooks somewhere.

When was the last time he felt excited about an idea or a project? Once or twice early on in his first year, but not since, until now, with the visitors' book. Next is a fantasy scene of a dragon and a unicorn fighting, in carefully intense colours. It's in the style of a children's book illustration; he was quite into that sort of thing back then. A nude of his then-girlfriend, Bella, in pencil. A close-up study of an acorn. They're not bad.

He reaches for the first portfolio again and spreads out a few of the pieces to compare. It's not easy for Jarvis to look at them. Art school shredded his confidence into a thousand tiny pieces and this lot really aren't good. What he's looking at is the destruction of all his young hopes and dreams. But what strikes him now, sitting here privately, occupying this strange new headspace he's found himself in recently, is not so much their artistic merit, or lack of – it's how the pictures make him *feel*. When he looks at the later ones he feels tense, jangly and a bit depressed. When he looks at the earlier ones, he feels happy and energised, kind of fizzy inside. He's always assumed that the pictures create the feelings. But now he wonders if it isn't the other way around.

The way he's explained it to himself, his parents, anyone who demanded to know why he dropped out after such a promising start, is that he had some talent, yes, enough to take him to art school. But once he was there, among countless talented others, under the scrutiny of teachers with impressive credentials and reams of letters after their names, his place in the hierarchy of brilliance was revealed. He was a big fish in the small pond of Hopley, but at art school, he was nothing more than whitebait.

Whatever the assignments required, Jarvis always failed to deliver. He wasn't cutting edge; he was laid-back, sensitive, dreamy, a bit of an anachronism really. He knew he could never be what they wanted, that he wouldn't get the marks he needed to pass his finals, that he was failing to make the connections that would get him shows and reviews after college. There was no point pursuing it; he'd never make it.

So he came home and said he wasn't bothered anyway, because it was really hard work. It *was* really hard work, but it wasn't true that he wasn't bothered. Without art, what could there be for him? The answer, so it had seemed, was the pub. Now Gwen and the bloody visitors' book have called that into question too. He remembers what he said to Gwen in the Swan: 'You never had any other ideas of what you wanted to do. You've found something you love. You're not exactly blazing trails in any other career…'

Well, the same is true of him, so where did it all go wrong? He's always assumed it was *him*, that he wasn't good enough, that he'd simply come to the end of his road. But maybe he drew the wrong conclusion. Maybe art school just wasn't the right place for him. Maybe there are lots of different ways to become an artist and that's just one of them. What if it wasn't a question of failure but simply a lack of fit? Look at Gwen: when he first met her, she seemed hopeless, full stop. But look at her when she's working on the visitors' book, or with his family. It's her boring, depressing home life that's snuffing all the life and colour out of her. Lack of fit. And in Jarvis's case… maybe he didn't ever need to give up after all.

He's itching for a ciggie so he stands up and leans out of the skylight – benefit of being so tall – and puffs away, easing the fear that's creeping into him at the thought of where this line of reasoning might lead. The sky is violet. A few stars are showing, reminding him of the stickers Gwen has plastered all over his church tower drawing. He laughs. That girl is seriously weird.

Yet he's had more fun with her in a couple of weeks than he did in eighteen months at art school with the cool young artists of the future.

He tosses the butt and watches it bounce over the roof tiles and land in the gutter. He winces. His mum won't like that. A normal woman would never see it of course – normal women don't check the guttering – but his mum is not a normal woman. 'High standards' doesn't even begin to cover it. Housework, career, morals, grooming – you name it, she excels in it. And Jarvis lets her down spectacularly on every single count. She still seems to like him though, so that's something.

He pulls the skylight shut – a chilly spring breeze is shivering its way in – and clears away the pictures. Enough soul-searching for one night.

CHAPTER NINETEEN

Gwen

On Thursday, Gwen wakes up so excited she can barely contain herself. She's going on a road trip. A whole day out. Away from Aunt Mary, away from the house, away from the Gwen she's become. Today she will be road-trip Gwen. She has somewhere to go, something to do and someone to spend the day with.

Naturally, when she told Aunt Mary of her plan, she was treated to a great deal of sniffing and numerous disapproving comments. But she didn't really listen.

She's nervous too. They'll be meeting Danny the artist, and Gwen's not good with strangers. The thought of it makes her pause in front of the mirror – not a place she usually lingers – and consider what sort of impression she might make as a representative of St Dom's. Not inspiring, if she's honest. In her usual layers and folds, she looks dumpy, insignificant. Her hair looks as if it's out to take over the world. Her skirt keeps slipping down and she keeps hitching it up: has the elastic gone in the waistband? She examines it; it seems fine. Then she wonders: has she perhaps lost a bit of weight? Over the last three weeks, she's done a lot more walking than usual. And although, during that first week, Hopley did a roaring trade in bourbons, she's slowed down lately. Now that she's getting several delicious meals a week, courtesy of Justine and the Swan, she doesn't rely on her emergency chocolate bars so much.

She opens her wardrobe and inspects the long-neglected items. Should she – dare she – try on her black jeans? She does, but they still don't fit. Her blue jeans though, which are slightly bigger, fit just right. Gwen hasn't worn jeans for ages. She tries a white shirt with little navy flowers on it and she actually looks quite nice. A single layer feels like *too* much of a departure from her usual look, so she puts on a navy T-shirt under the shirt and feels a bit more comfortable. She'll *carry* her cardigan – and no scarf. Gwen shivers but she's not cold; it's just strange to feel so *visible*.

Hair next. She brushes and brushes and wishes she'd thought of getting a haircut of some sort. It stands out in a static halo, invading the air around her head like alien tentacles. She plaits it, but she looks like an elderly peasant from a folktale. She puts it in a bun but looks like a Victorian governess. In the end, she clips it back on either side of her face but leaves it loose down her back. Now that her face is visible, the situation calls for a little mascara and lip gloss, and that's really as far as Gwen can bear to go. She rushes out of her room before she loses her nerve.

The smell of burned toast pervades the air again, but Gwen is ready. 'Thank you, that's *so* kind of you. I *really* appreciate it,' she says when Aunt Mary hands her a plate. 'I'll eat it on the way. Can I get you anything from Dungeness?'

'Chance would be a fine thing. There's nothing there. No shops. Bleak, it is. I don't know *why* you're looking so cheery. Visiting a nuclear power station isn't *my* idea of a nice day out. But there we are.'

'Visiting a…?'

'*Nuclear power station*,' enunciates her aunt, as if Gwen is deaf. 'There isn't, is there?'

'Yes. And you all done up like a dog's dinner. I hope you don't come back with radiation, that's all.'

Gwen hesitates. No shops and a nuclear power station? That doesn't sound like an artist sort of place to live. Is Aunt Mary winding her up? She must be. Still, that's beside the point. 'It's not really about having a nice day out,' she says (though it is). 'It's about meeting a potential donor. Anyway, you have a lovely day and I'll see you this evening.'

She escapes with her two blackened slices, leaving her aunt muttering about fool's errands. Then she walks to Jarvis's, tossing her toast on the way.

'You look different,' exclaims Jarvis when she opens the door. 'Nice. I like your shirt.'

Gwen blushes. 'Thanks.' They eat granary toast with butter and boiled eggs before setting off. The toast is so good that Gwen has three pieces.

'Mum was gutted she had to work today,' Jarvis says, grinning. 'She wanted to be here to wave us off, I think. She says to tell you have a lovely day. When we get back later, she'll grill us like sausages.'

'Fine by me,' says Gwen, thinking how nice it must be to live with someone who takes an interest. 'Jarvis, is there a nuclear power station in Dungeness?' But Jarvis doesn't know.

Justine's car is a little mint-green Fiat. Jarvis's legs are too long for it really; with his skinny build, he looks like a grasshopper, all concertinaed up inside. Gwen bites back a smile because he looks so earnest, adjusting the mirrors, checking she has her seat belt on, turning the key in the ignition. They cruise past St Dom's, turn right and head south towards the coast.

The day is mild and a little drizzly, which does nothing to dampen Gwen's spirits. She marvels that she's lived in Kent for two years but hasn't really *seen* it. She has no sense of the county surrounding Hopley. To be travelling, even when they hit the motorway, which is like all motorways everywhere, gives her an enormous sense of freedom. Here are cars, lorries, motorbikes, all on their way from A to B, going about daily lives or one-off trips. Here is life, no longer passing her by.

Jarvis puts the radio on but tells her there are CDs in the glove compartment. 'But they're all my mum's, so it's mum music,' he warns. Gwen doesn't care; she's never been exactly contemporary with her music tastes. She rummages and finds Tom Petty, singing along in her head about freedom when the chorus hits.

'I'm not going to talk much,' Jarvis warns her. 'I'm concentrating because I don't drive that often.'

'Fair enough,' says Gwen. 'You're doing wonderfully.'

The journey is no more than forty minutes. When they come off the motorway, Gwen feasts her eyes on vast, flat fields dotted with sheep and lambs, on huge skies with elaborate cloudscapes etched in a hundred shades of white and grey. She catches a glimpse of the River Rother and of dark-timbered red-roofed houses standing amongst burgeoning trees. Then they turn left and drive along a flat expanse punctuated by shining lakes and flocks of honking geese. The drizzle has eased and the sun's burning through, making the water and the white wings sparkle. She takes it all in, every bit of it.

When they get to Dungeness, Jarvis rolls to a halt, looking perplexed. 'What's wrong?' asked Gwen.

'I thought I'd followed his instructions right. He said the third house on the right. But there aren't any houses, so I'm wondering if I've come too far. There was that housing estate back there. Maybe that was it.'

He pulls over so he's not blocking the road, though everything is very quiet and they're the only traffic. 'Look, Gwendoline Poppy, you read it.' He's forwarded Danny's email to his phone and finds it to show her.

Gwen's sense of direction can best be described as haphazard, but she reads it carefully, determined to be helpful. 'No, I think you're right,' she says. 'He says to turn right after passing a red letter box. I saw one. And you did turn right.'

She gets out of the car and looks around. A warm breeze streams over her, and despite their confusion, she grins. There's so much space. A pebbly shore stretching as far as she can see to left and right and forward. A rim of denser blue than the sky on the horizon, which must be the sea. Dotted here and there on the shingle are old husks of boats, put out to pasture – or to pebble – and the occasional shed or shack which, at first, she thinks must be old boat sheds. It's bleak but beautiful.

'Wow, cool place,' says Jarvis, unfolding through the driver's door and stretching his legs while he gazes around, the breeze snatching at his dark curls. 'Strange but cool.'

'You know what? I think those are the houses,' says Gwen, pointing. 'I thought they were boat sheds at first but look, that one has a mailbox. And there's washing on a line.' A short line is indeed strung across a corner of a rickety picket fence, with one shirt, one pair of board shorts and one pair of underpants pegged on it.

Jarvis considers the unlikely-looking homes. 'Cool.' He slides back into the car and they carry on, slowly, counting house-like dwellings. The third is grey, as Danny said it would be, so they park outside and grin at each other.

'This is it, Gwendoline Poppy. We're going to meet Danny from Dungeness.'

When they knock at the door, a window cracks open above their head and a beautiful young woman wrapped in a sheet leans out. With her blond waves and the tops of her ample breasts showing above the sheet, she makes Gwen think of a mermaid who's come to live among the humans.

'Hi,' she shouts. 'I'm Merry. You must be the guys from the church.'

'Yes, that's us,' says Jarvis, looking slightly spellbound.

'Danny said you were coming. He's at the Britannia.'

'Oh, did we get the time wrong?' flusters Gwen, not wanting to seem intrusive or inept.

'No, you're bang on. He said to send you over.'

'OK. Thanks,' says Jarvis. 'Er, where...?'

'Oh, just keep going along the road. Follow it round. You can't miss it. See ya.' She disappears, leaving the window open.

Gwen and Jarvis look at each other, excitement or nerves mounting. Then Gwen smiles. 'The guys from the church.'

Jarvis frowns. 'It makes me feel like a Jehovah's Witness or a Mormon.'

Gwen grins. She can't think of a less likely missionary than Jarvis.

They get back in the car and follow the road round until they reach an area where there are two parked cars, a black-and-white lighthouse on one side and a pub on the other. 'Guess that's the Britannia,' says Jarvis. In the distance behind it looms a huge, dark shape. A nuclear power station; Aunt Mary was right. It's ominous, yet it can't detract from the odd, wild beauty of the shore. *What a strange place*, thinks Gwen.

They walk over, Gwen vastly glad that she's not doing this alone. Danny sits alone, easily recognisable from his gallery photo, staring into the far distance. On the table is a steaming pot of tea.

As they approach, Danny stands. He's taller even than Jarvis and has long black locs reaching halfway down his back and tied in a red band. He's about forty, with a dash of grey hair at his temples. 'You must be Gwen and Jarvis,' he says, holding out a hand.

'Hi,' squeaks Gwen, feeling a tiny bit star-struck. He's very handsome. 'It's nice to meet you.'

Danny's intense. He holds her hand firmly and stares at her, as if he's trying to read her soul. When he releases her, he does the same to Jarvis. 'Good people,' he murmurs at last. 'Good people.'

'Uh, thanks,' says Jarvis. 'Thanks for asking us to come and see you. We don't get out much, especially her.'

Gwen frowns. Now is not the time to be flippant. 'We love meeting people who are interested in St Domneva's,' she adds. 'It's amazing how many people it's made a difference to.'

'Sit, sit,' says Danny. 'I'll get you drinks. What will you have?'

'Oh no,' Gwen protests. 'We can get them. It's very good of you to see us.'

'You drove all this way. Least I can do. Jarvis?'

'A pint of the local. No, wait. I'm driving. A Coke.'

Danny's back in a moment with Coke for Jarvis and tea for Gwen. 'So, tell me about yourselves.'

If only there was something interesting to tell, thinks Gwen, letting Jarvis go first. He spills out a big jumble about the church and working in Speedy-Spend and Danny narrows his eyes. 'But that's not you,' he says, with a look that could strip paint. Jarvis goes pink again, so Gwen says what has to be said.

'He's an artist but he left art school and hasn't done anything since,' she explains. 'He says he wasn't good enough to make it, but he *is*, Danny, he's amazing.'

Jarvis is now so pink he's practically fuchsia. 'She doesn't know what she's talking about,' he mumbles. 'Whatever. *She* wants to be a writer.'

Danny shoots a swift glance at Gwen. 'We'll get to you,' he threatens, then turns his attention back to Jarvis. 'Where did you go to art school?'

Jarvis names the fancy London college and Danny winces.

'And why did you leave?'

'Because I wasn't good enough. I really, really wasn't.'

Again, Danny fixes him with that look. 'But really?' he says, and it's obvious to both Gwen and Jarvis that he won't let it rest.

Jarvis picks at some loose skin around his cuticles and Gwen resists the urge to swat his hands apart. 'Because I wasn't happy,' he says at last.

Wow, thinks Gwen. *I didn't know that.*

'I really did *think* I wasn't good enough,' Jarvis goes on, 'but a couple of nights ago I realised that might not have been the reason. I wasn't doing well on the assignments, that's true, but I've just started thinking, maybe it just wasn't the right place for me, you know?'

'And how long did it take you to work this out?' demands Danny, his dark eyes stern.

Jarvis progresses from fuchsia to magenta. 'Almost two years.'

'And now. What do you think now? Are you an artist?'

Jarvis's colour is so intense that Gwen starts to worry that he's about to have an embolism. He looks around desperately and for a minute she thinks he's got tears in his eyes, but it must just be the light. When he answers, it's not what she expected. 'I want it too much to let myself think I might be,' he sighs.

Oh bless. She understands. Completely.

Danny lifts his eyebrows. 'You realise that makes no sense? What you're saying is that you'll only believe yourself capable of doing things you have no interest in. What's the point in that? Talk sense to me now, man.'

'I *want* to be good. I used to be good. It's been so long I'm not sure anymore. I used to be cocky. Art school knocked it all out of me. I couldn't do anything right there. I lost all the joy of it.'

'Now I understand you. Good. Well, Jarvis, many things are needed to succeed as an artist, but there are two that are vital. Do you know what they are?'

'Talent?'

'Yes, talent. And the other?'

'Self-belief?' hazards Jarvis.

'You're in the ballpark, but that's a wishy-washy term, overused these days. Let me make it more specific for you. You need to be bulletproof.'

Gwen bites her lip anxiously. That doesn't sound like Jarvis at all.

'When you put yourself out there, people will pull apart everything about you. Your work, your appearance, your background, your politics,' Danny continues inexorably, like the voice of doom. 'When I started out, I was too black. Trust me when I say that you will be too white. I was too poor and foreign. You will be too middle-class and comfortable. The voices will go on and on. They will echo around your head at night. The same will be true for you, by the way,' he adds to Gwen and she wants to cry.

'Now let me guess. You're both gentle souls. You don't like confrontation. I am the same, at heart. Those are good qualities – they are what will make you a true artist, a true writer. But you also need to be tough. And if it doesn't come naturally, learn it. You cannot let yourselves be sidetracked by the criticism. Keep yourselves healthy, stay in tune with your own inner voice, work hard, harder than anyone you know. And never, ever listen to the voices that tell you that you're wrong, that you don't belong, that you can't do it.'

Jarvis scratches his head. 'That's full on,' he says, and at last, Danny laughs.

'I know,' he says. 'Merry says I'm too intense. But I hate to see young people thrown off their path because someone in authority says they're doing it wrong. There's no right way to do art. Or literature. Or life.'

'I, uh, I brought a portfolio,' mutters Jarvis.

Gwen looks at him, amazed. *Dark horse.*

'I don't want to take liberties – we're here to talk about the church – but…'

'Show me – now. Where is it?'

'In the car.'

'Fetch it,' Danny commands, and they both watch Jarvis slouch off to the car. 'You two an item?' asks Danny.

'What? Oh no. We're just friends.' Gwen laughs at the absurdity of it.

'OK then. Now, Gwen. Your turn. Tell me.'

CHAPTER TWENTY

Jarvis

As Gwen and Jarvis drive towards Rye, they're both silent. After an hour with Danny, Jarvis has more to think about than he has in two years. Gwen, beside him, seems similarly stunned. They park and find their way up a steep hill to a lookout point with benches at the start of a cutesy main street, where they promptly collapse.

Jarvis is in awe of Danny – and rather intimidated by him. It was a relief when it was Gwen's turn to get the interrogation. But talking to him was like getting a shot of something revitalising in the arm. He feels galvanised – a word no one ever associates with Jarvis. He hasn't shown anyone his work for ages, and he'll never forget his clammy hands and strong desire for a beer as he laid the case on the wooden pub table. Danny and Gwen looked through his portfolio; they both said good things. Their comments, his and hers, are ringing around his head. When they left, Danny promised to contribute to the roof fund and gave them a painting, for a raffle or auction prize. It's all packed up so they haven't looked at it yet, but they don't need to see it to know that it'll be the most valuable prize they'll ever have raffled at St Dom's. He also told them to go to Rye and check out his gallery, which they'd planned to do anyway. They'd promised themselves a whole day out: gallery, shops, lunch, exploring.

The gallery's beautiful. It's not large, but it's a lovely, light-filled space and manages to carry an impressive variety in its two rooms. One is dedicated to Danny's work, and Jarvis admires his range and scope. The other is filled with work by three other artists, and it's easy to see that they've been handpicked for quality and vision. It's a long time since Jarvis went to a gallery purely for pleasure, and he's forgotten how inspiring it is; approximately four thousand new ideas come streaming through his head just from gazing at the wonderful artwork around him.

After a while he hears Gwen chatting. Gwen. Chatting to a stranger. Without being forced. Wonders will never cease. Danny's assistant Renee looks very interested when Gwen introduces him – well, he knows he's a good-looking guy – and they chat for a while about art, then his stomach starts rumbling so it's time to go.

They have lunch on a pub balcony, overlooking the harbour. Perfectly content, they demolish steak pies while a salty wind causes trouble with their hair. Soon Gwen is as ungroomed as she ever was, and Jarvis wishes men could wear Alice bands without looking like total knobs.

'So, it's not turning out too badly, this visitors' book thing, despite me not finding my mystery woman,' he observes.

'We *will* find her for you,' says Gwen seriously. 'You've held a candle for her all these years. I'll think of something, Jarvis – you'll see.'

He smiles. Such an old-fashioned phrase. So Gwen. 'What about you, Gwendoline Poppy? I know there's no one on the scene now but was there ever? There must've been, right?'

'Of course. Two or three short-term ones, nice, but just not compatible enough to last long. And then Max. Maxwell. He was the serious one.'

'How long were you together?'

'Three years. All through uni, and then he dumped me about a month after we graduated. Said it was a new phase and we needed a fresh start with no ties.'

'Bummer.'

'Yes. At least, I thought so. I was devastated at the time; I thought maybe we were forever. But then after Mum and Dad…'

'Least of your worries?'

'Exactly. I mean, losing them put *everything* into perspective.'

'For sure. So what was he like, this *Maxwell*? I'm seeing suits and ties and glasses and a careful side parting.' Jarvis didn't like the sound of old Max. *A new phase, indeed. He'd met someone else, hadn't he?*

Gwen laughed. 'An uncannily accurate description. Apart from the suits; I mean, we *were* students. What can I tell you? We got on really well, liked a lot of the same things. We weren't exactly a rock-'n'-roll couple but we fitted together, back then. He was super-academic, sensible, steady…'

Jarvis gives a big yawn. 'Heard from him since?'

Gwen looks so downcast he wants to give her a big hug, but they haven't started doing the hugging thing and he doesn't want her to get the wrong idea. 'A letter, after Mum and Dad died. It was a nice letter, very genuine and sympathetic. He was very fond of my parents. But nothing since. He's not the type to, y'know, look back.'

'And do you still *hold a candle*? If he arrived in Hopley tomorrow begging for a second chance, would you fancy him now?'

Gwen frowns. 'It's never going to happen, so I've never thought about it. But probably not. I mean, after what happened… well, it changed me so much. I'll never be the same Gwen again. What about you, Jarvis? Anyone special in your past? Apart from the girl in lilac?'

Ouch. Jarvis doesn't want to think about *his* love life. Too many one-night stands after riotous parties. That whole mess with Bella and Tash… But, then again, it's Gwen. He can tell her stuff.

'I had a girlfriend before art school. We were together five years, from when we were seventeen. Yeah, I know, sweet and all that. But in the first month at college, I had my head totally turned by this other girl, Tash. She was stunning and edgy, and everything was so new and different and exciting that suddenly it felt like she was the sort of girl I *should* be with. So we got together, and a few weeks later I had to tell Bella.' He shudders. 'I should've done it much sooner – she came up to London to see me and we went out for lunch. God, it was horrible. I put her back on the train in tears. She was really heartbroken, and you know the weird thing? So was I, even though I was totally obsessed with Tash.

'Anyway. Tash and I dated for a few months, then I went home at Easter and bumped into Bella in the Swan and, well, it was just so good to see her. So, stuff happened. I know, I know. Then I went back to college and told Tash, so that was the end of *that*… Then there were a few girls that people tried to set me up with, but none of them lasted. Everyone had this idea of my type, you know. Like Tash – sexy in a really obvious way, tons of attitude and fire. But I think the real me was much happier with Bella. She was sweet, you know? Just easy to be around. And really pretty too.' He sighs. 'We were too young. It was too much too soon, and y'know, I'm a guy, so I'm stupid.'

'No wonder you weren't happy there,' says Gwen. 'It can't have felt good, hurting one girl after another… At heart you're a really kind person, Jarvis.'

'So my mum says. But I've never trusted myself with girls since. I let everyone down.'

'You're being too hard on yourself. You were young. Everyone makes mistakes, Jarvis, everyone.'

'I guess. Well, I wouldn't make *that* mistake again, that's definite.'

'If you had a second chance with Bella, you mean?'

Jarvis doesn't need to think. He's spent plenty of time brooding over his mistakes. 'No. I mean if I was with someone really special like that again. Not Bella though. It's like you said. I haven't been through anything like your nightmare, but failing at art school, losing myself afterwards, it's all made me a different person. We had our day, Bells and me, and it was great, but it's in the past.'

'Well then,' says Gwen with a little smile. 'We'd better crack on with finding your mystery girl. Otherwise you'll end up a sad old man propping up a bar.'

Jarvis sighs uncomfortably. 'Oh, I think that's inevitable.'

CHAPTER TWENTY-ONE

Gwen

Gwen is so happy after their day out that she honestly can't believe it. She hadn't thought it was possible to feel that way again after losing her parents. On the last stretch of the homeward drive, she imagines telling them all about it, and it's almost like being with them in reality. What a day. Beautiful weather and scenery. Stunning, ancient houses hundreds of years old, sagging under the weight of history and climbing roses. Talking to Jarvis as if they're old friends, like she talks to Amma. And, of course, Danny. So driven, so sure of his own path. She's chock-full of inspiration.

They get back to Hopley and it's dark, with a few silver stars dancing overhead. Jarvis pulls over in a layby next to the church and Gwen looks at him. 'Laptop?' she asks, and he nods. They run into the church to see if Danny's made his donation yet. He has – £3,000.

'Holy shit,' breathes Jarvis, and Gwen is too stunned even to tell him off for swearing in the church. Next, they check the emails and there's a note from him too:

Jarvis, Gwen,

Good to meet you today. Check my donation if you haven't already. I hope it's a pleasant surprise for you and your vicar. Every autumn I tithe – I divide a share of my profits between three or four different charities. No point waiting until autumn – you should have it when you need it. Now.

Keep in touch. Stop painting/writing for one reason only: because you no longer love it and it makes you miserable and bored. No other.

Salutations,
Danny Martinez

'Unbelievable,' murmurs Gwen.

'Three grand. And a painting,' says Jarvis. 'Go on then, update the chart. I know you want to. Then let's go – I'm starving.'

He's right, she wants to update the chart. And it's so satisfying to colour in such a substantial block. 'We've raised £5,870,' she announces. 'Only £32,130 to go.'

'It's not looking *quite* as desperate as it was.'

Gwen nods. She'll email Danny to thank him when she's not so tired and has figured out exactly what she wants to say.

Justine's just home from work so Jarvis throws a couple of pizzas in the oven. They tell her all about their day and Danny's amazing donation. 'We've raised £5,870. Only £32,130 to go,' says Gwen again. She needs to keep repeating it until she believes it.

'That's just wonderful. You're both doing a really tremendous job. I couldn't be more impressed.'

Gwen and Jarvis exchange a misty look. Her praise means a lot to both of them for different reasons.

Once he's fed, Jarvis goes out to the car and lugs in Danny's painting. With the aid of his dad's Stanley knife, they peel away the layers of stiff cardboard to see what he's given them. Gwen, Jarvis and his parents stand in a row in the kitchen, awed. It's a huge oil canvas, one of the paintings they saw on the website. It's the one of the church nave, with the ocean on either side of it. The colours are rich and unexpected: a red sea; a purple, green and gold church. It's like a fantasy, a stained-glass window and a landscape all rolled into one. They leave it propped up in front of the fridge for the rest of the evening and move around it reverently. When the clock chimes nine, Gwen shakes herself and starts gathering belongings. She's never wanted to go home less.

The following morning, work seems greyer and more spirit-drenching than ever. The office isn't busy at all and that almost makes it worse. Not working on the visitors' book if she were really needed elsewhere would be one thing. Not working on it to sit here staring at the walls is pointless. But after all the fresh air yesterday, she fell asleep as soon as she hit the pillow, and her dreams were strange and busy. At least a day doing nothing gives her a chance to get her head around everything.

Jarvis: more talented than even she suspected and coming around at last to the idea of trying again. Danny: telling her that he lost his parents in Cuba when he was *fourteen*. Heartbreaking.

He went off the rails for a while, he told them, then came to London when he was eighteen. 'I had to find my own way to be a man,' he told her, 'and my own way to be an artist. Art saved me.' Despite all sorts of discrimination, stories that were painful to hear, and a running theme of no money, he wiggled his way into the art world on his own terms, one hard-won inch at a time. And look at him now. A successful gallery, love, a bohemian home in a beautiful place… And he didn't get any of it by living in Aunt Mary's spare bedroom.

'Look at this place,' he said, pointing at the sweeping, pebbly shore. 'Light like you've never seen. Rare plants and birds. Dark blue sea – never seen it quite that colour anywhere else. Bleak as hell in winter but no less beautiful.'

'It's wonderful,' Gwen sighed.

'Now look that way.' He pointed to the power station. 'Think of it like the bad things in life. They'll always be there, looming on the horizon. You keep your head turned *that* way.' He placed his hands on either side of Gwen's face and physically turned it back towards the sea and the sky. 'At all times.'

Gwen knows what he means. She's spent too much time looking at the blots on the horizon, until they've engulfed her. It's time to try a new view of things.

Jeannie shuffles over to lift an ancient directory off the shelf behind Gwen's desk. Gwen has offered to show her how to use the internet, but Jeannie declined. 'Can I help you with anything?' asks Gwen.

'No thank you,' says Jeannie.

'How's your week been?' Gwen tries.

'Fine.'

Gwen resumes thinking. They had so much fun in Rye. Ice cream, the bookshop, the harbour, photographs of every single historical building. Jarvis kept winding her up, saying, 'Oooh look. An ancient kerbstone. An ancient lamppost. An ancient leaf.' *Idiot.* It's one of the most inspiring places Gwen's ever been. She wanted to capture it all. Gwen's goal now is to have more days that make her feel like that.

I'm ready, Amma, she writes, emailing her friend from her personal account. *I'm going to get a job and move out. I'm not leaving Hopley until the church is saved, but I need to start looking now. I have no idea what to try. Suggestions please.*

Amma replies ten minutes later. *Finally. I'm so happy... Heritage? Libraries? Museum? Admin as a means to an end? Publishing? Give me three weeks. I think I'll have a good idea by then.*

Odd. Why in three weeks? That's very specific. Those all seem like good ideas right now, to Gwen. She opens a job website and starts looking.

CHAPTER TWENTY-TWO

Vicar Dave

On Sunday after church, David wants nothing more than to hurry home. It's been an intense morning, with the Barretts wanting to know if their grandson can be married at St Dom's for free. With the roof falling in, for heaven's sake. Bill Brody offered some criticisms of his Easter sermon that he's apparently been mulling over ever since. And Agnes Soames and Effie Parker had a falling out over the flowers, which he hopes he resolved gracefully. It's so often like this on Sundays. Issues and antagonisms that have bubbled away in the background come to the fore, and sometimes ministry and the word of God seem like the smallest part of his duties.

First though, he must visit Mrs Dantry. She wasn't at church, she's ninety-two and she lives alone. He wants to be sure she's OK.

'Oh yes, Vicar, thank you,' she coos when she answers the door. 'My grandson brought me this Kirk Douglas box set so I've been watching his films all weekend. Such a handsome man, he was. I'm halfway through *Spartacus*. Would you like to join me?'

'No thank you, Evelyn. I'd better get back. I'm glad to see you're well.'

'Oh Vicar, how's Colin getting on?'

'Who?'

'Colin. And that funny-looking girl. With the fundraising?'

'Oh. Jarvis and Gwen. Very well, thanks, Evelyn. Surprisingly well.'

He goes home, smiling, and arrives to find a very unusual state of affairs: he and Annie have the house to themselves. 'Where's Wendy?'

'At the church, with Jarvis and Gwen. She really liked Gwen when she met her that time. Gwen offered to help out sometime if we needed it so…'

'Do we need it? Is something wrong?'

'Yes we do, and no, nothing. But we can use some quiet time, David, you and I. I hardly see you, and while I love you for your caring nature, I do occasionally need to have my husband to myself once in a while. So I've made scones and I've got the special-occasion teapot out and we're going to sit on the deck and chat, just the two of us, until they bring Wendy home.'

'I honestly can't think of anything nicer. But do you think they'll be alright with Wendy? Do they know that she can be…?'

'Yes, they do. They'll be fine. They're only two minutes away if there's a problem. I stayed a while when I took her there, and it's so peaceful with the two of them working away. Wendy seems calm around them.'

'Then let's make the tea.'

Ten minutes later, David settles into a chair outside, his wife beside him, tea steaming, to enjoy the dart of birds on the feeder and the profusion of spring flowers filling the flower beds. The sense of luxury is overwhelming. He hasn't had an unexpected interlude of leisure in the longest time. '*Oh thank God,*' he says with feeling, reaching for Annie's hand. 'This is just lovely, Annie, thank you.'

'You work too hard. I know it goes with the territory, but honestly, David, you have to take care of yourself too. God didn't give you a spectacular wife for you never to see her, you know.'

He laughs. 'I know. I'll have to remember that. More time relaxing with you. Part of the Divine Plan.'

'Exactly. So Jarvis and Gwen told me about this artist donating £3,000. Would I be right in guessing you've let William know about that?'

David grins. Of course he wasn't able to resist telling the archdeacon. 'How well you know me, wife. I *may* have dropped him a quick email, telling him that we've raised nearly £6,000 in three weeks. Just to keep him in the loop.'

Annie laughs, a sound that lifts his heart. 'It's only courtesy, *I* know. Do you think we'll get there after all? The full £50,000?'

'I don't know. What they've achieved is remarkable and it's still only April, but there's a long way to go. I'm not sure how many more donors they'll find.'

'I hope we can stay. Not only to prove William wrong about St Dom's but because…' She waves her hand around at their garden, their home.

'I know. I feel the same. But I'm certainly not giving up hope. If this whole experience has taught me anything, it's that help can come from the most unexpected sources.'

'Oh I know. Two months ago, would you ever have imagined leaving *Jarvis Millwood* to care for Wendy? But he's changing, David. Belatedly growing up.'

David nods thoughtfully. 'I think they both are.

CHAPTER TWENTY-THREE

Gwen

Two and a half weeks have passed since their day in Dungeness and it seems as if the universe is playing with Gwen, sending her one challenge to her new-found positivity after another. First, they can't find any more decent leads. Then, when they do, everyone is horrible.

Gwen found a phone number for a Mr D.P. Beddons from Slough. She tried to pass it over to Jarvis, but he was having none of it, and actually, she realised, if she was going to get a job, she had to get over this fear of talking to people. So she rang him and explained, and he shouted and swore, asking how *dare* she phone a stranger out of the blue asking for money and didn't she realise people like her were the scum of the earth, disturbing decent people during their five minutes of peace and quiet, and he hoped she'd just **** off and die. Gwen put down the phone in shock, close to tears. Oh God, she'd never make another phone call again.

Jarvis made her a cup of tea while she recounted Mr Beddons' outburst and he put the mug down in front of her with a puzzled face. 'So why did he leave his phone number then?' he wondered. It was a good point.

After three hours Gwen was recovered enough to carry on, trying to relegate Mr Beddons to a looming smudge, like the

power station. Later that day she tracked down a number for
Shirley Ray, who'd left her place of work as a contact – quite a
lot of people seemed to do that. She'd written for her comment:
Many happy memories. That seemed promising. So Gwen picked
up the phone again.

'No thank you,' was Shirley's tight-lipped response and she
put the phone down. Gwen thinks the universe might give her a
little something for being brave enough to use the phone. Perhaps
Shirley is long-lost kin of Aunt Mary.

Jarvis has had two similar responses by email, and a few people
just haven't got back to them at all. None of this takes away from
the wonderful experiences they've had and all the money they've
raised in a relatively short time, but neither does it chip away at
the outstanding amount they need to raise. Over £32,000.

It's May. Even once they get the money, suitable builders must
be found and approved by the church authorities. Then the work
needs to be done. It all takes time. Gwen starts to dream of St
Dom's, flooded by rainwater. She sees herself and Jarvis and Vicar
Dave all getting carried away in different directions on the tide,
along with rafters and roof tiles and all her notebooks.

Then something wonderful happens. Really, really wonderful.
So Gwen is cross with herself for feeling a little bit sad. Jarvis gets
an email from Danny, offering him a job. Renee is leaving the
gallery to go home to France, it transpires. The gallery has a little
studio above it, where the assistant can live, so Jarvis won't have
to wear himself out travelling back and forth every day. Danny
wants someone passionate about art, for whom it won't be *just* a
job but a potential foot in the door. Someone personable and not
too strait-laced. Hard to believe there could be a job for which
Jarvis is perfect, but this seems to be it.

Best of all, it's only four days a week, Thursday to Sunday. So
Jarvis can, as he points out immediately, travel home after work

on Sunday, and drive back on Wednesday night. They'll still have three days a week for the visitors' book. Really, it's perfect, and he deserves it so much.

But Gwen can't help worrying. She can see why Jarvis got all caught up in the visitors' book living in Hopley with nothing to do but while away every night in the pub. But when he's living half the week in gorgeous Rye? He'll be doing a real job, making money, meeting new people – arty people. Surely the visitors' book, and the weird girl he was hanging out with, will fade to a distant memory? Danny's bound to display Jarvis's work sooner or later, and Jarvis will be plunged into an exciting new world – not like horrible art school, but one where he's genuinely at home. And Gwen *wants* all that for him. It's just that she'll miss him.

Meanwhile, *she's* applied for three jobs and been rejected for all of them. What if she's stuck here in Hopley for good, living with Aunt Mary and working at the surveyor's? The visitors' book will come to an end. Jarvis will be gone. Her life will be thoroughly bleak again.

'At last,' cries Jarvis beside her. 'Something positive.'

'What is it?' asks Gwen, trying to pull herself together. It's too soon for gloom. Jarvis's job doesn't start for a month and who knows? They may have saved the church by then. Gwen might have a job herself.

'You know that journalist on Twitter?'

'Purple Marcella?'

'That's her. She's messaged me back. It's been so long I thought she wasn't going to bother, but she's been away on a retreat apparently. Anyway, read it.'

In a nutshell, Purple Marcella has donated £100 to the fund. 'Well, that's nice – better than a poke in the eye,' observes Gwen. And their quest has captured her imagination and she'd like to run a story on St Dom's, and on Jarvis and Gwen, she's written.

It's a lifestyle mag about making the most of our moments. We cover craft, days out, nature, psychology and wellness, creativity, that kind of thing. I'm looking for a feature urgently – we had to pull one. Any chance I could come with a photographer and interview you both tomorrow? Any chance you've got an event coming up that I could reference? Our readers love an event.

'That's good,' exclaims Gwen. 'At least, for the church it's good. Not for me. I don't want my photograph to be in a magazine. And we've got no event for her…'

'No,' says Jarvis thoughtfully. 'The party will be ages away, if we even raise the money. But we *could* have. I was thinking about Danny's painting. We can't raffle it. You know St Dom's raffles. We'll sell twelve tickets – ten of them to my mum. That's rubbish. It must be worth hundreds. At least. We need an auction, Gwendoline Poppy.'

'But will people bid sensible money at an auction? St Dom's people I mean?'

'No, they won't. I was thinking that – we need your brain on this. Now this purple woman is asking about an event – seems like it's time we came up with something.'

Jarvis Millwood and his unsuspected depths of ingenuity. 'An art-themed auction,' says Gwen slowly. 'We'd have to advertise it outside the congregation. Maybe put an ad in a local newsletter or something. Or do a leaflet drop.'

'God, I haven't done leafleting since I was thirteen. Never say never though.'

'You should paint a picture for it too. We can't have an auction with only one prize. And we'll have to rustle up some others. Oh! And to make more of an event of it, we could have an art workshop with none other than the St Dom's artist in residence.'

'I didn't know we had one. Who is it?'

'You, you imbecile.'

'Oh no, I can't hold an art workshop.'

'Yes, you can.'

'Then you have to write a short story to sell in the auction.'

'Who on earth would want to bid for a short story?'

'A short story signed by St Dom's writer in residence? I would. You're doing it, Gwendoline Poppy, otherwise no workshop.'

'OK,' sighs Gwen. What's one more humiliation after all these job rejections and being on the receiving end of Mr Beddons' wrath and the horror of appearing in a magazine?

'I'll write back to her and say yes. What's tomorrow? Tuesday. Good. Neither of us is working.'

'Or ask her to come Thursday. She could just interview you. You're much more interesting anyway.'

Jarvis shoots her a disdainful look and reads aloud as he types: 'Tomorrow is fine. Any time is good. We are planning an event, tell you tomorrow.'

'Oh, Jarvis?'

'*What*? I'm not doing it when you're at work.'

'Not that. Just, can you ask her to come in the afternoon please?'

He retypes. *Any time in the afternoon is good.* 'Why? What's in the morning?'

'I'm getting my hair cut.'

Jarvis smiles but says nothing.

They work away for another couple of hours with nothing exciting happening except for a message back from Purple Marcella saying that she and her photographer will be at St Dom's at three the following day. Gwen swallows. This is suddenly all feeling a bit much. But it has to be done. Some coverage in their magazine could make a real difference to the church.

'Fancy a quick drink in the Swan?' Gwen asks when they start clearing their things away.

'Love to, but I can't. I'm in the middle of something – a piece of work. I really want to get it finished this week.'

'That's OK,' says Gwen, disappointed and proud of him at the same time. Already in the evenings, he's applying himself to his art. Which is a good thing. But it means he has less time to work late at the church, or to call into the pub when they finish. His focus is already shifting.

CHAPTER TWENTY-FOUR

Jarvis

For the past few days, Jarvis has turned his back on all socialising, even with Gwen. He *should* be working on pieces he can show to Danny when he starts work, and it's not like he's not excited to get serious about his art again – he's still in utter disbelief that such a gigantic piece of good fortune has landed in his lap. But there's something more urgent at hand. He promised to make Gwen a T-shirt.

After telling her about Bella and Tash, he's been thinking about what she said: that he was young, that everyone makes mistakes. He likes that better than his old assessment of it, which is that he's useless and can't be relied on. From now on, Jarvis has decided, he won't make a promise he doesn't intend to keep. He even took a whole evening to reflect on the job offer – perfect as it is – just to be certain he wouldn't say yes, then change his mind and let Danny down. But of course he took it. Working with Danny is a dream of an opportunity, and he doesn't even have to move away altogether. He knows Hopley's not much to get excited about, but he does love his family, lame as that probably is, and there's St Dom's and Gwen… stuff to feel good about. Stuff that's made him start to think maybe he's not such a waste of space after all.

Anyway, he's struggled to think of a design for Gwen's T-shirt ever since she asked for one, but since their trip to the coast, ideas have been coming and he's been doodling. Doodling has turned into sketching and the sketches have multiplied. There's Gwen eating ice cream, Gwen looking out to sea with her hair windswept, Gwen wearing her solemn listening expression. He's bought the T-shirt, a plain one in a rich purply-blue, like her eyes. She's always in subdued colours, but he reckons it'll suit her. He only hopes it'll *fit* her – always a dangerous call that one, with girls. Now to finalise the design.

He works in his room – the first time his desk's been used as anything other than storage for fags and video games in years. He's almost there with the main design. It's a picture of Gwen, but stylised, almost cartoon-like, a picture of a girl with huge swirling hair (he's taken some liberties with that, obviously, to make it look good) bent over a desk, wielding a pen. There's a lamp behind her, and ink flying and a ream of finished pages drifting into a pile on the floor. Her face is largely hidden but it's unmistakeably Gwen – you can see the corner of huge specs and a bit of her wide smile, which is becoming more familiar all the time. On the page that cartoon Gwen is writing on, you can read some words: *Anything is possible*... Jarvis is particularly pleased with that. It's like a private message from him to her, as well as a great slogan for a T-shirt. And only he would write a slogan upside-down. Cool. He works on the sketch for a while, refining it so it'll work well when he screens it onto the fabric. Can't have too much detail or shading...

At last it's there, and he's pleased with it, but he still doesn't know what to put on the back. All Jarvis's T-shirts have an image on the back. He thought about St Dom's, because she got so excited about the chart he drew, but picturesque as it is, he doesn't want to stick a church on a T-shirt. He usually puts something light-hearted on the back, like his beer-swilling chipmunk, but a drinking joke doesn't really say *Gwen*. He can't put anything rude or she'll never wear it. He sighs and stops for the night.

The next morning Jarvis goes to the church, but true to her word, there's no Gwen. He gets to work and realises how much progress they've made. Another few weeks and they'll have been through the whole book. He's not sure how he feels about that. It *was* the point of the exercise after all, but still. A text comes through from Gwen. *I'll be there by one. Don't do anything I wouldn't do.*

Ha. He settles down. He's done all of 2014 to the present, then he did 2013, and now he's just getting started on 2012. Let's see how much he can get done before Gwen gets here.

An hour later and he's found nothing. This seems to be the way of it lately. He really hopes they haven't had all the luck they're going to have. Bored, he checks the email account. Here's something. Ann from Aylesford has written back to Gwen.

Dear Gwen,

Thank you for getting in touch regarding St Domneva's. I remember it well. A very happy day amidst a very difficult time. It was a hard transition – from useful, working member of society to retiree, waiting out the rest of one's days. Especially for a woman, I think, with the added significance that working for a living always held for me and all the stereotypes that abound regarding older females. I expect you're too young to know about any of that yet. Anyway, you'll be pleased to hear that I've got over my 'depression' and have found a new way to view myself and my life. I miss the school of course, but they're very forbearing and allow me to visit. I try not to go too often and become a nuisance. I now spend my days in a number of ways I consider helpful to others and pleasurable to me. Would you think very badly of me if I said that the latter consideration is often the more important of the two?

Anyway, you didn't write in order for me to witter on. You wanted to know if I could help. And the answer is yes.

Giving back has always been very important to me, and St Domneva's has given me so much – more than I could tell you in one email. It mustn't close. I'm glad people like you and your colleague Mr Millwood are doing what they can. I salute you. Please find on your 'JustGiving' page a brief note from me together with my donation for £500. It may be a drop in the ocean, but I hope it makes a difference.

Sincerely yours,
Ann Wilson (Miss)

PS Apologies for my delay in replying. I don't check my 'emails' very often.

What a doll. Jarvis would love to write back and thank her but that has to be Gwen's job. She'll be so pleased. Nor will he colour in another £500 on the church tower. It would be more than his life's worth. He does, however, update the spreadsheet.

A while later, he hears Gwen arriving. It's only a door opening and some footsteps, but he fancies he detects her unmistakeable air of fluster.

'Gwendoline Poppy.' He beams, turning round. 'At last. Time for lunch.' Then he sees her and his jaw drops. 'Like, wow!' he says. 'You look *amazing*.'

Gwen goes red. 'Really?' she asks, looking uncertain, hanging her head. It's typical Gwen body language, but the haircut is sensational. It's still long – he won't have to change his T-shirt design – but a good few inches are gone, and that suits her. She looks like she's got hair, rather than the other way around. There are a couple of layers around her face so it's not such a *monster*, and she's had some highlights if he's not mistaken – nothing dramatic, just some chestnutty glints that make it warmer and more vibrant. It really suits her. Her eyes look brighter too.

'*Yes*, really. It suits you so much.'

'Oh good.' Gwen wilts with obvious relief. 'It's so different I couldn't tell. But I thought, it couldn't be worse, could it?'

'It's better,' says Jarvis, priding himself on his tact. 'Come on – I'm starving.'

'You're always starving.'

They have salmon salad and boiled spuds courtesy of Justine, who gushes over Gwen's hair and is as excited about the interview as if she were doing it herself. Then they race back to the church. Vicar Dave is meeting them at 2.30 p.m. and Jarvis wants Gwen to see Ann's email first. A reply is sent and the chart is duly coloured in. Jarvis has never known such delight to be caused by filling in small boxes.

Vicar Dave looks slightly stunned as they discuss the forthcoming interview and their ideas for the art auction. He wears that look a lot around Jarvis and Gwen these days. He probably never thought for a minute they'd get their arses in gear. You can't blame him. They decide to do it in a month's time or thereabouts. Jarvis will have to ask Danny if he can swap a gallery day that week as they'll need to make it a Saturday to stand a good chance of pulling a crowd. He emails right away.

When Purple Marcella arrives, she's a diminutive woman with purple hair. 'Marcella Manek,' she barks, shaking hands all round vigorously. 'Father Indian, mother Irish. Born in Jaipur, lived here thirty years. Can't fault it, bar the weather. Right, let's do this.'

She seems to be in a terrible hurry. Jarvis had imagined that someone working on a magazine called *Magic Moments* might be a bit more relaxed.

'We'll do the photos first. You never know when it's going to rain.'

The photographer, Andrea, does a quick recce around the church to scope out the best spots. Then she takes a number of shots of Jarvis alone, Gwen alone and Vicar Dave alone. Then the three of them. Then Jarvis and David, then Gwen and David, then Gwen and Jarvis. By the lychgate, in the church doorway, under the yew tree… after forty minutes, Jarvis is exhausted.

Then they retreat to the office, shivering – Andrea wouldn't allow any jackets for the photos and there's a stiff breeze even though it's May. Marcella fires questions at them while Gwen determinedly makes tea. Andrea brings out a laptop and starts editing the images while Marcella records the interview on a Dictaphone. Gwen's umming alone will fill quarter of an hour. But when the job is done, Marcella softens. She wraps her hands with their long magenta nails gratefully around her mug then reaches for a biscuit. There are choc-chip cookies and lemon shortbread – Gwen's gone posh with the biscuits.

'This is all great material, perfect for the magazine,' she says. 'We're quite new, only a couple of years old, but we have 30,000 subscribers so I hope it gives you some useful coverage. Thanks for seeing me so quickly. It'll go in the July edition; we're very late for that. But they had to pull an article because they found out this knitting tutor had been having affairs with her students for years, all very dodgy.'

Jarvis chokes a little on his shortbread.

'So the deadline's, like, yesterday. I'll write it all up and file it tonight. How're the images coming, And?'

'Good,' says Andrea without looking up from the screen. Jarvis looks over her shoulder, fascinated to see how she squares off photos that already look perfectly straight to him, increasing or decreasing the saturation of various colours, discarding pictures with a fed-up sounding 'out of focus' even though they look anything but to his untrained eye.

'So it'll be on the shelves next month,' Marcella continues. 'In time to make a difference, perhaps. Let me know as soon as you get a date for that auction, Jarvis. Message me right away.'

Jarvis promises, and eventually Vicar Dave has a chance to ask about her previous visit to the church and her lovely comment in the visitors' book.

'Do you remember that lovely little shop that used to be here, Namaste? The owner was a friend of mine from uni. I was visiting her. Shame she had to close, she loved that place.'

'Mahira?' asks Gwen. 'She was *lovely*. I loved that shop and I used to go to some of her workshops. Are you still in touch with her?'

'Yes I am. I love her workshops too; she's so gifted. She once realigned my aura in just forty minutes.'

Jarvis blinks.

'Oh please will you say hello from all of us?' says Gwen. 'We all miss her, and even one of our donors asked after her. She'd only been to Hopley once, but she remembered Mahira.'

'I will,' says Marcella, downing a cookie in two bites. 'She'll be happy to hear that. Right, got to go. I'll send you some complimentary copies when it's printed. Good luck, troops.'

CHAPTER TWENTY-FIVE

Gwen

The following day is Wednesday. Gwen and Jarvis are just finishing lunch in the Swan when Gwen's phone rings. 'It's Vicar Dave,' she says, surprised, because they only saw him that morning.

'Gwen? Are you nearby? There's a man here to see you.'

'A man?' echoes Gwen.

'A Bryan? Says you contacted him about the visitors' book?'

'Good grief. Well, we're just about to head back, as a matter of fact. Can he wait five minutes?'

She hears a muffled question and an even fainter reply. 'Yes,' says Vicar Dave. 'He says he's got bags of time.'

'There's a man. At the church,' Gwen tells Jarvis when she's hung up.

'Your ex?'

'Don't be daft. A Bryan apparently, about the visitors' book. Jarvis, do you think it's Travelling Bry? After all this time?'

'I can't remember any other Bryans, can you?'

'No.' She frowns. 'But why didn't he email back? Why would he just turn up?'

Jarvis shrugs. 'Because he's Travelling Bry. Let's go.'

They race back to the church where they find Vicar Dave and another man sitting in a pew, chatting companionably. 'Ah here they are,' says the vicar, standing up.

The other man is unmistakeably Travelling Bry. He's small, mousey and a bit dishevelled. He has a backpack almost as tall as he is and a patchy beard. He looks up with the brightest smile. 'Gwen Stanley, I presume!' he cries, hastening from his seat to shake hands.

Gwen can't help it; she goes all shy again. It's so unexpected. Seeing him there, when she'd thought he was disregarding them, is so *nice*. And because of the hours she's spent spinning stories about the names in the visitors' book, it's a bit like meeting a fictional character, as if David Copperfield or Bella Swan has just stepped out of the page. Or, in Bryan Bolan's case, out of the laptop screen.

'Twenty-six and terminally shy,' says Bryan, still smiling as if she's an old friend. 'Aspiring writer. Grieving but putting the pieces back together. I read your email and honestly, I could have been hearing from my younger self. I'm so pleased to meet you.'

'I'm pleased to meet you too. Thank you for coming.'

'And you must be Jarvis Millwood, fellow fundraiser and friend of Gwen's.'

'In the flesh,' says Jarvis, with a grin and a handshake. 'Good to meet you, man. Your website's very cool. You've seen some places. Hopley being the *most* exotic of course.'

'Of *course*. Can a weary traveller beg a cup of tea and a chat?'

'Of course, yes, yes,' frets Gwen, going into Mother Hen mode. 'Come through to the office. Vicar Dave, will you have one?'

'I've got places to be, thanks. But I'll see you soon. Mr Bolan – thanks so much for stopping by and for what you're doing for us. Gwen, you'll need to colour in another brick on the church tower.'

Bryan looks quizzical.

'He means our progress chart,' Gwen explains. 'Oh. Does that mean you're donating? I'm sorry, I shouldn't ask. We haven't even sat down yet.'

'It's fine,' says Bryan easily. 'Yes, I certainly am. I'll tell you all about it over this cuppa.'

Jarvis hoists the backpack onto his shoulder, which Gwen thinks is very courteous of him, and he nearly collapses under the weight. Bryan must be stronger than he looks. Jarvis is pink-faced and puffing by the time they reach the office and drops the bag just inside the door. 'You travel the world with *that*?' he demands in horror.

There are still some of the good biscuits left from yesterday. Gwen arranges them on a plate while Jarvis makes tea, and the three of them sit around the table. Marcella yesterday, Bryan today… St Dom's is becoming quite the hub. As it should be. As it used to be.

After small talk and biscuits, Bryan begins his story.

'I wasn't kidding when I said your email was like hearing from the younger me, Gwen. I was a very shy young man. Excruciatingly so. Only child. I loved reading and the natural world, but I grew up in Sunderland and they're a pretty tough crowd there. The popular activities, when I was a kid anyway, were team sports and crime. I had no talent for sports and no inclination for mugging old ladies, so you can imagine how well I fitted in at school. And, as you see, I'm no Marlon Brando. I was always small; my mother told me I'd grow into myself, but she was wrong in that regard. Girls laughed at me, guys beat me up… are you reaching for the violins yet?' Bryan laughs and scoffs another choc-chip cookie. 'These are *good*,' he mumbles with a blissful expression.

'Bryan, I'm sorry to interrupt, but have you eaten lately?' asks Gwen, leaning forward in concern. 'Only you seem really hungry and wouldn't you rather have a meal? There's a really nice pub just down the road.'

Bryan hesitates, halfway through reaching for a piece of shortbread. 'I *am* hungry. Haven't eaten for a while. But I don't want to take up too much of your time. You're busy, and I just showed up – don't want to impose.'

'We've got plenty of time,' says Jarvis. 'If a man's hungry, he's got to eat. But I'm not carrying that backpack.'

They lock the backpack in the office and relocate. Inside the Swan, Bryan orders a hearty hunter's chicken with extra potatoes, and Jarvis and Gwen, who've already eaten, order desserts to keep him company. Between mouthfuls, Bryan continues.

'So I was pretty unhappy is what I was getting at. Thought I'd never have friends, that life would just happen to other people, not to me. But I was lucky – like you, Gwen – I had great parents, and they wouldn't let me give up, encouraged me to go to university. I went to Durham. Different world. Where loving books was a plus, not a liability. Three years flew by and I started to dream. Of travelling the world, working in ecology, saving the planet. My dream job was elusive, so I worked in insurance in Bristol as a stopgap. The work was boring, but it was nice trying a new city, living down south. And then I met Rachel.

'I honestly couldn't believe I'd found a beautiful girl who would love me. But she did, and we got married, and I was the happiest man alive. She got pregnant really quickly so I stayed in the insurance job and we put travelling the world on hold, but we didn't mind. Our daughter Miranda was our heaven and earth, and we were only in our twenties. We'd travel when she grew up and left home, we always said. But it didn't work out like that. Rachel got cancer – ovarian – and after six years struggling against it, we lost her.'

Gwen can feel tears threatening. Such a nice man, such a happy family. Why did such things have to happen?

'I'm skipping over this awful bit. I haven't come here to bring you down – quite the opposite. But it was hell. I don't need to explain. Eventually Miranda went back to uni and graduated with a first and got a job in Paris. And I was alone again, treading water. Still in the same damn job.' Bryan laughs, shaking his head. 'They'd been good to me you see, with time off and so on when Rachel was ill and after. Even now I'm grateful for their decency. And it was stability among such cataclysms of change. Time passed. Too much time.

'Eventually I realised that Rachel wouldn't be happy with how I was living now. I could actually *hear* her, telling me off, telling me it was time for a new start.'

Gwen fidgets. She can't bear to interrupt him, but she knows exactly what he means.

'So when I turned fifty, I set off on my first trip. Thailand and India, the first two places Rachel had wanted to go. I kept a journal – letters to her, really, bound up in a book. I saw so many amazing things. Huge, awe-inspiring sights that changed me forever, and little exotic details that massed up like a treasure trove. I can't explain to you what it meant to me. So far from England, unable to speak the language, not even sure what I was eating half the time, I'd thrown myself on the mercy of the wide world and it caught me like a safety net. Rachel would have loved it. Miranda loved my emails to her.

'When I came home, Miranda visited. She was the one who encouraged me to blog. She set up my website and taught me how to add the photos. Two months later I did Australia. I was meant to stay a month; I think I was gone just over a year. I made it to the Great Barrier Reef and that was it. I started doing conservation work for UNESCO and I didn't want to leave. And I wanted to tell you this, Gwen. Once, I was lying in the water of one of the reefs. It was really warm and shallow, like being in a bath. I was all alone and my arms were outspread and I was thinking about Rachel and feeling sad that she couldn't be with me, sharing this, when I felt a tickling on my little finger. I assumed it was just a fish passing by so I kept drifting and wishing... The tickling persisted, and it's not like fish to hang around so I opened my eyes and turned my head, and guess what it was?'

'What?' Gwen glanced at Jarvis, whose mouth was open.

'A tiny little seahorse. It had curled its tail around my finger, and it was just hanging out there.'

'Wow,' breathed Gwen.

'Yes. It was just exquisite, hanging on to me like I was part of the reef, part of the natural world. Which of course we all are, if we only remember it. And I remembered that seahorses mate for life. It came to me just when I was missing Rachel so much it hurt. It was a message that she was still with me. Always will be. I don't know if you guys believe in things like that, but that's what it meant to me, and I'll never forget it.'

'Oh.' Gwen's eyes brim with tears. 'I do believe it. That's so beautiful.'

'Our loved ones don't leave. This world is *so* big and *so* miraculous. Your parents are with you, sharing everything you do. I wanted to tell you. I read your email when I was in Greece. I started to write back, but the Wi-Fi was terrible there. I knew I was coming back to Britain in a few weeks, so I thought I'd wait and come and see you myself.'

'Thank you so much.' Gwen can only whisper. That a complete stranger would take such trouble to comfort her. What would she rather her parents witness and share? Seahorses and sunshine and joy? Or fear and shrinking and Aunt Mary's cooking? If Bryan's right and they're right there with her, they haven't been having much fun lately. 'I've been trying lately, really hard. The visitors' book has really helped, and Jarvis has been amazing.'

'I have?' Jarvis looks pleased.

'Of course. You know you have. I've had more fun in the last few weeks than... well. You've been so kind to me. And now you've got this amazing job and you're painting again and you've inspired me.'

Jarvis scratches his head. 'Cool.' Then he turns to Bryan. 'Still surprised when I inspire anything other than an urgent need to drink, to be honest.'

He's so self-deprecating, thinks Gwen. He doesn't know how much he has to offer. He needs to find his mystery woman. Maybe she'll make some enquiries when he's not around. Wouldn't it be wonderful if she could find her and bring them together?

'Can you stick around a few days?' Jarvis asks Bryan. 'I could listen to your travel tales all day. Or are you catching a plane tomorrow?'

'I can stay a bit, if you're sure I won't be in the way? I'm in the UK for a month or two so I can spend some time with my parents, then I'm off to Paris to see Miranda, and Malaysia after that.'

'*Do* stay,' agrees Gwen. 'We're holding an art-themed event on the first of July with an auction and a workshop. We'd love you to be there for it.'

'I can do that,' says Bryan, looking pleased. 'Maybe I'll go up north in a couple of days, spend a few weeks with my folks, then come back here. I'll tell Miranda about it, see if she wants to pop over and support you. I won't bother asking Mum and Dad. Mum won't go anywhere without the old man, and *he* firmly believes that if he goes anywhere south of Middlesbrough he'll melt.'

'And we're having a party later in the summer,' adds Jarvis. 'When we're all done with the visitors' book. To thank everyone who's donated, or even just talked to us. You should come for that.'

'I'll certainly try. And I should tell you about my donation. Conservation is a huge focus of my travels, you've probably gathered. Wherever I go, I work – I get a job that will help. I don't want to be just a tourist, a consumer. The beautiful world and its special places saved me. I save what I can. So I've given £5,000 to St Dom's.'

'*Five…*?' wheezes Gwen and chokes on her lemonade. Jarvis whacks her on the back. The guy hadn't eaten in ages, he lives out of a backpack and there are holes in his shoes. How has he got £5,000 to give away?

'Woah, man, are you sure?' asks Jarvis, more coherent than Gwen. 'I mean, we appreciate it, but that's a lot of money…'

'I'm sure. When Gwen wrote to me, I remembered St Dom's at once. It's strange the places that stand out, when you travel as much as I do. It's not the famous landmarks but tiny corners of the world that I'll never forget. St Dom's has to be saved. And I've plenty of money. All those years gainfully employed in insurance.' He winks.

'Well, *thank* you,' says Gwen, overwhelmed. 'For everything. It's just – it's just *wonderful.*'

'Let me buy you both a drink,' says Bryan, getting to his feet and patting his belly. 'That food was great. I think I need some chocolate cake now.'

'You wouldn't think a little guy like that could put away so much,' observes Jarvis, watching him amble to the bar.

CHAPTER TWENTY-SIX

Jarvis

Jarvis is working his notice at Speedy-Spend. Now more than ever he feels the disconnect between his best life and how he's been living. It was tolerable spending days here when he was utterly hungover. The counter propped him up when he was too tired to stand erect and the alcoholic haze in his brain meant it didn't really matter where he was. Plus, there wasn't anything better to do anyway. Now that he's excited about his art again, about starting his new job, about St Domneva's, it's so much harder to be here.

He's been combatting the boredom by handing out fliers for the art event to customers, but then his boss told him to stop. It's against company policy to 'promote a personal agenda' apparently. But he can pin one up on the notice board. After an hour, he notices there's a very obscene diagram scrawled on it. But likewise all the other leaflets on display so at least it's not personal. The joys of living in Hopley.

The week after Bryan appeared was slow but positive. A few more people contacted, two donations coming in of £30 and £150 apiece. Bryan stuck around for three days, then disappeared up north to see his parents. 'See you for the auction,' he promised as he hopped onto a train, blithe as if his backpack was full of marshmallows.

Thanks to Bryan, he knows what to put on the back of Gwen's T-shirt now. Two seahorses, to represent Gwen's parents, together forever and still with her too. In his mind's eye, he doodles a cheeky-chappie boy seahorse and a long-lashed girl seahorse sitting at a table, sharing a bottle of wine. Ha. He can get some booze on there – his signature theme – but she can't object because it's classy.

He's so distracted that he forgets to scan Mrs Millis's oranges. Instead of taking them quietly like any normal person, she says – shouts actually because she keeps forgetting to switch her hearing aid on – 'You haven't scanned my oranges, young man. I'd have been going home with free ones if I wasn't an honest person.'

And wouldn't that have been the end of the world? thinks Jarvis, taking them back and scanning them. Of course, his boss overhears. 'That's the third time today,' he points out, looking outraged. 'We're not a food bank, Millwood. Just because you're off to some fancy job doesn't mean you can do what you like around here. This is a business and we want A-game focus. *A-game focus*. Can you give us that?'

Jarvis takes a deep breath, preparing himself to apologise and all that blah. But instead… 'Not really,' he says.

'Not… not…' sputters Keith, who is six inches shorter than Jarvis and very red-faced. Jarvis isn't convinced that managing the Hopley Speedy-Spend affords him maximum life satisfaction.

'Not really,' repeats Jarvis kindly. 'I'm very bored and I've got a hundred better things to do and I'm finding it very hard to concentrate.'

'Well.' Keith's voice is quite shrill now. 'Perhaps you're just not an A-game sort of person, Millwood. And we don't employ anything less here.'

'Hmmm,' says Jarvis. 'I see.'

'In fact, I don't like your attitude at all. I think we can do without you. Don't bother finishing your notice, Millwood, and don't expect a reference. Go on – get out.'

Finding it hard to conceal his glee, Jarvis rips his tabard off over his head and shimmies out from behind the till. 'You'd better take over, Keith. There's quite a queue building up. Take it easy, man.'

He tosses his tabard onto the counter and slopes to the back room to fetch his hoodie, fags and battered copy of *Cloud Atlas*. Then he emerges into the sunshine and lights a cigarette. A free man. He's off to draw seahorses.

On impulse he turns towards the part of town which boasts Hopley's few small offices and finds the surveyor's. It's actually the ground floor of an old house, dating from days of the town's former grandeur. A receptionist with her hair scraped back so tightly her features are all pulled back into the oddest shape looks up from her phone.

'I'm here to see Gwen Stanley,' announces Jarvis.

'Name?'

'Mr Millwood.'

'What's it regarding?'

'A survey.'

'Which property?'

'A new one.'

The receptionist sighs and picks up the phone. 'Jeannie? Is Gwen Stanley there? Can you tell her there's a Mr Millwood here to see her about a survey. Oh, OK.' She points down a corridor. 'Second door on the left.'

'Thanks. Do you like art? Take one of these. In fact, take a few, bring your friends.' Jarvis hands her a sheaf of fliers and winks his most charming wink.

He finds Gwen in the corner of a dingy office with one high window and an elderly woman at the next desk. They both look as if they're about to fall asleep though Gwen perks up when she sees him. 'What are you doing here? Why aren't you at work?'

'I got fired,' he says, beaming. He fills her in and she cracks up. 'I wish I'd get fired,' she mutters then.

'You could just leave. Get a better job. It's not like you're living your dream life at your aunt's place.'

Gwen sighs. 'I know. Look, Jarvis.' She turns her computer screen – it's one of those big old Compaqs – for him to read an email. It's from her friend Amma. She's secured a great job with a London law firm. She's starting in July and she's found a two-bed flat near London Bridge. *Will you come and live in it with me?* Amma's written. *You know you're dying a death at your aunt's place. You know you'll find a job if you come to the Big City. It'll be awesome, like uni again, but with money. Please come, Gwen, I miss you…*

Jarvis swallows. The thought of Gwen not being in Hopley when he comes back from Rye every Sunday is weird. But of course she can't stay here forever – there's nothing for her. He grabbed *his* big opportunity. And this is Gwen's, no doubt. 'Gwendoline Poppy, that's *amazing*. You'll do it, right?'

'I think I have to,' she says, looking scared. 'I need a proper job, a proper life. London's the best place for jobs, and if I've got to brave the Big City, I'd rather do it with Amma. It would be so much fun to live with her again.'

'I'm so pleased for you.'

'Thanks. Only, do you think I can do it? Find a job there, keep it all together? I mean, London's pretty intimidating, and I'm a bit out of practice at, y'know, life. I've got a cushion, financially. But London's so expensive. I could eat through all my money in no time if I don't find a decent job. And I'm not exactly a high-flier, am I?' She gestures around the dusty office with its antiquated technology and Jeannie, pecking away at her keyboard with two fingers.

'Are you kidding? This is a solid admin background, useful for any job. You've got your degree, your interest in literature and, most of all, the visitors' book. You can add fundraising to your CV, dealing with all kinds of people, press and PR experience, event organisation – the list is endless.'

She smiles. 'I never thought of it like that.'

'Well then, no wonder you haven't had any luck with your job applications. Come over tomorrow with your CV and I'll go through it with you. Or better yet, Mum will. You'll see. You'll get a job in five minutes flat. Look out, London, Gwendoline Poppy's coming.'

She lets out a deep breath and shakes her head in disbelief. 'That's it then, all this is coming to an end.'

Jarvis perches on the edge of her desk. 'Yeah, but it had to. I'll miss you though. You know, I'll be working weekends, and that's probably when you'll be free so…'

'I know.' She looks touchingly glum.

'But you can't stay in this one-horse town just to hang out with me on weekdays, thrilling though that may be.'

'I know. Do you think we'll lose touch, Jarvis?'

'No way. I'll come to London on a Monday or Tuesday and meet you for lunch. Monday lunch – it could be our thing.'

She smiles, though neither of them knows how things will pan out in reality. 'You're a good friend, Jarvis.'

'I know. You're so lucky. OK, I'll leave you to it. Email Amma. Say yes.' He lopes out, leaving a flier on Jeannie's desk.

CHAPTER TWENTY-SEVEN

Gwen

Going back to Aunt Mary's gets harder every day. The silver lining to this is that it counters Gwen's great, great fear about moving to London. Whenever terror sets in at the prospect, she asks herself if she could honestly stay here much longer. And the answer is always no. She spends Saturday at Jarvis's, working on the visitors' book and perfecting her CV with Justine's help and, at the end of the day, finds herself literally dragging her feet in the hallway, not wanting to go home.

Justine notices. 'Do you want to stay the night, Gwen?' she asks, looking concerned.

'No thanks,' sighs Gwen. 'I told her I'd be back for dinner. I don't want to be rude.'

'Some other time then. Why don't we fix a date? How about tomorrow?'

'That would be lovely. Thank you. She's not all bad… I mean, she must have a heart or she wouldn't have let me live with her. It's just…' Gwen wants to explain so she doesn't seem too pathetic. Probably she *is* a bit pathetic, but she's taken such big steps lately and Aunt Mary is the one person who doesn't seem to notice or care. 'Everything's changing,' she says. 'I'm applying for jobs, I'm moving to London… but when I walk into that house, I feel exactly as I've done the whole time I've been living there. Like this heartbroken, paralysed person. As if all of this' – she waves her hand around to encompass her friends, St Dom's and life in general – 'is just a dream. Every time I walk through the door, I want to put on armour.'

'That's intense,' says Jarvis, leaning against the wall.

'I don't like it.' Justine shakes her head. 'You're making some very big life changes, Gwen, in the aftermath of a tragedy no young woman could take on the chin. You deserve to be supported and encouraged, not criticised and pulled down.'

'It's only a few more weeks. Amma takes over the flat on the tenth of July. I'll probably go that day. She'd be pleased and why wait? The art event will be over, we're bound to be finished with the visitors' book by then…'

'I have a suggestion.' Justine looks thoughtful. 'Say no if it doesn't feel right of course, but it strikes me that that's a month and a half, in fact. Quite a long time to live somewhere that you're actively unhappy. Why don't you come and stay here instead?'

Gwen's jaw drops. 'For the whole time? All those weeks?'

'You're here all the time anyway,' points out Jarvis, sliding down the wall to sit on the floor.

'Oh, but I can't put you out, Justine. I'm sorry, I shouldn't moan.'

'Gwen, it wouldn't put me out. George's room is sitting there empty. It's not the most feminine environment, but it's clean and tidy and it's temporary. You might be happier and more productive when you don't feel you have to face the music every night.'

She would, there's no doubt about that. For a minute she imagines it. To be part of a family again. To be relaxed in the evenings, as well as happy and busy in the days. Granary toast for breakfast. Then she slumps. She can't do it to Aunt Mary. 'It would seem so pointed,' she says aloud. 'As if I'm saying to her: "You're awful company and they're great. Your home is drab and miserable, and theirs is lovely and fun." I'd feel just terrible.'

'That's about the size of it though, right?' says Jarvis from the floor.

'Well *yes*. But that makes it worse, doesn't it?'

'It's difficult,' allows Justine. 'You're a kind girl and she deserves consideration. But perhaps you should think about yourself a bit, Gwen. You've had so much unhappiness. I think London will be brilliant for you, but a new city, a new job, is quite an undertaking. You need to build your strength up before you go, not have it worn down. Look, if you want to come, just know you're welcome. But if you're happier to let things lie for this last stretch, I understand completely.'

Gwen has learned over the last two years not to be demonstrative. Her aunt actively shrinks from physical contact, and when Gwen has tried to give her a hug, on her birthday or Christmas, she always makes some personal comment – 'Oh, your hair could do with a wash,' or, 'You've put on more weight, haven't you?' But now she hugs Justine tightly, as she used to hug her mum. 'Thank you,' she says sincerely, looking into her eyes. 'Your kindness has helped me so much.'

'Bye, Jarvis,' she adds, stepping over his legs.

Gwen walks home in a gauzy, purplish dusk, her head whirling. Justine is right – six weeks until she moves to London. That's a long time to feel uncomfortable and unwanted and *crushed*. And there's a lot to do during that time. The visitors' book to finish, the auction to arrange, Jarvis's mystery lady to find, job applications to make... Oh, and she'll have to get her stuff out of storage.

On the edge of the estate, Gwen stops. Her things are still in storage. She has a sudden memory that's been buried deep under the months of grief and missing her parents. Aunt Mary hurrying her to pack up so the move could be done and dusted. And then announcing that there wasn't room in her house for 'all that rubbish' and that Gwen would have to put it in storage.

Gwen was too numb to argue or even see anything strange about it and there it's been ever since.

There are only about eight boxes, not a huge amount to show for the lives of three people, a happy family. She feels a sudden yearning to see everything again. These are the sorts of tasks that face her now. She tries to imagine a day looking at her parents' things and then returning, emotionally raw, to Aunt Mary's razor tongue. She can't. She just can't. It occurs to her that she hasn't actually told her aunt that she's leaving yet.

She walks slowly through the depressing little estate. Aunt Mary doesn't have to live like this. She might not be the richest woman in the world, but Gwen knows for a fact that she could easily afford a more charming little place on the nicer side of town. But charm doesn't matter to her aunt. Nothing seems to. She never goes out. Just cleans and cooks and watches mindless television. Is she depressed? No. Gwen knows depression. It robs you of energy, and you need energy to be as sharp as Aunt Mary eternally is.

At the front door, she's assailed by a great, sweeping dread that makes her want to cry. Gwen feels eight years old all over again, arriving at school, bullied by Melissa Parsons. But she's twenty-six. *It's not for long*, she tells herself sternly as she unlocks the door. *Only six weeks.*

'Hi, Aunt Mary, I'm home,' she calls, kicking off her shoes.

'Quiet. I'm watching something.'

Gwen goes into the lounge and sits down, watching patiently while a husband and wife scream at each other on the TV set. She's pretty sure they had exactly the same argument the night before, and last week too. When the credits roll, her aunt grudgingly turns down the volume and looks at Gwen. 'Well?'

It's not the most inviting start to a conversation, but there are things to be said. The more Gwen puts it off, the worse it'll get. 'How was your day?' she asks, to be polite.

Her aunt snorts. 'A thrill a minute. Twelve dead flies on the windowsills. Do *all* the insects in Kent have to come here to die? Wouldn't hurt you to grab the dustpan and brush once in a while. There'll be more now summer's coming.' She sounds gloomy, as if summer is the plague.

'Sure thing,' says Gwen. 'No problem. Hey, why don't you come to church with me tomorrow? You could meet Jarvis, and Justine and Bradley.'

'*Jarvis*,' mimics Aunt Mary in a sneery sort of 'posh' voice. '*Justine and Bradley*. Very nice, I'm sure.'

Gwen is at a loss how to respond. Are they particularly posh names? What difference would it make if they were? Aunt Mary sounds like a narky teen. 'I just thought it might be a change. It would be lovely to take you, seeing as I've spent so much time there lately.'

'Pff. I don't need reminding of that.'

All over again, Gwen feels that she's done something very wrong, though she has no idea what or why. She takes a deep breath.

'What do you mean?' she asks softly. 'You sound a bit annoyed. Was there something you felt I should be doing instead?'

'Well, it wouldn't kill you to do a bit around the house you know—'

'I do,' counters Gwen mildly. 'Every morning before I go out, I do an hour. And the house is very, very clean.'

'I suppose standards aren't what they were in my day. And it wouldn't kill you to get a proper job either you know. Or do you expect to doss about on two days a week in my spare room forever?'

Gwen is starting to boil with the unfairness of it. She's told Aunt Mary about the jobs she's applied for, which proves what she's always suspected, that her aunt hardly listens to a word she says. But she can't get wound up now. She's just been given her opening.

'I have been applying for full-time jobs lately. I did mention a couple,' she can't resist adding.

'I can't take in everything you say. So where are these jobs then? Around here?'

'A couple in Kent, a couple in London. I didn't get them though.'

'Of course not. Done nothing but mope around here for the last two years. What did you expect?'

Gwen squints. She's being told to apply for jobs, but also that she's so rubbish there's no point applying for jobs. *Again, Gwen, stick to the point.*

'Anyway,' she continues. 'I want you to know that I'm really, really grateful to you for having me here after Mum and Dad died. I wasn't dossing actually. It's been… a really hard time and I couldn't get myself together. But now I have. I think I'll get a job soon, and Amma's moving to London and we're going to share a flat. I'm going on the tenth of July.'

A long silence. Gwen fidgets. Isn't Aunt Mary going to say *anything*?

'So I'll have the house back to myself at last then.'

'Yes. I'm sorry if I've been a burden. I probably haven't been the most cheerful company. Although things have been getting much better lately. Well, I'll miss you, Aunt Mary.'

Her aunt turns the TV back up and stares intently at an advert for vacuum cleaners. Gwen frowns. OK, it was a lie, but it was a white lie, designed to smooth over their appalling relationship and this big transition. Is she not even going to answer?

'Aunt Mary?'

'You're always with those Millwoods these days, and that dodgy vicar, so it won't make much difference. It's been no picnic for me either, you know. Another person coming and going at my age, when all I want is my peace. July, you say? I suppose I can manage until then.'

'You won't have to,' says Gwen, without thinking. 'I'll be staying with the Millwoods until it's time to go to London. So you'll be shot of me disturbing your peace tomorrow.'

To Gwen's surprise, Aunt Mary does look briefly stricken. 'I didn't mean it quite like that,' she said. 'I just meant… it's been an adjustment for us both. And probably not the right thing, you know, long term.'

'Oh, I do know!' exclaims Gwen, eager to take advantage of the temporary thaw. 'I am sorry, Aunt Mary, for any trouble I've been, and I'll never forget you taking me in.'

'Well… hush now, my programme's back.' On screen, a handsome young man in hair gel deals his girlfriend a ringing slap across the face.

'I'll leave you to it. But even if you don't fancy church tomorrow, please come to this. It's an art auction we're arranging. It's for the whole town. Jarvis is giving an art workshop and I think it'll be really good.' Gwen puts the flier in her aunt's lap and goes to bed.

The next morning, she lies in bed a long time, disbelieving. Has she really done that? Is she really moving out today? Hopefully Justine hasn't changed her mind. Gwen goes downstairs and sees a note from her aunt on the table.

Out of bread. Gone to shop.

It's scrawled in black felt-tip across the flier for the auction. Gwen goes upstairs to pack.

CHAPTER TWENTY-EIGHT

Jarvis

Jarvis is worried when Gwen doesn't show up at church. It's not like her. After the service he shambles into the office, but before he can get started, a message pings through on his phone. His mum:

Gwen's here x

Never one for a long text, his mum.

Has he forgotten some plan they made? He's been doing much better at remembering stuff lately. He wanders home to find his dad carrying a large wheeled suitcase up the stairs and Gwen crying in the hall.

'I can't believe I've done it,' she keeps saying. 'Oh Justine, have I done the wrong thing?'

Jarvis can tell they won't be working on the visitors' book for a while, so he drifts in and starts making hot chocolate. Girls like hot chocolate. He chucks in a slug of rum while he's at it. Soon, he, Gwen and his mum are sitting round the kitchen table while his dad takes himself off to mow the lawn.

Turns out she's moved in. He's not too sure what she's upset about. It doesn't sound as if there was a big row or anything. She told the old trout that she was moving to London, and staying here before that, and apparently not much was said. Perhaps that was it, the indifference. He lets his mum do the soothing and philosophising.

'I'll go and get the rest of your things this afternoon, Gwen. I'm sure Mary will want to meet me, seeing as her niece is staying with us.'

'I really don't think she cares,' moans Gwen. 'After all this time. Are you sure it's alright that I came? I'm so sorry – I should've checked with you first.'

'Gwen, I haven't changed my mind overnight. Yes, I'm sure, so cheer up now. You've got your big London adventure to look forward to, and in the meantime, you can really enjoy your last weeks in Hopley. How much stuff do you still have there?'

Three boxes of books, a tote bag and a small TV apparently. It makes Jarvis realise how little a presence she must have had in that house for all this time. He can see that his mum is thinking the same, but she puts a positive spin on it. 'I can easily manage that alone. You two go off to the church for a couple of hours. Take snacks; I'll do dinner this evening.'

Perhaps his mum is hoping that Gwen will perk up once she resumes normal activities. And she does. He can actually feel her calm down as she starts poring over the pages, kettle boiling, birds singing outside. He finds an email address for Larry Sinclair, Worcestershire, and sends off the usual. Otherwise, it's uninteresting.

He starts perusing the spreadsheet to see if they've left any loose ends so far and one name jumps out at him. Greta Hargreaves. It takes him back to that very first day when he rocked up hungover and exhausted, and Gwen was so obviously fed up to have him there. He snorts. Where would she be without him now?

'What?' asks Gwen, looking up.

'Nothing.' She went babbling on about Greta and Coleridge and how her village sounded tiny and perhaps they could find her… He knows what will cheer her up once and for all. He makes a few enquiries on the internet and thinks for a bit. 'Let's go to Devon,' he says.

'What, now?' Gwen looks startled.

'Course not. At some point. Let's go to Winthrop-St-Stanhope. Look for Greta the poetry geek.'

'Really? You think it's worth it? You don't think she'll be dead?'

Ah. If she is, that won't cheer up Gwen at all. 'Well, she *might* be,' he says carefully. 'I mean, I suppose anyone we contact might be, in theory. But people do live a really long time these days so she might *not* be too. It's up to you. If you want to check it out, we'll go. If you don't, we won't. I've looked in the phone book online and she's not there, but that doesn't mean she's not in the village.'

'Exactly. She might be ex-directory or something. I want to go, Jarvis. I want to find Greta.'

By the evening, Gwen seems to have come out of her shock. She's smiling and talking at the dinner table, excited about their trip to Devon. 'We should probably wait until after the art auction though – there's so much to do.'

'Devon's a long way,' cautions his dad.

'We'll stay the night,' says Jarvis. 'No, don't get excited, Gwendoline Poppy – separate rooms.'

'*Jarvis!*' his dad exclaims. 'I do apologise for my son, Gwen. I'm not sure he's really mine.'

Sunday dinner is roast lamb with all the trimmings and lashings of gravy. By the end of it, they can hardly move. Shortly afterwards, Gwen decides to have an early night.

'Good idea after an emotional day,' approves his mum. 'Sleep well, Gwen. If you need anything just holler.'

Jarvis runs up to the attic to get the finished T-shirt. He knocks on Gwen's not-quite-closed door. 'It's perfect timing that you've moved in today.' He grins. 'I've got a present for you, and now it's kind of a celebrate-your-liberty thing.'

'A present?' Gwen is sitting on George's bed gazing into her book boxes. 'What for, Jarvis?'

'Because you asked for it.' He brings out the T-shirt from behind his back and watches her expression shift into bewilderment. Has she forgotten the day she asked him to make her a T-shirt?

'Jarvis. You remembered! You made me a T-shirt.' She *hasn't* forgotten.

She spreads it out on the bed. 'Oh my God. Is that me? That's me, isn't it, writing my stories? Oh, Jarvis, it's fantastic. I look like a *heroine*. I've never felt like one, but I might when I wear it. I love the colour by the way.'

Jarvis decides not to mention he chose it to match her eyes. It might sound a bit sappy, and it's not like that. 'Turn it over,' he urges.

She does. And for a fleeting moment, she goes deep red and looks almost… shocked. But quickly the expression clears and she looks up at him with the biggest smile. 'It's my parents, isn't it? My parents as seahorses, because of what Bryan said.'

He nods, feeling a bit soft around the edges when he sees tears come into her eyes. 'So you remember they're always with you. Is it OK, Gwen? I wanted it to be… y'know. Really good.'

To his astonishment she gets up and throws her arms around him. 'It's really good,' she mumbles into his shoulder, her voice all muffled. 'It's perfect.'

CHAPTER TWENTY-NINE

Gwen

Gwen has slept the deepest sleep she can ever remember and wakes feeling light, floaty, almost joyous. That's odd. She rolls over, luxuriating in the unfamiliar feeling of… relaxation. What's going on? She sits bolt upright and it all falls into place. Of course. She's at the Millwoods'.

She looks around the room at George's brown-checked duvet cover, IKEA wardrobes, his set of golf clubs propped in the corner. Strange to see her hairbrush, her faithful old TV set and her books in this masculine setting. It all comes back to her: packing her few possessions and trundling off to Jarvis's, wheeling her suitcase, leaving a note on the kitchen table.

She looks at the clock. Seven. If she knows Jarvis, he won't be up yet, which means that Gwen has time to make a cup of tea and drink it in bed, reading a book. That's just about her favourite thing in the whole world, but Aunt Mary didn't approve of morning idling and the sharp comments deterred her.

She pads down to the kitchen, feeling a little self-conscious in her dressing gown, but the Millwoods greet her cheerfully as they bustle around sorting out their breakfast. She spends two glorious hours relaxing in bed, periodically startling and thinking she should go and scrub an already-spotless sink, or quickly dress to avoid criticism, then remembering that's not her life anymore. Eventually she takes a shower in George's en suite and dresses in jeans and her new T-shirt (which she can't help thinking looks really nice with her new chestnutty hair and her dark blue eyes).

She loves it. She was a bit startled when she saw the back. For a split second she thought it was a romantic symbol and that Jarvis was making some sort of declaration... but then she realised it was a reference to Bryan's story and her parents. How amazingly thoughtful. Gwen goes downstairs for breakfast.

'How does it feel?' asks Jarvis, shuffling in behind her, hair sticking up and feet bare.

'Like I've escaped from Alcatraz,' says Gwen happily. 'Toast?'

It's a good day at the church. First, Annie and Wendy call in to say hi. Then Gwen finds a Twitter handle in the book, which she hands over to Jarvis because she's not on Twitter. Then there's another knock at the door.

They turn to see a neatly dressed man with 1930s hair, carefully parted at the side, and an immaculate moustache. 'Hello,' he says, looking nervous. 'Gwen and Jarvis, I presume? I'm James. James Varden.'

Jarvis looks vague for a minute, but Gwen has every one of their contacts catalogued in her brain. 'As in James Varden and Harry Bramley!' she exclaims. 'You left your address in the book and we wrote to you.'

'On the bee notepaper,' adds Jarvis, catching up.

'That's me,' says the man. 'I hope I'm not disturbing.'

'Oh no. Come in, sit down. Tea and biscuits?'

'She won't let you leave without some,' says Jarvis, 'so I'll just put the kettle on now.' He mooches over to the sink.

'This is very kind.' James sits down and looks at them attentively, sitting very upright, smoothing out his trousers.

'It's so lovely you came to see us,' says Gwen. 'Can we help you with anything or did you just want to say hello?'

'The latter really. And to see this old place again. How is the fundraising coming along? I do hope you're getting the support you need.'

'Pretty well. That is, we've still got a long way to go, but we've got an event coming up that we hope will give us a boost, and a lifestyle magazine's doing an article on us, so there's every reason to be hopeful. Look, here's our progress chart. Jarvis drew it.'

He leans forward and studies it intently. 'I see. Well, I would like to contribute to the cause. Is a cheque acceptable?'

'Our favourite thing,' says Jarvis, bringing tea.

'Thank you, that looks delicious. Let me write it straight away.' He takes a chequebook in an immaculate burgundy leather casing from his jacket pocket, followed by a navy fountain pen. Gwen admires his taste. The rip of a cheque, the flourish of a fountain pen – so much nicer than clicking and screens. She really wasn't made for these times. Nor was James, by the look of him. He's only about fifty but his manners and dress seem much older, weighted.

He scribbles and recaps his pen, hands the cheque across the table – £2,000.

'Wow!' cries Gwen and launches into a flurry of thanks and are-you-sures.

'Yes, really, thank you,' says Jarvis. 'This is very kind, and we're so grateful. You've taken us just past the halfway point. What a milestone.'

James sighs. 'Only too happy to help. This place is – was – very special to Harry and me. He… he's passed away now, you see.'

'Oh no.' Gwen can't believe it. Only yesterday Jarvis said that any of their contacts might be dead in theory, and now it turns out that one of them is. 'I'm so sorry. Was he your partner?'

'Yes. Although I find that rather a cold word, don't you? He was my everything. The love of my life.'

Gwen lays her hand on James's arm, even though he's formal and self-contained in a way that would normally put her off. She knows how he feels. Obviously it's a different sort of a relationship, but her parents were *her* everything. The poor man. 'When?' she asks softly.

'A year ago.' He bows his head and for a minute she thinks he's going to cry, but he's far too gathered-together for that.

'That's hard,' she murmurs. 'I'm so sorry.' Jarvis mumbles his condolences beside her.

'We had a difficult start, you see, when we got together. I don't mean in terms of our relationship – we had our ups and downs of course, but nothing significant. But coming out was hard for both of us. It was twenty-five years ago.' He shakes his head. 'We both came from very conventional families, families with expectations.'

'How did you meet?' asks Gwen.

'We met when we were both living in London. Harry was an antiques dealer, just starting out, and I was a research consultant for a TV station. We both enjoyed our work and loved London, we both dreaded our occasional trips home, even though we loved our families, because of the endless questions about when we were going to meet a nice girl and settle down. Neither of us liked to disappoint, you see. But neither of us could figure out how to tell them.

'Fast forward another year and we knew it was serious. It was too big a reality to keep secret anymore. Harry told his parents first and they were utterly distraught. Then I told mine, and it was no better. My mother had spent her whole life dreaming of my wedding and the grandchildren she would have. I felt terrible. I took all those milestones away from her.' He sighs and shakes his head.

'And your dad?' asks Jarvis.

'Not happy, let's just leave it at that. It was like a bad script from a TV show. But he came around. They both did. To be fair, both sets of parents really tried. But they weren't relaxed about the situation, and family dinners were always tense affairs. It was sad.

'Despite all that, we knew we'd made the right choice. I wish you could have met Harry. I was the serious one; he was the joker. He never made jokes at other people's expense, or took them too far, but he had a lovely sweet, merry way about him. He had wonderful taste, more flamboyant than mine, and because of his business he had some wonderful quirky things – a silver cuckoo sugar basin; an old 1950s telephone in powder blue. Our flat became a treasure trove.

'We first came here around the time we were moving in together. We were both exhausted so we took ourselves away for a weekend on the coast, and on our way back we stopped off here. We *loved* St Dom's. Harry raved about the windows, the gravestones, the crypt. I got all excited thinking it might be a great location for a programme I was working on… After that, we came back every few years. It was one of our favourite places.

'The last time we were here there was a visitors' book, so I wrote in it. I put our address – old-fashioned as I am. Harry told me off for that later, but now I'm glad. That particular day your vicar came hurrying around the corner. We were hugging and we jumped apart at once. Gut reaction – some people just can't take the PDA. But Reverend Fairfield introduced himself, asked all about us, just made *friends*. Which is all anyone wants really, isn't it?

'Before long Harry was bending his ear about the architecture, and we were swapping life stories, and he said a few things that really put things into perspective for us. We weren't young men by the time we met Reverend Fairfield, but his calm philosophy went a long way towards healing the old wounds. This place gave many gifts to Harry and me. So it's our turn to give one back.'

Gwen's eyes are full of tears as he finishes his story. James reaches out for a biscuit, and Gwen's glad that Jarvis brought individual plates. James doesn't look like a shared-plate sort of person. 'I'm sorry you lost him, man,' says Jarvis. 'And I'm glad Vicar Dave said some cool stuff to you guys.'

'Thanks, Jarvis. Now, you've heard my life story. Tell me about you. And is there anything else I can do to help?'

When he's gone, they look after him thoughtfully. 'Poor guy,' says Jarvis.

'I know,' says Gwen. 'I know how hard it is. I hope I'm starting to move on at last, but it's early days for James.'

'Hey, he lives in London, right? And you're moving there. Maybe you can keep in touch.'

Gwen smiles. What a lovely thought, that she might have another friend in the city besides Amma.

'And as for you moving on,' adds Jarvis, 'I think you're doing an awesome job.'

Gwen feels like a newborn lamb most days, just learning to walk, all wobbly. It's only at the end of the day, as she sinks into George's comfortable bed, that she realises that she wasn't at all shy when James turned up. She was actually happy to meet someone new. Perhaps she is getting better at last. Perhaps she *is* doing an awesome job.

CHAPTER THIRTY

Jarvis

The next day, James pops in on his way back from visiting Vicar Dave. He's staying in a nearby B&B for a while and they've set him the task of finding a venue for the art event since the church isn't conducive to holding an art workshop. Already he looks much happier.

When he's gone, Jarvis makes a start on May 2011. Here's something.

> 10th May. This church is one of Kent's true gems. We had our wedding day here in 1983 and it holds nothing but happy memories for us. 'Love never fails.'

The contact given is: The Everdenes, Whitstable. And there's an email address. He shows Gwen.

'That's good.' She beams. 'How lovely, they got married here. I bet they'll help.'

'Let's hope they're not divorced now.'

'Cynic,' Gwen scolds. 'They weren't divorced in 2011 and look – "Love never fails". It's from Corinthians. I bet that was the reading they had at their wedding. A popular choice, so they're probably quite conventional, but a lovely one so I bet they're nice.'

Jarvis shakes his head in wonder. 'Gwendoline Poppy. It never fails to amaze me how much you can work out about people from a handful of words in a book.'

'Maybe these Everdenes will give us £25,000 and solve everything.' She looks worried for a minute. 'What if we don't make it, Jarvis? There's so far still to go and we're nearly out of contacts to try.'

'Don't talk crazy, woman. Back to it.' He sends the email and gets back to the book but finds nothing else of use today. Gwen's right. They're running out of people to try. He's just about to suggest they call it a day and head for the Swan when Gwen exclaims.

'Oh my God.'

He looks at Gwen, who's staring at the book, all white-faced and startled-looking. 'What?'

'Oh my God. *Jarvis.*'

'*What?*'

'Wait, let me check I'm not seeing things…' She squints at the page with an expression of wonder.

Who's there? Idris Elba? Elton John?

'Jarvis, it's your girl in lilac,' she says, turning to look at him at last. Her pansy eyes are shining with excitement. 'Tell me again what she said to you that day?'

He wasn't expecting *that*. The words have been etched on his heart for three years, but for some reason he has to think for a minute. 'She said, "Wow, that's beyond gorgeous." And then she said, "What a fab picture. It makes me feel… radiant."'

'That's it – I thought so. Well, look at *this*.' She pushes the visitors' book over to him at last and he reads an entry from 2014.

3rd May. Beyond gorgeous. Everything about this church is radiant. I wish I could stay.

The name is C.P. Allerton, Dover, and there's an email address.

'It's *her*,' insists Gwen, hoarse with excitement.

'Why are you looking at 2014? I've already done it.'

'I *know*. But I've tried everything else, Jarvis. I looked up Karla Freja Silburg in the online phone book for Copenhagen, but I couldn't find her. I even emailed Amma because she used to have a Danish pen pal years ago. But Amma wrote to the old address and never got a reply. There's *no* way to find Nancy from Ohio so I thought I'd have just one more look in case you missed something. And *look*.'

'I can't believe you went to all this trouble.'

'Are you *kidding* me? Jarvis. You're my *friend*. Honestly, I thought you seemed like a bit of a pillock when I first met you, but you're seriously the nicest guy I've ever met. You've made me laugh for the first time in years, you've had me round for countless meals, you encouraged me to write, you made me the best T-shirt ever and now I'm living in your house. So yeah, I reckon you're worth a bit of trouble. And I want you to be happy. Email her, Jarvis, email her.'

'You do it. I feel a bit… it's a bit sudden. We have to ask her about the church anyway, otherwise it's just creepy. And if she does reply, well, we can go from there.'

'I get it. You're nervous. I would be. It's pretty momentous, isn't it? Imagine, Jarvis, your dream girl, after all these years. OK, I'll send the email. Probably best you don't get your hopes up anyway, in case the email's defunct or she just doesn't reply. You're right. I'm sorry. I'm getting way too excited.'

Wow. She *really* wants him to meet this girl. A guy could be a bit offended about that. Not Jarvis, obviously. Jarvis is way too laid-back. But another guy. 'Thank you, Gwendoline Poppy,' he says quietly. 'I can't believe it means so much to you to make me happy. You're a really lovely person.'

'You're welcome. Right, are we done for today? Shall we have a drink on the way home to celebrate?'

He laughs. 'I was about to suggest the same thing when you made your great discovery.'

They head out, Gwen chattering all the while. 'What do you think C stands for? It could be Chloe. Or Clara. Or Claire. Jarvis and Chloe – that's sounds nice. Jarvis and Clara. Jarvis and Claire.'

Jarvis and Gwen, thinks Jarvis suddenly – and randomly. And disconcertingly. *What?*

'Gwen. I thought you were going to stop being so excited.'

'Oh yes, sorry.' She subsides and he feels bad.

'I can't believe I missed that,' he says. 'I was so focused on finding women, women's names, that I only looked down the name column. I never thought there'd be a clue in the comments. What a fool. Although, it might *not* be her. It could be a guy.' He laughs. 'It could be Colin or Chris or Carl…'

'Oh don't,' scolds Gwen. 'It's her. It's too much of a coincidence. *And* she said she wished she could stay longer. There was a reason she didn't go back and talk to you, but she left you her email so you could find her, with a bit of ingenuity. Well, it only took you three years.'

Jarvis sighs. Has he really been pining all these years only to find that her email address has been right under his nose the whole time? It seems a long time to waste on a phantom, an unobtainable dream. Although she might be about to get a lot more real. He remembers her beautiful face, her long blond hair. That gentleness and warmth that emanated from her. He should be happy. He should be sick with excitement and hope. But it seems to him that now, Gwen is more excited about it than he is, and all he can think is that he doesn't know this person at all. They might have everything in common or nothing. She's a complete blank.

Everything happens very quickly after that. The following day a large Jiffy bag arrives containing six copies of *Magic Moments*.

Eagerly they leaf through features about making your own textile dye from vegetables and summer flower collages to the article about St Dom's. Gwen moans and groans about the photo of her. The wind had lifted her hair just as the shot was taken and she's looking startled but smiling. Jarvis thinks she looks great. Obviously, *he* looks smouldering. There's one of Vicar Dave inside the church and a photo of St Dom's as a backdrop to the whole text, which runs across two pages.

On Thursday, the magazine's in the shops, and Jarvis's phone goes crazy, ringing and buzzing throughout the day with people asking about the event and wanting to donate. The money starts to trickle in – a tenner here, a fifty there – until they've raised £500 in two days and no longer bother closing the laptop; they just leave it open on the donations page and glance up every few minutes to refresh it. Gwen's jumping up to colour in the chart so often it's practically cardio. They keep track of every single person who's helped on the spreadsheet, and Jarvis hasn't forgotten that he promised those early contacts a party.

They haven't heard back from C.P. Allerton and Jarvis doesn't think he's disappointed. He was *longing* to find her when he started this thing, but maybe the moment's passed. If it *was* her, he'd probably get nervous, he's built her up so much in his mind.

The occasional larger donation appears among the small ones, and by Sunday evening, their grand total has somehow scrambled up to £37,000.

'Only £13,000 to go,' murmurs Gwen, gazing at the church tower that Jarvis drew all those weeks ago, now with far more bricks coloured in than left uncoloured. 'We have to do it, Jarvis, we have to.'

'We will.'

'But we're not really going to make £13,000 at the art event, are we?'

'No,' he concedes. 'But there's still Greta to try. The magazine's still bringing in donations. We have a few pages left in the book. Remember, Bryan gave us five grand. Danny gave us three and James gave us two. We only need a couple more like that and we've made it. But if all that's not enough, we'll have a... I don't know, a bake sale or something. A hundred of them if we have to. We'll do it.'

'But, Jarvis, you're going away tomorrow.'

'I know.'

He hasn't forgotten. He's borrowing his mum's car for the week so he can take all his stuff down to Rye. He'll travel back and forth by train once he's settled. He starts work officially on Thursday, but it's Renee's last day on Wednesday. Jarvis is going to have a training day with Danny on Tuesday, then a day in the gallery shadowing Renee on the Wednesday, then on Thursday, in at the deep end. He's terrified. He's been in the habit of thinking of himself as useless for a long time now. But things are changing. *He's* changing.

'But, Gwen, me being away half the week won't stop the money coming in. I'll be back on Sunday evening. I'll want to hear *exactly* how much dosh you've raked in while I'm away. In fact, I want you to text me the day's total every afternoon when you finish.'

Gwen smiles bravely. 'I will. And you're right of course. It's going to be tremendous, Jarvis, your first week I mean. I'm so glad you're having proper training and everything – you'll love it. In fact, I got you something. A good luck present.'

She hands him a beautifully wrapped package in shiny paper. He opens it to find an expensive sketchbook and expensive watercolour pencils.

'You've got so much art stuff I didn't know what to get you. But you said the other day that you want to try experimenting with different media and I've never heard you mention these so...'

'Gwen. Clever you, they're perfect. No, I've never used them, but I'm totally up for giving it a go.'

'Oh good. I was worried after I bought them that they were a bit girly or whatever. But I thought, it's something you can easily carry when you're on the move, not like an easel. Because you'll be travelling every week.'

'You're a star. They're great. Thank you so much. I'll use them this week and show you when I come back, even if it's rubbish, OK?'

'Good. And I'll push on with the short story for the auction while you're away. I still don't think anyone will bid for it, but hey, I'll humour you.'

'Good woman.'

He looks at the coloured pencils. Maybe he can try some illustrative work again – it's been ages. He wonders how they'd be for portraits…

They wander home at six. His mum is making him a farewell dinner. Lalie's come home for it, though George 'can't swing the time, sorry, bro'. George can't carry off the term 'bro' and he shouldn't try.

At the door they're greeted by the rich, winey scent of Jarvis's favourite stew. There are more presents. Lalie gives him a vintage shirt in pale turquoise linen. 'Honestly, Jarvis, you can't start a new job in T-shirts and hoodies.'

Jarvis holds it up. It's seventies style, with long, flared cuffs and a pointed collar. He can see it working with his black jeans. He has to hand it to his sister, she has some taste. 'I actually really like it, Lalie. Thank you very much.'

She mimes fainting with astonishment. 'Marvels will never cease,' she comments and kisses him on the cheek. There hasn't been a Millwood sibling display of affection for some years.

His parents' gift is a backpack. 'For all the back and forth,' his father explains. 'You won't need a suitcase every time…'

'Especially for travelling *back*,' his mum adds, smiling through suspiciously glittery eyes. 'To us.' And she disappears into the kitchen. The whole going-to-work-in-a-gallery thing takes on a surreal, rose-tinted tone in the face of his family's delight. They're *proud* of him. Who'd have thought?

CHAPTER THIRTY-ONE

Gwen

Jarvis is gone. He loaded up the little Fiat with art supplies, freshly laundered clothes and bedding this morning. Then he hugged everyone, laughed at Gwen and his mum for being losers when they got a bit teary, and drove off into the sunset. Or the bright light of noon.

It's mid-afternoon and Gwen's in the church, but the stillness is too still, the silence too quiet. She has a vivid, painful recall of her first day here, wanting the visitors' book all to herself, hoping Jarvis wouldn't show up. Now it's just not the same without him. There are only three months of the book left to peruse and Gwen wants to get through them this week. Time is of the essence. The church isn't safe yet, and for St Dom's sake, for Vicar Dave's and Annie's and Wendy's, she has to plough on.

Vicar Dave drops in with some post for Gwen and Jarvis. One is a postcard from Bryan from up north, a picture of some dramatic mountains with creamy gold light breaking over the summit. She pins it up on the chart for Jarvis to see when he gets back. And there are two cards. The first perplexes her until she sees the name at the end.

I heard that you emailed Mum and Dad. I grew up hearing stories about their wedding day and got dragged along to see

St Dom's several times over the years. It's a lovely place and indirectly responsible for me being here I suppose. So here's a little something to help.

Rose Bold (Everdene as was)

It contains a cheque for £300. *So* nice.

Gwen opens the other card and a shower of photographs falls out. There are wedding photos of a very eighties-style couple, the young woman with enormous blond curls and poufy sleeves and a dark-haired groom wearing a Don Johnson-style linen suit and a lilac tie. They are at St Dom's, roof intact, stained-glass windows casting little mosaic-like lights on the sunny path below. A vicar, one of David's predecessors, smiles over the proceedings. There are also pictures of an older couple, both bespectacled, clutching each other's hands and smiling. She is grey-haired, he is balding, but they are unmistakeably the same people. There's a cheque for £400.

Dear Mr Millwood and Ms Stanley,

Thank you for your email. We're so very glad that you reached out to us when dear St Dom's is in trouble. As you gathered from the visitors' book, it is one of our favourite places, the scene of our wedding day and the start of our big adventure. As you can see from the enclosed pictures, we are still going strong after thirty-four years. Douglas is my best friend and that's the secret. We could not bring this to you in person as we are having some car troubles, but we hope to visit soon.

Good luck, and best wishes,
Irene and Douglas Everdene

Gwen feels a little emotional. That's what *she* wants, she realises. Eventually, one day, when she's sorted the rest of her life out. She colours in the chart, then takes the cheques to the bank immediately, both for security and for something to do. The visitors' book used to be a glorious distraction from a grim reality. But now her mind keeps drifting off into fears about the future and without Jarvis beside her, telling her to 'calm down, wench', they seem to be multiplying. The walk helps and she decides she must have a decent walk every day to keep herself from going loony bins.

The following day she feels a bit brighter. Jarvis is gone but not for long, and life is still a thousand times better than it was a few weeks ago. She powers through six weeks of the visitors' book though with no exciting results. She's brought her notebook today and alternates working on the book with working on the short story she has to finish in good time for the first of July. She's writing a short mystery about two people who get lost on a hiking holiday and about their daughter, waiting back home. She's made them lost, rather than dead, because in her story, at least, she wants them to come home.

And then an email drops into the church inbox. Gwen looks up and her heart thunders a little bit. It's from C.P. Allerton.

Gwen had sent the usual email from herself and Jarvis, regarding the church. But she'd added a PS just from her. She thought it would sound better coming from a girl.

PS This might sound strange, but on the day you visited, did you happen to pass a young man painting a picture by the lychgate and say a few words to him? It's a long story and I hope it doesn't sound sinister – it's really not at all. I just wondered. I'll explain if you're at all interested in getting in touch. Gwen.

At first, she'd felt really jittery about it and checked the emails compulsively. But gradually she relaxed and Jarvis didn't bring it up and now, because it's over a week since she wrote, she'd rather forgotten about her. But here it is. A reply at last. Gwen clicks on it and reads.

Hi Gwen,

Thanks for your email and sorry for the delay in getting back to you. I've just got back from a week's holiday in Spain and spent the last couple of days catching up with work emails. I was glad to hear news of St Dom's. Yes, I remember it well for a number of reasons. And oddly, yes, I remember the (rather attractive) guy with the easel. Intriguing! Why? I would love to donate to your cause. I'll head over to your JustGiving page this evening when I get home. Writing this slightly furtively, in case my boss is on the prowl. I'd love to see that old church again. Would it be very odd if I came to visit and maybe said hello?

Best wishes,
Christine Allerton

Gwen lets out a deep breath she's apparently been holding. It *is* her. *And* she thought he was attractive. Jarvis and Christine. Christine and Jarvis. It's not Romeo and Juliet but it's OK. And presumably musicality of names is no predictor of romantic compatibility. She sounds really nice and that's the important thing. Just from one email Gwen feels she knows her a little bit.

She writes back at once.

Dear Christine,

Thanks so much for replying to us. And thanks for your promise to help – I'll look forward to receiving your donation. As for your question, it's not at all odd to want to visit again. Several of our donors have turned up out of the blue and it's been lovely to meet them. FYI, we're holding an art-themed event including an auction on July first, here in Hopley. I attach the flier in case you're interested. Otherwise please come any time and we'll be delighted to see you. As for my cryptic question about the artist, he is my colleague in this endeavour, Jarvis Millwood. I'll explain more when we meet.

Best wishes and many thanks,
Gwen

Goodness. She feels all jittery again, so she closes the laptop firmly and returns to her story.

Later that evening she remembers that she needs to go through her storage unit before she moves to London. She meant to ask Jarvis to do it with her, but what with arranging the auction and writing the story and applying for jobs, she totally forgot. She could ask him to do it when he's home, but he'll only have a couple of days and there'll be so much to do…

She trails into the kitchen, preoccupied. Justine, ever perceptive, wants to know what's wrong. How different from life at Aunt Mary's.

Gwen explains her dilemma. 'I really don't want to do it alone and there's not much time left now. You wouldn't be willing… by any chance… would you?'

'Gwen, of *course* I would,' exclaims Justine. 'I'm honoured that you'd want me with you for such an important job.'

'Thank you.' Gwen is so relieved. 'Thank you so much.'

'Do you want to do it tomorrow? It's just that I'll be in work for the rest of the week and I've a busy weekend planned so it would be next week then.'

Gwen chews her lip. That's a little daunting. But next week is the week before the auction, and if Justine has a free day, maybe it's meant to be…

'That would be great,' she says. 'Tomorrow.'

CHAPTER THIRTY-TWO

Jarvis

Jarvis has never known time to go so fast. One minute he's travelling to Rye. The next he's training with Danny and then with Renee. The next he's working in the gallery. And suddenly, not one but two working weeks are behind him and it's Friday night and he's on the train back to Hopley for the weekend of the auction.

His watercolour pencils and sketchbook are in his blue-and-grey rucksack, but the muse is not with him tonight. His brain is absolutely teeming with all his new experiences. He remembers once, on holiday in Italy, paddling in the sea. He looked down and saw a shoal of tiny fishes flurrying around his ankles, darting hither and thither, with a restless, relentless kind of energy. That's exactly what the inside of his head feels like now. He leans his buzzing head against the cool train window and closes his eyes. All he can see are scenes from the past two weeks.

He remembers arriving on the Monday afternoon, finding a place to park, lugging his stuff through the busy streets and carrying it all up the stairs to his new flat. Renee had cleared it out ready for him and stayed with a friend in town for her last couple of nights so he could settle in at once. He hadn't taken much, but no doubt it'll become homier in time.

He remembers Danny talking him through his vision for the gallery, the vision that had brought him this far and the vision that would take it forward. They talked art and people and purpose. In typical Danny style, it was all very intense. It was his way of getting Jarvis on board, of making sure that the gallery mattered to Jarvis as much as it did to Danny.

The last two hours of the day focused on Jarvis's own art. Danny inspected the new canvases Jarvis had brought and was pleased. But not pleased enough. He gave him an in-depth critique which, under other circumstances, an aspiring artist might have paid a fortune for. Unlike his feedback at art school, it made sense to Jarvis. It inspired him to get started on something else and do better. It even made him laugh.

He remembers putting on his new shirt on Wednesday morning to go downstairs to work in the gallery with Renee and feeling glad of it whenever a customer came in. His sister was right: he needs to look like a grown-up. At lunchtime that day he texted her, asking if she could pick up a couple more for him in different colours. He remembers spending the whole of that evening learning all about the artists on display, and the individual paintings. He even got out of bed at one point and padded down to the gallery in his pyjamas, to remind himself of some details he'd forgotten. He wants to do a good job. He doesn't want to let Danny down.

Now, with two working weeks under his belt, it's starting to become familiar. It's not second nature yet, but there's a shift, and he knows he can do this. *Even so*, Jarvis thinks as the train rolls into Hopley station half an hour late, *it's good to be home.*

He walks home from the station. They've held dinner for him, and he's greeted with a shower of hugs and questions. As with his going-away dinner, there's an extra guest, and to his complete and utter disbelief, it's his brother George.

'Holy crap, George. Haven't you got a meeting to go to? A form to fill? The world to save? What will happen to all those wheels without you there to keep them turning?'

'Very funny.' George looks the same as ever – neat Ralph Lauren ensemble, little frown. 'Our mother said I have to come to your auction or I'll be disinherited, so. Very intriguing, though, my little brother saving a church. Don't worry, I'm only staying one night.'

'Thank God for that,' says Jarvis, cuffing George on the arm. George nods seriously.

And there's Gwen, in her big old specs, with her lovely glinty hair and her pansy eyes shining. Is that blue eyeliner she's wearing? She's beaming and brimming with news which she says can wait until he's eaten. So they all sit around the table and talk about tomorrow. He learns that they've had two more donations today and their total stands at £38,575. James has procured the Swan as their venue. Ed the landlord said he's more than happy to cordon off half the beer garden for the workshop – Jarvis groans; he forgot he has to give a workshop tomorrow – and half the lounge bar for the auction. Vicar Dave is keen to be the auctioneer, and Ed has said the first round is free so he hopes they won't get a good turnout.

'And what are we auctioning altogether?' asks George.

Gwen explains that the *pièce de résistance* will be Danny's painting. There's also Jarvis's painting and her story. She adds that she and Justine decided that three items wasn't much of an auction so she donated a couple of things from her boxes from home – two bottles of her father's very expensive wine (she's keeping the rest) and a small oil painting of some onions, a glass carafe and, improbably, a string of pearls. It's the one painting of theirs that she never took to. And Justine has baked a three-tiered clementine cake which looks like a dream of a cake, the sort you'd find in a patisserie in Paris or London.

'Still,' George says, frowning. 'Six prizes. It's still a pretty small auction. Pity you can't rustle up one or two more.'

Jarvis rolls his eyes. Gwen, of course, looks worried.

'I was thinking the same,' she admits. 'I've been racking my brains and I just don't *know*. I thought of asking Danny if we could auction off a day behind the scenes in the gallery, but he's already done so much for us I don't want to ask for more.'

Jarvis frowns. 'Yeah, I feel the same. It's a good idea though. Pity we can't ask George if we could auction off a day at his office.'

'Why can't you?' asks George, adjusting the starchy collar of his neat checked shirt.

'Because you're an *accountant*,' Jarvis points out. 'We don't want to kill them with boredom.'

'I've got it!' cries Gwen, looking at Jarvis in a way that makes him sense impending doom.

'Oh no.'

'No, really. I think it could be great. Did you ever see that programme *Down Home*? No? Set in small-town America? An advertising exec from the big city ends up moving there and hating it at first, but then there's this handsome—'

'Wait,' George cuts in. 'Isn't that the plot of every single Christmas film on TV? My wife watches them,' he hastens to add.

'Well yes. But anyway, in this series there was this young girl with a spinal condition who needed an operation and her family didn't have the money, so the town chips in and they have this hay ride—'

'Gwendoline Poppy, we are not going to arrange a hay ride in Hopley.'

'No, *listen*. After the hay ride, they hold an auction of the town's eligible bachelors.'

'Oh!' gasps Justine, with a gleam in her eye that strikes fear into Jarvis's heart. His father is looking as nonplussed as George.

'*All* they had to do was take the woman out to dinner and make small talk for an evening. But they raised some serious money for the operation, and Shelley's spine got fixed, and she could tap dance again. Anyway, that's beside the point. The point *is*, Jarvis, you're single and you're good-looking and—'

'No. Absolutely not.'

'But why not? It would be fun.'

'Oh, would it? I don't see *you* volunteering to be sold off like it's the Roman Empire. Have you *seen* the women in Hopley?'

'But there'll be out-of-towners too. No one expects romance to blossom – it's just for a laugh. They do it in America all the time.'

'Gwendoline Poppy,' growls Jarvis, feeling his face flame, 'we are not in America.'

'Oh come on, bro,' George says, laughing. *Again with the bro.* 'It's your big project. You still need to raise over ten grand. Every little helps, right?'

'It *does*,' agrees his mum. 'It absolutely does. And I've got *two* handsome sons which would take us to a total of eight items in the auction, which is quite respectable *I* think…'

'Wait, *items?*' cries Jarvis. 'You're calling me an *item* now? I'm not a piece of meat you know. Dad, tell her that's just wrong. Wait. *Two* handsome sons?' He turns to look at George, who's blinking fast. It's almost worth doing it if George is roped in too. That's hilarious. Of course, they *could* make a stand together, brothers united against the forces of Crazy Womanhood. But they've never really been that close.

'I don't think she means me,' says George. 'I'm married.'

'Oh, we could say that in the intro,' says his mum breezily. 'Lot number seven, an evening with George Millwood. Now don't get too excited, ladies, this one's married. Good food and conversation only.'

'What are they supposed to get out of a date with *me* then?' asks Jarvis, half amused, half appalled.

'They can *flirt* with you, dear. They won't be stepping on anyone's toes.'

'But I go back to Bristol tomorrow night. I won't be *around* to take anyone out,' argues George in his accountant's voice and wearing his accountant's expression.

'So take them for a quick drink before you set off. We can announce that up front too. It's just *fun*, George.'

'Dad, you're not OK with this are you? Do you realise your wife's gone mad?'

'There's usually method in her madness,' he says unhelpfully.

'Oh God,' groans Jarvis, sinking his head into his hands. Trust him to befriend a weird girl with an inexplicable taste for heartwarming American TV drama. Then he looks at George again. His brother looks close to tears. Oh, to hell with it, this is brilliant.

CHAPTER THIRTY-THREE

Gwen

When Gwen wakes on Saturday morning she lies in blissful relaxation for about 8.3 seconds before it hits her: the day of the auction is here. Jarvis is home and it's Saturday, and it's their last real chance to raise significant money for the church.

It's brilliant to see Jarvis again. There's something different about him, she noticed last night. It's a new confidence, a new light in his eyes, as if, at last, he's a man of twenty-seven instead of an overgrown teenager.

And Gwen, well, *she* heard yesterday that she's got an interview for a job in London on the eleventh. Her very first day in the city. It's an admin role for a heritage property in West London. A beautiful, historical house open for the public to enjoy is one of Gwen's favourite things. It will be right up her alley. When she told Jarvis about it last night, he was so pleased and proud of her; it was sweet.

But an even bigger achievement, Gwen thinks, was going through her storage unit. She and Justine had gone that Tuesday, as planned, and Gwen had been dreading it. Even stepping inside, switching the light on, felt momentous. There were a lot of tears. But there was a lot of laughter too, to Gwen's surprise. Memory after memory came out of those boxes, and as sad as it made her, she also felt lucky that she'd had such a happy childhood, that it had all been so good once.

And it really wasn't bad now either, she realised. She had Amma and London ahead of her, wonderful friends in Hopley, and a real sense of achievement and contribution there, thanks to the visitors' book. Compared with the past two years, it was technicolour.

At first it was difficult to decide what she wanted to keep and what she could say goodbye to. Justine suggested she keep anything that would be useful in her new life and anything that was simply too precious to let go. 'Go with your feelings,' she urged. 'You don't need to justify anything, one way or the other.'

Using these criteria, Gwen ended up with two roughly equal piles. A lot of her university stuff, to her surprise, she didn't want to keep. She'd thought she would; it had been such a happy time. But Oxford was behind her and London was ahead, and her old stuff wouldn't suit her new life. But a lot of the things from her parents' house fell into both categories – useful *and* precious. Seeing old friends like china and paintings made her feel excited about making a new home with Amma. She would fill it with a mixture of the sentimental and the brand new for a fresh start, she decided.

The whole exercise took less time than she'd expected, though extra time was needed for tea and tears. Luckily Justine had brought a flask.

Now Gwen is in a fizz of nervous excitement. What if the event today goes wrong? What if no one comes? What if no one bids even ten pence for her story?

She bolts into the shower and spends longer than usual grooming – she wants to be a positive reflection on the church. At breakfast, the kitchen is buzzing with excitement. George looks pale and keeps re-knotting his tie. Yes, he's wearing a tie. Jarvis is wearing his vintage shirt and looks… really great. Justine is cooking and singing, and even Bradley keeps checking the time and saying, 'Big day, folks. Big day.'

They get to the pub at 10.30 a.m.; the event is due to start in half an hour. Vicar Dave, Annie and Wendy are there, helping Ed arrange furniture and string fairy lights. Vicar Dave shakes Jarvis's hand and welcomes him back to Hopley. Gradually people start to arrive, and by 11 a.m., not only is there enough of a crowd to make it worthwhile, but they're still coming in. Gwen and Jarvis's determined leafleting must have done the trick. Ed hits the stereo, there's a bit of a debate about the optimum volume, and then they're off.

Vicar Dave makes his welcome speech, recapping on the saga of the church roof and the significance of getting it fixed, the visitors' book project, and Gwen and Jarvis's efforts to raise funds. There are plenty of people there who aren't church-goers and interested murmurs run around the pub. Gwen thinks it must be nice for Vicar Dave to have an audience that hasn't heard it all a thousand times before.

'The art workshop will take place outside in the beer garden in ten minutes,' he says. 'For those of you not participating, feel free to mingle, chat, order drinks – and to make a donation if you wish of course. We've come so far, but we have £11,425 yet to raise, and without it, we can't save St Domneva's. The auction items are on display over here – all bar the two mystery lots – so please feel free to inspect them ahead of the auction.' He climbs down from Ed's music stage to a cheerful smattering of applause.

'Gwen, where's your story?' asks Jarvis. 'You need to put it up there with the paintings and the wine.'

'Oh yes.' She pulls it out of her bag: a sheaf of A4 pages, neatly printed.

'That won't do,' says Jarvis.

'You haven't read it.'

'No. And whose fault is that? But I'm talking about presentation. You want people to bid *money* for this, to feel inspired, not look as if you're handing over office supplies.'

'It's too late to do anything about it now. I don't have time to go and print it on pink leopard-print paper.'

'Do you *have* pink leopard-print paper?'

'No.'

'Thank God for that. Wait, James. Can I borrow your pen a minute, mate?'

James is wandering past, talking to Annie. Jarvis collars him and borrows the classy fountain pen Gwen so admired.

'Here, sign it,' says Jarvis, handing it to Gwen. Gwen signs the manuscript with a flourish. James is released and Jarvis looks around for further inspiration. Three children are playing chase around the table and he grabs one of the little girls.

'Hey, Lily, can I have your hair ribbon please? It's an emergency.'

'It's my best one.'

'Well *yes*, that's why I need it to save the day. I'll buy you another one.'

'My mum will think I lost it and be cross.'

'I'll talk to her.'

Lily chews her lip. 'A new ribbon and an ice cream?' she barters.

'Done. Hand it over.'

Lily's ribbon is long, satiny and emerald green. Jarvis takes the signed story and rolls it into a scroll, tying it with the ribbon. 'There.' He looks pleased with himself.

Gwen takes it over to the auction area, and Ed places it reverently on a small table covered with a snowy white cloth. It's displayed between Jarvis's landscape and Danny's vibrant painting of St Dom's and the ocean, with a gravitas Gwen is quite sure it doesn't deserve.

But she can't feel embarrassed for long. There are too many people to greet. Bryan is back, with his tall, elegant daughter Miranda, who's come for a long weekend from Paris.

'I was overdue a visit to my father and, after all, I only live over the water.' She gestures in a vague channel-ward direction. 'We're neighbours.'

Gwen wants to grill her about Paris, somewhere she's always longed to visit, but there's also James and the receptionist from the surveyor's office and, to her great astonishment, her colleague Jeannie. 'I'll miss you, Gwen,' she says sadly and Gwen is amazed. Perhaps company, companionship, doesn't have to be all about words.

A few of the old people from the church come creaking in, grabbing chairs and settling down with a gasp and a great air of curiosity. Jarvis's pals Royston, Andy and Whacko turn up and lean at the bar, nursing pints as if it's any normal day, except that when they see Jarvis, there's a lot of back-slapping and fist-pumping. There are people who've come because of the article in *Magic Moments*. And then a stranger walks in, a stranger who can only be one person.

It took all of Gwen's self-restraint not to tell Jarvis that Christine was coming today, just in case something happened to stop her and the day would be spoiled for him. She figured it would be more romantic like this too. Christine stands just inside the doorway, looking around. She's wearing a red-and-white flowered dress and high-heeled red shoes, and her long blond hair falls to elbow length. Gwen hurries over. 'You must be Christine.'

'Yes. Gwen? How lovely to meet you.' They shake hands and then Christine kisses Gwen on the cheek. 'Sorry, I know I don't really know you, but I feel as if I do after our emails…'

'Me too. I'm so glad you came. Can I get you a drink? Some nibbles?'

'A glass of white wine would be lovely. Only let me pay for it.'

'No, first drink is free, courtesy of Ed the landlord. Come with me.' They start chatting easily, and Gwen is glad to have this chance to vet Christine before she meets Jarvis. She shows her the auction display, the chart that Jarvis drew.

'So is he here?' Christine asks, taking a sip of her wine and looking a little pink.

'Outside giving a workshop.' Gwen points through the window to where Jarvis is sitting at one of the wooden pub tables, along with three attendees and another four on the next one.

'Yes. That's him!' Christine's tone is one of delight. It's easy to see that Jarvis made the same impression on her that she did on him. 'So tell me: why did you email me three years later asking if I remembered him?'

Gwen doesn't want to present Jarvis as some pining, lovelorn weirdo so she understates the case. 'You came up in conversation one day when we were talking about all the visitors to the church. He said that you'd spoken that day… I think he thought you'd come back out again and that he could talk to you more. But you left the other way. I just wondered if the two of you might like to… have another chance to meet.' Better to present herself as an interfering busybody.

'Yes. I remember it clearly. I don't mean to sound vain or anything, but I had the feeling that if I passed him again, he'd ask me out.'

'And you didn't want to?'

'I did, but I had a boyfriend.'

'Oh.' *Of course. The obvious explanation.*

'Things weren't good between us, not at all. I was looking for an out, but I didn't want to put that on someone else. I knew it was over, but until I'd officially extricated myself, I wasn't going to date.'

So Christine is a decent person too. It seems a foregone conclusion that in a year or two Gwen will be attending Jarvis's wedding, hopefully at St Dom's, beneath an intact roof.

'And is he… nice? A good guy?'

'The very nicest. And are you with anyone now?'

Christine gives a little smile. 'Not at the moment.'

There we are then.

Just then there's a commotion outside. One of Jarvis's partici-pants is Wendy, and the person next to her has started painting in green. Wendy springs from the table, knocking over a water glass and stands at a safe distance, shivering. Jarvis calmly mops the water up, rearranges his students so that all the people wanting to use green are on one table – leaving just himself and one other person on the other table, using mostly red. Then he goes and chats quietly to Wendy for a while until she's ready to re-join the group.

'He's so patient,' says Gwen admiringly.

'I like him already,' says Christine.

An hour later, the workshop is over. Jarvis shambles in looking exhausted but chuffed, a smudge of blue paint on his cheek, a smear of yellow on the back of his hand. Gwen wants to go and hear all about it, but Christine can only stay a couple more hours. So she hangs back and watches as his eyes fall on the newcomer and widen, as the penny drops and his face lights up.

'Go and say hello,' says Gwen to Christine. She goes to mingle, and every so often she glances across to see them talking intently – and laughing. Good – that's good.

Vicar Dave, looking slightly giddy from all the activity, clambers back onto the stage and taps a wine glass for attention. No one hears, so Ed does the job by blowing a klaxon he keeps behind the bar for those occasions when things get too rowdy.

'And now it's time for the main event!' Vicar Dave announces. 'Our special auction. All proceeds will go straight into the fund to mend the St Domneva's roof. Without further ado, lot number one. A painting inspired by St Dom's, by Danny Martinez, the successful artist. Rye-based by way of Cuba, Danny has exhibited in Soho, Belgravia and Montmartre, to name but a few. Danny's work already commands high prices in the art world so let's see if we can do it justice here in Hopley…'

Somehow, during all the milling around, chairs were marshalled into rows. Gwen is sitting at the front, and when she looks round, she's surprised at how many people are packed into the little pub, listening attentively. They seem more in number than when they were standing about chatting. She's reminded of a school assembly.

The bidding starts and Gwen snaps to attention. This is the whole point of today after all. Vicar Dave's head bobs one way and then another, as he keeps up with the bids, clearly determined not to miss a single one. He looks like an avid fan at a tennis match, and his face is taut with concentration. The bidding creeps up to a thousand and then past, and Gwen heaves a great sigh of relief. If Danny's painting had gone for less, it would have been really embarrassing. At last it sells for £1,700.

Twisting round again to see who on earth would pay such a sum in Hopley, she realises it's been bought by Miranda. Gwen can see people congratulating her, then her slender figure threads its way to the front to shake hands with Vicar Dave. *Now there'll be a little bit of St Dom's in Paris*, she thinks. How lovely.

Gwen waves at Jeannie across several rows and grins at Jarvis, who gives her the thumbs up and swipes theatrically at his forehead. Yes indeed. Phew.

'Lot number two,' announces Vicar Dave at last. 'Another gorgeous work of art by up-and-coming artist Jarvis Millwood. I think most of you know this gentleman, who is currently working with and mentored by Danny Martinez. He is St Dom's very own artist in residence. A beautiful painting of the Kent Downs at sunrise. Jarvis, as you know, has been tireless in his work to save the church over the last months so please bid generously, ladies and gentlemen. Don't let his efforts have been in vain.'

Jarvis's painting sells for £800. 'Wow,' he mutters, coming over to Gwen. 'My first sale and it's a big one and I won't get a penny. Can I change my mind and keep the cash?'

Gwen rolls her eyes.

It's been bought by a features writer from *Magic Moments*. 'Marcella wanted to come,' the journalist explains, 'but she couldn't make it. I only came to cover the auction, just a small piece, as a follow-up to the article. And now look. Parting with large sums of cash wasn't in my brief,' she adds ruefully. 'But it's beautiful, Mr Millwood, I couldn't resist. Good luck with your career.'

Then Gwen's parents' painting is sold to Mr Hennessey, one of St Dom's regulars, for £300. 'Why didn't he just donate that in the first place?' wonders Jarvis in outrage. But Mr Hennessey doesn't care about the church, he's heard explaining loudly, he just likes a nice piece of art. And what's nicer than onions and pearls?

Gwen's story goes under the hammer next. When she hears Vicar Dave describe her as St Dom's heroine and writer in residence, Oxford graduate and rising literary star, she wants to die. He gives a little precis of her story to whet readers' appetites and then he's off. At first, the bidding is for £5, £10, and Gwen is mortified. It's almost as bad as she feared. Of course no one's going to pay significant money for a few sheets of paper, a story that they can read in under an hour and then, most probably, throw away, but still, compared with the sums raised by the previous lots, it seems like such a puny contribution. Why did Jarvis make her do it?

But the numbers gradually rise and eventually it's 'Sold! To the lady at the back' for a very respectable £90. Gwen can hardly believe anyone would part with £90 for her story. It's not the biggest contribution they've had to the roof fund, but it's another little block on the chart after all. She turns around again but can't see who's bought it, and Vicar Dave moves on to the wines, which are sold for £60 per bottle.

'Not that we encourage the stereotype of the drunken artist,' he warns. 'These are special bottles to be saved for celebration of artistic achievement.'

Justine's cake sells for £50 – 'Because every creative endeavour is best fuelled by cake' – and then Vicar Dave's face lights up.

'And now the two mystery lots, to close the auction,' he says, beaming. 'Ladies and gentlemen, we are auctioning off an evening with our artist in residence, Mr Jarvis Millwood, and an evening with his brother, Mr George Millwood. These two gentlemen have sportingly agreed to give up their time to entertain one lucky lady or gent to the best of their ability. And aren't they a handsome pair? Come up please, Millwood boys, so the audience can see you both.'

They clamber, scarlet-faced, onto the stage amid catcalls and wolf whistles. Gwen has to smile when she sees the contrast between them. Jarvis's curls, neatly brushed this morning, have gone wild again from the excitement, and with his paint smears and louche air, he's quite a contrast to buttoned-up George with his neat shirt and tie and immaculate hair.

The audience go wild, and the Millwood brothers stare at their shoes – beaten-down old trainers in Jarvis's case, polished loafers in George's. Vicar Dave auctions off George first, with plenty of reminders that he's married – expectation management – and an evening with George raises £360.

Jarvis shrugs at Gwen with a look of comical astonishment. The funniest thing about it is how genuinely proud George looks. James, who raised his hand every now and then to push the bidding up, plays at looking disappointed while Mrs Croxley, who runs the local bakery, proudly claims her prize. 'With our son Sam off in New Zealand, we miss the company of young men,' she explains. 'Frank and I will have George over for dinner the next time he visits.'

Then the bidding for Jarvis begins, and it's fast and furious. The receptionist from the surveyor's office and Mrs Dantry appear to be slugging it out, but when the bidding slows down, Christine enters the fray. Eventually, she wins the date with Jarvis, as well as some serious scowls from Mrs Dantry, all for the modest price of £600. *She must really like him*, thinks Gwen. And Jarvis looks relieved when he sees who he'll be spending an evening with.

The audience start to stand and stretch their legs, laughing and joking, teasing the Millwoods and Christine and the Croxleys. Then Vicar Dave shouts a few last remarks over the milling heads.

'Thank you all so much for coming. My colleague Mr James Varden will be bringing a basket round in a moment so please, if you have any spare change or notes, James is the man to see. And please tell your friends about St Domneva's. We've done wonderfully well today but we're still not *quite* there…'

James moves through the crowd, nodding and smiling. He looks so much better, thinks Gwen, just for having company and something to be involved in. She knows all about that. She looks for Jarvis, but he's deep in a heart to heart with Christine, so she goes to find Vicar Dave to ask who bought her short story. He smiles and points. Gwen looks to see Aunt Mary standing at the edge of the crowd, wearing her coat and clutching the scroll.

'No?' queries Gwen, looking at the reverend in shock.

He nods. 'Yes.'

Gwen crosses the pub. 'Aunt Mary! You came. I'm so pleased. It's lovely to see you.'

'Is it? I'm glad. I wanted to see you before you leave, Gwen. I wanted to say, well, I'm sorry. I could have made it all much easier for you, I realise. But I… *couldn't*. You wanted things from me that have gone from me.' She looks horribly awkward and Gwen takes pity on her.

'You don't have to explain. You gave me a roof, and I'll always be grateful. And now you've bought my story. I'm so surprised and grateful.'

'It seemed like a helpful way to have something to remember you by.'

'Will you read it?'

'Yes.'

'I'm glad. Will you come and meet the Millwoods? And my other friends?'

'No thank you. I need to be getting back now, but I wish you luck. I got you this.' To Gwen's utter astonishment she extracts a gift-wrapped box from her pocket and hands it to Gwen.

'You got me a going-away present?'

Her aunt shrugs, looking embarrassed.

'Thank you so much. That really means a lot.'

Gwen rips off the paper and opens it to see a necklace with a pendant in the shape of a puffin. The gold is fake and overly yellow and the puffin is an odd shape. It's cheap and ugly, really quite horrible, but Gwen will treasure it. She won't *wear* it, but she'll treasure it.

CHAPTER THIRTY-FOUR

Jarvis

By the time James has done the whip-round, and Ed throws in half the bar profits, the auction has raised over £5,000. It's been a roaring success by anyone's standards, and when Vicar Dave sees the progress marked on the chart, he looks quite tearful.

'We're almost there,' he whispers. 'We might really be able to fix this roof.'

'Save St Dom's,' Gwen sighs happily.

'Keep you and the girls here in Hopley,' adds Jarvis. Suddenly the implications of what they've been trying to do these last months come crowding in on him. What Hopley would be like if its loveliest building fell derelict. What it would be like here without cheerful, wise Vicar Dave. One more month to raise another £6,305. How?

It's a problem that Jarvis refuses to ponder as he enjoys his celebratory dinner with his family and Gwen on Saturday night, as he texts Christine to arrange a date and all throughout Sunday, the date itself.

He could hardly believe it when he walked into the pub yesterday and saw her there, the girl he's remembered so often and so longingly over the years. She's every bit as pretty as he remembered, and he wasn't wrong about her being gentle and sweet. He could hardly believe Gwen had really done it – tracked her down, brought her here. It feels a bit like being in a dream. A good dream.

Christine stayed the night of the auction with a friend in Willbury, only about ten miles from Hopley. So Jarvis meets her for brunch there before she leaves. But this isn't the date she bid £600 for. This is their getting-to-know-each-other date, the one he would have taken her on three years ago if he'd had the chance. It has a surreal quality, but they have a good time and talk for hours. Christine lives in Dover, which is less than an hour from Rye, so they can easily meet up when Jarvis is there. He'll take her to some shoreside restaurant on the south coast – somewhere much fancier than anything Hopley can boast. *That* will be the date she bid for and won.

He drives back from Willbury feeling strange – all starry-eyed and happy about Christine, yet with an odd feeling as though he's forgotten something, which nags at him distractingly. *What is it?* he wonders as arrives back at the house. The admin for the roof fund is all up to date. Did he promise to help his dad with something? But he can't think of anything.

Back at home, he spends a couple of hours with Gwen drawing up a plan of action. It's a one-point plan so far: go and see Greta. They agree on a date, then he realises that it's 6 p.m. and he really needs to head back to Rye.

The week flies by. He works hard in the gallery, paints in the evenings and explores his new part-time home after work and on his breaks. It's enchanting. The architecture is a mish-mash of Georgian, and Victorian, and even older styles he can't name: cottages with sagging roofs and roses clambering all over them. Ancient fortified gates, canons, blue plaques everywhere. He can't pass one without remembering Gwen's delight as she exclaimed over memorials to authors he's never heard of. Jarvis has never been so busy.

On the Wednesday night, he takes the train to Dover and meets Christine at an elegant French restaurant he's found on the internet. He splashes out on Prosecco and three courses, not because he's trying to be flash but because this is their official auction date and he wants to be worth it. Plus, it's romantic. It's a lovely evening, though Jarvis isn't back in Rye until nearly midnight. If this becomes a thing, he'll have to get a car sooner rather than later. And then it's Sunday again. He works until four – they close early on Sundays – and catches the train to Hopley.

Welcome back, Jarvis and goodbye, Gwen. She's off to London the next day. How weird that this period in their lives is really over at last. They go to the Swan, just the two of them for a good-luck drink, and Jarvis gives her his going-away present.

The gallery stocks gifts by local artisans and he used his staff discount to buy her a silver necklace with a pendant of a beautiful shell wrought in silver. 'I bought it before I knew your aunt had got you a necklace too,' he explains. 'Hopefully you like this one a bit better.' Jarvis knows for a fact that that gold puffin came from Speedy-Spend and cost £3.50. He used to wonder, when he worked there, who would ever buy them. Now he knows.

'Oh, Jarvis. It's beautiful. You really, really didn't have to but thank you. I love it, and it'll remind me so much of the visitors' book, you know? Because it comes from your gallery, and you wouldn't have ended up working there if it wasn't for Danny… and it'll remind me of our lovely day out too.'

The next morning, Jarvis and his dad load up the big car with all of Gwen's things. Even *with* the boxes she's brought from storage, it doesn't seem very much to start a whole new life. Still, it's enough to fill the car so that there's only room for Gwen and his dad.

'I wish I could come,' frets his mum. 'I'd love to help you settle in, Gwen, make sure you're all cosy.'

'I'm not Scotch mist!' his dad declares, indignant. 'I will carry the boxes in and make sure she's settled.'

There are hugs all round, and Gwen's in tears as she gets into the car and buckles up. Jarvis is feeling a bit misty himself. He and his mum watch as the car disappears down the road then go inside and sit at the kitchen table by unspoken agreement.

'House feels empty,' remarks his mum. Jarvis nods. 'I'll go up later and strip the bed in George's room. Give it a quick clean. It'll be ready then if George wants to come and stay. Or Gwen.'

'Do you think she will? I mean, London's going to keep her pretty busy, isn't it? Especially once she starts working.'

'I suppose it will. But you never know.

Tuesday and Wednesday pass slowly. Jarvis plods over to the church both days, checks the emails, finds one donation of £100. There's a note from a woman named Lisa, saying:

£10 of this is from Dad, the rest is from me. He's a nightmare but he's mine.

Jarvis has a suspicion and checks the emails. Sure enough there's an email from Jase Norris – ah so that was a letter L, not a number one – which says:

Oright Jarvis. I'm on the dole again so not much spare but have a tenner from me. My girl Lis will do it. Good luck. Jase.

Jase, who was reunited with his long-lost daughter after saying a prayer in St Dom's. After the turn of luck Jarvis has had lately, he doesn't find it surprising at all. Ten pounds from someone on the dole. Amazing. He replies with a heartfelt thank you then forwards the note to Gwen and tells her about Lisa's top-up. She'll be over the moon.

Then Vicar Dave calls in and remarks how quiet things are without Gwen.

'They are,' Jarvis agrees. 'And she wasn't even a noisy person.'

It's quiet all round in Hopley. No more sibling visits. Bryan has gone to Paris with Miranda, and James has gone back, albeit rather reluctantly, to London. On Wednesday evening, as Jarvis is travelling back to Rye, a text comes through from Gwen. She's been offered the job. She starts next week.

Well done, woman, he texts. *You're amazing, GP. Sounds really cool.*

A heritage house in West London. What could be more Gwen? The news is wonderful, and everything that she deserves. Yet somehow, in his mind, Gwen belongs here in Hopley, working to save St Dom's. She's texted frequently over the last couple of days: the flat is amazing, Amma took her out for celebratory cocktails, they're going clothes shopping on Regent Street… It all sounds fantastic, and he's so glad for her. But it's so different from Gwen's old life in Hopley that it makes him feel she's a million miles away, instead of fifty.

CHAPTER THIRTY-FIVE

Gwen

London is a whirl. It's a crush and a blaring and a bright streak of light. It's summertime hot and stuffy. Gwen has never felt so simultaneously frightened and exhilarated. It was one thing to come here as a student, for a day trip, with a friend. Then it was all giggles and Ben and Jerry's. But to immerse yourself, to try to build a life here… it's like being smacked by a wave.

Since Gwen arrived, her feet haven't touched the ground. As promised, Bradley helped her to carry all her things into the flat. Amma was there waiting and hurled herself into Gwen's arms the minute she saw her. God, Gwen had forgotten how good it is to spend time with a girlfriend. Bradley stayed for a cup of tea and a guided tour of the flat… 'I'll need to report back to Justine. In detail.' They offered him lunch, but he wanted to get back, so Amma and Gwen caught up on everything while Gwen unpacked.

Her bedroom is tiny – but Amma's is tinier. Gwen protested, but Amma has the slightly nicer view, of next door's courtyard garden, while Gwen looks out over a main road. She doesn't mind. It's so different and unlikely being here at all that it would take more than a courtyard to make her feel at home. From Jarvis's texts, she's learned that another shop in Hopley is closing down: one of its two hardware shops. She can't feel personally saddened – she never shopped there – but it's a shame that the town keeps diminishing. London, in contrast, is so *thriving*. Even so, she keeps having flashes of memory – the quiet lanes around St Dom's, her trip to Rye, the flat fields of Kent, silvered by drizzle or lit up by the sun.

That first evening, Gwen and Amma went out for a celebratory dinner, then cocktails in a courtyard bar in the shadow of Southwark Cathedral. Gwen's interview wasn't until 3 p.m. the next day so she could let her hair down a little. Over margaritas, Gwen heard all about Amma's new job, the medium-sized firm with the amazing reputation that Amma's over the moon to be part of and where she fully intends to blaze trails. Also, Nolan, the clever Australian whom Amma was dating in Bristol. They kept it casual because she knew she'd be moving to wherever her career took her. Now she misses him and hopes he'll end up in London too. Amma and Gwen have been in touch regularly since they left Oxford, but even so it feels as if they could talk forever.

The job interview went better than Gwen could ever have imagined. She got lost three times on the way, utterly baffled by the Tube, and arrived in a frazzled state due to her high-octane journey. She wondered how she could ever hold a sensible conversation with London flashing past outside the windows, snatching at her senses, making it hard to concentrate. But concentrate she did, and at the end of the interview, they asked her when she could start. 'Um, tomorrow?' she answered, wanting to seem keen but privately hoping for a few more days to settle in first. They agreed on a week on Wednesday, giving her a full week to acclimatise to London, hang out with her best friend and prepare herself for this new adventure.

'And shop,' pleaded Amma. 'Your clothes are just… no.'

She's right. Gwen's wardrobe is a concoction of things that are too small, things that are too big, student garb that was never fashionable in the first place and a well-worn Halloween costume. Amma takes her to Regent Street and insists on not only smart clothes for work but some fun things too, cool sneakers and Converse for combatting the hard pavements of London on the weekends and even a party dress or two.

'*Why?*' demands Gwen.

'Because,' says Amma.

Amma's job doesn't start for another couple of weeks so they make the most of these days together. It's like being on holiday, albeit somewhere very noisy, dirty and stressful. They walk, they explore different parts of the city, they visit galleries and spend hours in Foyles bookshop. They go to Hampstead and meet James for lunch. From a second-hand furniture shop near the flat, Gwen buys two old pine bookcases so her books have a proper home at last.

It's as though all the colour and variety and vigour that have been missing from her life these last two years have been stored up and emptied all over her now. She spends her days with her eyes wide and her heart pounding, and her nights staring sleeplessly into the city dark, which isn't very dark at all. Night-time is processing time, and sometimes Gwen wonders if she'll ever sleep again. But then morning comes and she's off, pulled along by the current, by the adrenaline rush. Occasionally she feels out and out panic; her life has become so utterly unfamiliar. But then it gets pushed aside as Amma proposes some new distraction and another day passes in a mix of euphoria and exhaustion.

She misses Jarvis terribly. She tells herself it's just that she's not used to having someone in her corner, but that's not entirely true. Certainly the two years with Aunt Mary were a low point. But before that she had her parents, every step of the way. Then, at Oxford, there was Amma. And now there's Amma again. No, the missing is fairly Jarvis-specific. But then again, they *have* spent a lot of time together recently, so that's probably just normal.

The best thing about her new job isn't that she'll get paid, nor that she'll be working in an office at the back of a lovely historic house with a view of the large and leafy garden, nor that she'll get a staff discount in the visitors' café which serves, her interviewers assured her, exquisite chocolate cake. No, it's that she doesn't have to start until Wednesday, which means that she can meet Jarvis on Monday, before she starts. He promised that on her first Monday in the Big Smoke, he would come and take her to lunch, see the flat, meet Amma. The thought of it has been like a cornerstone throughout that first crazy week.

So Gwen meets him at noon at London Bridge station. It's only a week since she saw him, but it feels like longer because so much has happened. When she sees his familiar lanky figure loping through the crowds, she feels as if she's being steadied by an anchor in the middle of a swirling tide. His face breaks into a slow grin when he sees her, and he gives her a big hug. 'You're wearing the necklace,' he observes. Gwen's been wearing her silver shell all week, like a charm. She holds it solely responsible for her getting the job.

First, they walk. Gwen shows him the parts of her new neighbourhood that she's been able to map out so far. Then they go to Covent Garden for lunch and exchange news. Danny is pushing Jarvis hard with the painting, holding the possibility of being displayed in the gallery out in front of him like a carrot. 'Much better,' he says every time. 'But not yet.' It is, Jarvis admits, forcing him to raise his game, a little more every week.

'I don't really care how long it takes,' he says. 'It's just so good to be working again, and though Danny is fierce about technique and vision, he never tells me what to paint, or how. I'm working on stuff I really care about.' And Danny's decided to stock Jarvis's T-shirts in the gift section of the gallery meanwhile. Jarvis will get a cut of every one they sell. 'I can work on them when I'm in Hopley and when I have a bunch finished, I'll take them down with me. Gives me something to do when I'm at home. It's quiet there without you, Gwendoline Poppy.'

'I'm so proud of you,' says Gwen. 'Have you got photos? Of the paintings you're working on?'

Jarvis shows her several of various pieces. One is a portrait of Christine and it is, of course, quite lovely. 'How's it going with you two?' Gwen asks.

'Good. Really good. She's a great girl, everything I imagined really, which is surprising, let's be honest. We're taking it slowly because, well, we live in two different places so it's not like we can see each other every day anyway. But also because we want to do things right, you know? Not get swept away and go all crazy.'

'That's smart, Jarvis. I'm so pleased. Say hi to her for me, won't you?'

'I will. We often say how lucky we are that you brought us together, you know.'

After lunch they go back to the flat and she shows Jarvis around. Then Amma comes home and they go to the courtyard bar for a beer. Gwen loves having her two best friends together, hearing them chat and banter. Jarvis eventually leaves at 7 p.m. and the girls walk him back to the station. They're quiet as they walk back to the flat.

Then Amma says, 'Mmmmm-mmm.'

'What?' asks Gwen, looking around as if there might be a cream bun speared on a railing.

'That Jarvis.'

'Amma, he's with Christine now, remember? And I thought you liked Nolan?'

'Not for *me*. For you. I'm just saying, he's nice to look at. And he's nice inside too. I'd be jealous except that I'm so completely awesome I obviously command best friend status forever. Which still leaves a vacancy.'

'Of course you do. What *vacancy*?'

'Boyfriend, partner, lover, whatever. He could be that.'

'What? No. I've told you, we're just friends. He's my second-best friend in fact.'

Amma frowns. 'I'm not sure about that, Gwen.'

'Amma, no. I've *never* thought that way about him, and now isn't the time to start. He's with someone else. He pined for her for *three years*. The visitors' book brought them together... it's romantic. It's fate.'

'The visitors' book brought *you* together. *You* brought *them* together.'

As they arrive back at the flat and climb the stairs, Amma is quiet and Gwen hopes she's done. But, waiting for the kettle to boil in the tiny kitchen, Amma resumes.

'But have you never thought that way about him because you just *don't*, or because you've never let yourself? Because you'd only known each other a few days when he told you about Christine. So even before you found her, she was always in the picture. Which made him off limits in some way – for a nice girl like you. Except he didn't know her, and even now they've had what? A handful of dates? Whereas you and Jarvis spent three solid months together and both your lives transformed. Are you really telling me you're immune to that? He's gorgeous, he's kind, he's talented and he's finally got his shit together. You can spend seemingly endless amounts of time together without ever getting tired of each other. He thinks the world of you – anyone can see that...'

'You think he thinks the world of me?' Gwen sinks onto one of the stools at the tiny kitchen counter, cursing the fact that she's told Amma quite so much about her life in Hopley. Her friend's memory is laser-like and, being a lawyer, she can build a convincing case.

'Gwen. Look at that T-shirt he made you. Which you wear almost every day by the way, despite the fact that you have tons of fabulous new clothes. Look at the necklace he gave you. Oh, and then there's the way he looks at you. I'm OK with guys having female friends, I really am. But if I was Christine, I wouldn't want my new boyfriend looking at another woman like that.'

'Oh, Amma, that's rubbish. He doesn't look at me any way.' Gwen feels herself going hot. She really, really can't believe that Jarvis likes her that way. Which means that she can't afford to consider whether or not *she* might like *him* that way. Oh bugger. She stares at the countertop, appalled.

'Early on,' she says, gathering her wits, 'the first time we had lunch at the Swan, I was really reluctant. I couldn't imagine spending a whole lunchtime with him, and I thought he must have some ulterior motive for asking. He could see I was unsure and he said – I remember vividly – that it was safe to say that he would never fancy me and I would never fancy him.'

Amma shrugs.

'*What?*' demands Gwen.

'So Jarvis is prescient, is he? Psychic? Never been wrong about anything in his life? Because no one *ever* ended up falling for someone they weren't attracted to from the first moment? I give you exhibit A, Gwen – Maxwell. For the first month we knew him, you thought he was – and I quote – "an arrogant tosser with a flat bum". Which he was, I might add, but you still ended up dating him for three years.'

'OK, but… but… Jarvis is with *Christine* now. And he's *happy*. They really like each other, Amma. It's not like she's really horrible and I can hope they break up.'

'OK. Well, I've said enough.'

'Yes, you *have*,' retorts Gwen with feeling.

'I'm just saying. Tea?'

CHAPTER THIRTY-SIX

Jarvis

Jarvis has never been so roundly happy in his life. Before art school, yes, he was happy in the way of any young guy from a decent family: taking each day as it came, taking everything for granted. Then came art school and the destruction of his dreams, the shattering of his high opinion of himself. Then came the hazy years, drunk, aimless, all bravado and no inner life at all. Now he loves his job, he's working harder than ever at his art and he's sold three T-shirts in the first week they were on sale (giving him a grand total of £27 in his pocket but it's not about the money). He's dating a beautiful girl. Things are easy between them – none of the fraught emotional ties he had with Bella, none of the frenzied desperation of Tash. Christine is mature, gracious and she plays no games.

Best of all, today is the day that he's driving to Devon to meet Gwen to hunt for Greta Hargreaves. It feels great to have some genuine, official visitors' book business to pursue once again, and it's two weeks since he's seen Gwen though they've texted every day. She's completely overwhelmed by her new job of course. Despite all she's done for St Dom's, she's still struggling to take herself seriously as a professional after her two blank years, but it doesn't sound to Jarvis as if there've been any major disasters so far. OK, so she absent-mindedly posted a pile of account sheets on her way home one day, only realising they were gone when she got home and sat down to work on them; she found herself looking at a pile of letters instead. But everyone does stuff like that when they're tired and everything's new. She didn't get fired: she's all good.

When she took the job, they were fine about giving her the two days off that she'd arranged with Jarvis for Devon. He's going to meet her at Newton Abbot station – Gwen is taking a direct train from Paddington.

Jarvis gets there in plenty of time and sits in the car, texting Christine. She asked him, over their last drink together, whether she should be worried about him spending two of his days off with Gwen; about the two of them staying the night in Devon.

'God no,' he told her. 'Don't get me wrong, I think Gwen's fantastic, but not like that. We've only ever been friends. We're only staying over because it's a long way and it could take a while to find Greta. Separate rooms *obviously*. It's church business. The last loose end we have to tie up.'

It's quite a sobering thought really. After this, there's the party to arrange – the one Jarvis dreamed up to thank the donors, the one Vicar Dave saw *in his vision* – and they've settled on a date at the end of August. But Jarvis can do that on his own, with a bit of help from Vicar Dave. And he'll have to, because Gwen's in London and up to her eyes in work.

'You're *not* worried, are you?' he checked with Christine. 'You really don't need to be.'

'No, I'm not. I just had to ask the question, because the two of you get on so well. I know you wouldn't cheat on me – and Gwen wouldn't stitch me up either.' Which is true. So everything's good between them but a little text here and there can't hurt, he reckons.

Arrived NA. Waiting for Gwen. Hope you're having a great day xx

And there she is. Gwen. Emerging from the station and looking all about, then spotting the Fiat and grinning and waving. She's wearing all new clothes. A summer dress, some lemon-yellow Converse, a light jacket. And the silver necklace he gave her. He gets out to hug her and stow her overnight bag in the boot. 'How was the journey?'

'Heaven! Two and a half hours just to sit and read. First time since I started work. How was yours?'

'Fine. Boring, really, with no company. But all good. Shall we go?'

It's a thirty-minute drive into the countryside to reach Winthrop-St-Stanhope. They check into their B&B and ask their host if she knows Greta, but she tells them she's only been there a year. 'It's flown by, and I spend more time talking to people who are passing through than the ones who actually live here.' Which makes sense.

They kick off with a late lunch in a little country pub on the edge of the village. Again, they ask about Greta but no luck. Maybe she isn't a pub-goer. They explore the little village, keeping a weather eye out for places where they might find people who know her. The first and most obvious is the church, but it's locked and there's no sign of anyone around. There's a gorgeous-looking bistro with wooden floors and dripping candles. It's closed, but a sign on the door says, 'Open at 6'.

'Dinner tonight?' suggests Jarvis.

'Ooh, *yes*,' says Gwen, eyes sparkling.

They try a cutesy gift shop, a dental practice and a bakery. Each time, Gwen conscientiously offers all the variables of how to pronounce Greta's name. Gretta. Greeta. Hargreeves. Hargraves. No one knows her.

Dispirited, they sit on a bench on the village green and look around. It's 4.30 p.m. already. Just as well they're staying the night, or they'd be running out of time; shops close early around here. Jarvis texts Christine.

We've asked a bunch of people but no luck so far x

She replies a moment later.

Don't give up. Good luck x

Then Gwen sits up straight. 'Over there,' she exclaims, pointing.

'What am I looking at?' Jarvis can only see mossy rooftops and trees fulsome with leaves.

'I think I can see a green cross. It must be a chemist. Now that's a good bet, isn't it? We know she's old, so she may well be on some sort of medication.'

'You're smart, Gwendoline Poppy. Come on.'

They hurry across the green only to find that the chemist closed at 4 p.m.

'So frustrating!' exclaims Gwen. 'This wouldn't happen in London.'

'Listen to you, Big City girl. But look, there's someone inside.' Jarvis can see a figure moving around the murky depths of the little chemist, which is one of those old-fashioned ones selling make-up brands no one's ever heard of and toiletry gift sets. Maybe Greta comes here to buy her Yardley soap. He taps on the window.

The figure comes to the glass. A middle-aged guy with glasses. 'We're closed,' he mouths.

Jarvis and Gwen nod and gesture randomly and look pleading until the man unlocks the door.

'Thank you,' exclaims Gwen. 'We just need to ask you a question.'

Quickly they explain their business and the pharmacist looks thoughtful. 'Normally, I'd have a dilemma about whether to tell you anything. You both seem like nice, genuine young church people, but you can never be too careful these days and in any case I wouldn't give out a patient's address.'

Again, with the church people? thinks Jarvis.

'In this case though, it's a bit academic. You've missed her by a week.'

Gwen gasps. 'She died last week?' Without thinking, Jarvis puts his arm around her.

'No, she didn't die. She's gone into a home. She's had all her meds transferred over there. She used to live in Acorns, the big house just along the lane there, but she's been on her own for years now, and she didn't need all those rooms. She's gone to a place in Dorset; I can't remember the name. I'm sorry, I really can't, or I'd write to her and ask if she wanted to contact you.'

'That's kind of you. Well, thanks anyway.'

That's sad, thinks Jarvis. It was Greta who'd broken the ice between them really. That first day, when they were poles apart, sizing each other up with little enthusiasm, it was Gwen's analysis of Greta's comment in the book that had got them talking, that had made Jarvis realise there was more to Gwen than met the eye.

'At least she's not dead,' says Gwen. 'Though being in a home doesn't sound like much fun, does it?'

'Maybe it's a really nice one,' Jarvis speculates. 'With really cool old people and brilliant staff and a big garden for strolling in. Maybe she plays poker and has loads of visitors and she's having the time of her life.'

'I hope so.' Gwen smiles, and he gives her a comforting squeeze.

'Want to go and look at the house? See if anyone's around who can tell us more?'

'Yes, why not? Thanks, Jarvis.' He takes his arm away because to walk along the lane like that would be... well, a bit weird really.

Acorns is five minutes away. A very big house in very poor repair – you can see that at a glance. It's lonely looking, surrounded by dark firs, windows blank and sightless, a SOLD flash plastered across the For Sale board on the drive. They wander closer, drawn by a mutual compulsion to approach the door, even though they know the house is empty. Jarvis gives a half-hearted rap of the knocker, but there's no answer of course. They start to edge along the side of the building and find themselves peering through a window into a bare, dusty room. Empty shelves, dusty corners, bare walls… but there's a television and it's on. 'That's weird,' says Jarvis. And feels a vicious prod in his back.

'Hands up!' says a voice close behind them.

Jarvis flings up his hands and spins, hoping he doesn't have to protect Gwen, because he's not that buff really.

'I didn't say you could turn round,' barks the voice, and Jarvis finds himself looking – down – at a tiny old lady wielding a shovel, jabbing the handle end in his direction.

'Peace,' he finds himself saying, though he's always styled himself as more of a rocker than a hippy. 'We don't mean any harm. We've been looking for Greta Hargreaves and we've only just found out that she's gone. We're gutted. Just curiosity, no bad intentions.'

'Why were you looking for her?'

'Um, it's kind of a long story.'

'I've got time.' The woman, who looks like an angry gnome, or one of those goblins in *The Lord of the Rings*, taps Gwen, who's still facing the wall, on the shoulder with the shovel handle. 'You can turn around too, girlie.'

Gwen turns gingerly, as if trying not to anger a spitting cat. 'Hello,' she says, 'I'm Gwen. And this is Jarvis.'

Between them they recount their story for what now feels like the hundredth time, though they've never told it standing up with their hands in the air before. When they reach the end, the diminutive vigilante's face cracks into a smile. 'Well, isn't this your lucky day?' she says.

'How so?' asks Jarvis cautiously.

'Because I'm Greta.'

*

Sure enough, she takes a key from her back pocket and opens the door. It's actually colder inside than out in the summery afternoon.

They follow her in and she goes to turn off the TV. 'I leave it on so there's sound when I come back from my walks,' she explains, leading them down a hall with wallpaper peeling along its length. She opens an understairs cupboard. 'There are some camping chairs in there somewhere. Would you bring two into the kitchen, please, young man?'

Jarvis leans in and a smell of damp assails him. He finds the chairs and hauls them out, covered in cobwebs. In the kitchen, Greta is filling a kettle while Gwen hovers in the middle of the room. There's no table and only one chair. Jarvis brushes off the camping chairs and opens them out.

Greta takes three mugs from a cupboard. 'I've got Earl Grey and that's it,' she says. 'No milk. Any takers?'

'Yes please,' they murmur, like children facing a particularly stern teacher.

She sloshes boiling water rather haphazardly over teabags. Jarvis winces, foreseeing a trip to the local burns unit. 'Let me,' he says, grabbing the mugs. Greta lowers herself into the one good chair.

'I *love* St Domneva's,' she says. 'I got married there and christened my first son there, many, many moons ago.'

'You lived in Hopley?' asks Gwen.

'For the first thirty years of my life. The day I went back to see the church, the day I wrote in the book, was my first return there in many moons. I'd been feeling a little down in the dumps. Husband dead, children scattered to the four winds, a common enough story. Life had become very lonely, very stale. I felt I was just waiting to die, and I was only seventy-two back then. Visiting St Dom's shook me out of it. It reminded me in stained-glass technicolour of the wonderful life I'd had – and that I had a lot of life still to live.

'I sat for a long time, steeped in memories. I'd always been a bit different I suppose. I went to university when it wasn't automatic that a woman would. I got a first in English literature from Exeter. I wrote a couple of books that got published.'

Jarvis can sense Gwen's interest pique but neither of them wants to interrupt.

'I ran a community centre for refugees back when most people my age were deeply suspicious of refugees. All that on top of bringing up four children. Sitting in St Dom's that day made me think I hadn't done too badly. I realised that Fergus, my husband, would have hated to see me give up. I came home to Devon and threw myself into village life. I founded a book group, I began writing again, I started a community centre for the elderly. I had a lot of longstanding friends who got involved, either more or less reluctantly. Life was very full again for a good few years, thanks to the inspiration of St Dom's.

'But lately it's taken… a downwards turn again. Some health troubles. And all those friends are gone now, either dead or moved in with relatives or into care. I'm only eighty-two but I'm the last one. Over the last while it's dawned on me what a shocking state the house has got into. Fergus and I didn't do much to it over the years, and I just never *thought* of it after he'd gone. One day, I was here, alone, twiddling my thumbs, trying to muster the enthusiasm for one last new phase, when I looked around. Really looked. And I knew it was more work than I had money for, or could stand to have done. So I arranged to go into a home.'

'Couldn't you go and live with one of your children?' asks Gwen.

'All four have offered – two of them convincingly. But they all have such busy lives, so far away. They have a grandchild or two apiece, and busy careers still. I won't be that parent, the one who expects other people's lives to be arranged around me. I don't want to cramp their style, as the saying goes. It's a decent place, the home, and I know they'll visit me; they're good kids. Ha. Kids! They're all in their fifties. Anyway, I'm going the day after tomorrow. That's why the place looks like a ghost house. I'm all packed up.'

'The pharmacist in the village told us you'd gone,' says Jarvis. 'Last week.'

Greta snorts. 'He's got the dates mixed up. He's the most absent-minded pharmacist I've ever known. It's a wonder he hasn't given my heart meds to some young woman in the village and someone else's birth control pills to me.'

Jarvis laughs. 'That's why we were snooping around. We'd never have done it if we'd known you were still here. You caught us red-handed.'

Greta grins. 'Sorry about that. As if I could have defended myself if you *had* been bad 'uns. But I've had to accept such growing helplessness, such sad inevitabilities. Thievery felt like one indignity too many and my temper took over.'

'Kudos,' says Jarvis.

'But is it what you really *want*?' Gwen is frowning, doing her Gwen thing. 'The home? You seem so… independent. Such an individual. Will you really be *happy* there?'

'I'm not sure about that, dear. You're right, I do like to do things my own way, dance to the beat of my own drum, so to speak. And it does bother me that I might not be able to do that there. But you have to accept certain things as you grow older. I've had enough happiness in my time. And I don't have it in me for another bold new beginning.'

'I… I don't think it's rationed, happiness,' murmurs Gwen.

Greta sighs. 'Perhaps you're right, dear; perhaps you're right.'

They talk for a long time. About books and writing and London and Rye, about Greta's work with refugees and the elderly. Jarvis can tell that Gwen's not happy with the ending to Greta's story, but you can't march into a stranger's home and tell them what to do, can you? They talk about Hopley – what a sorry state it's fallen into and their hope that it might come back to life now, with the almost-saving of the church. Of course, Greta doesn't know Vicar Dave but Jarvis wracks his brains for the names of the elderly parishioners. 'Mrs Dantry?' he suggests.

'Good God. Evelyn Dantry? Is she still alive? She's a few years older than me. Is she well? Is she compos mentis?'

'Yes, apart from being convinced my name is Colin. She lives in sheltered accommodation near us. It's a compromise, my mum says. She has some care and someone to keep an eye on her, but she's still independent. Still goes to church and sees her friends and mixes up people's names.'

'I'm glad to hear it. Anyone else?'

Jarvis names Mrs Soames and Mrs Bowler but she doesn't know them. 'Perhaps they got married after I left so I don't recognise the names.'

'Oh and there's Mrs Parker, Effie, our next-door neighbour. She's about your age. She comes to breakfast sometimes.'

'The name Parker doesn't mean anything to me, but Effie. Now then. Does she by any chance have a sister called Felicity?'

'Yes!' Jarvis is glad that he's taken in at least some of Effie's ramblings over the years. 'An older sister, right? She lives in Australia now.'

'Well I never. Felicity Prior, as was, was one of my closest friends in school. Effie was her little sister. Used to tag around after us and steal our sweets. Fancy you knowing Effie. I don't suppose you have her phone number?'

Eventually twilight starts to gather around the old, cold house and Jarvis glances out of the window. 'We'd better get going. We're going for dinner in the village, Greta. Would you like to join us? We'd love to treat you.'

'Oh no, dear,' says Greta, but not before they've seen the spark of wistfulness in her face. 'I'd love to – you've no idea – but it's a long time since I was out past eight. I get so tired, and the doctor says I mustn't fight it, so it's early nights all the way for me. But thank you. It's very exciting to have an invitation.'

'Then what about tomorrow?' presses Gwen. 'We're leaving mid-afternoon, so what about lunch? Or brunch? Or breakfast?'

Greta considers. 'I hear brunch is all the rage now. I rather like that idea, if you're sure I wouldn't be an encumbrance.'

And so it's arranged.

'I hate leaving her there,' mutters Gwen as they walk away from Acorns. 'It's so cold and gloomy.'

'I know. But she's been managing like that for however long, and it's only for two more nights. I know you don't like the thought of the home, but at least she'll be warm and cared for there. And her kids will visit. *We* could visit, if you like.'

Gwen stops and looks at him with an unreadable expression. 'Thanks, Jarvis. You're a really, really wonderful person.'

Back at the B&B, they go to their respective rooms to freshen up, and Jarvis, elated by finding Greta, replies to a text from Christine asking that very question.

Yes, he texts back. *She's awesome. Tell you all about it when I'm back xx*

As he presses send, it occurs to him that he could phone for a quick chat and feels an unaccountable dip in his spirits. Why should a harmless text from lovely Christine spoil his mood? Jarvis sinks onto the bed with a deep frown, his shoulders rounding with preoccupation.

Because it makes him question some things, he realises. Like why is he looking forward *quite* so much to dinner in that candlelit bistro with Gwen? And why, now that they've found Greta, did it not even occur to him that they could head home earlier tomorrow, if they wanted? That hasn't even been a consideration.

He wouldn't dream of cutting short his time with Gwen. Is that the *usual* way to feel about a girl who's not your girlfriend? And how have his two favourite words in the whole world somehow turned out to be 'Thanks, Jarvis' – when Gwen says them? Jarvis gives a weighty sigh. He told Christine she has nothing to worry about, and he really, really doesn't want to be a liar.

CHAPTER THIRTY-SEVEN

One month later...

Gwen

The party to celebrate the saving of St Dom's is early on a Sunday evening. An odd time for a party, perhaps, but then a church do was never going to be rock 'n' roll, according to Jarvis. A lot of the guests will be elderly, so a 6 p.m. start should have them home in plenty of time for bed. And it means that Jarvis doesn't have to rearrange another working week.

Work has kept Gwen from helping to organise the party, but she came to Hopley yesterday so that she and Justine could get everything set up. And she's taken tomorrow off; she doesn't want to have to rush away the moment it's all over. Amma arrived this morning, in time for Sunday lunch with the Millwoods – 'I've heard great rhapsodies about your cooking, Justine' – and she'll head back tonight. They're joined for lunch by Effie-next-door and none other than Greta Hargreaves, who's staying with her.

It's wonderful being back in the house where friendship and delicious food brought Gwen back to life. And strange, being there without Jarvis. It's been a whole month since they've seen each other. Their frequency of communication has eased off, which was inevitable, she knows, but it still feels sad. The absence of the visitors' book, of their shared purpose, leaves a big hole in her life, no matter how she tries to fill it with work and fun evenings with Amma.

The last time Gwen saw Jarvis was their trip to Devon, which she cherishes as a special memory. For one thing it was refreshing to get out of London's frenzy and back to a gentler part of the world. For another, they found Greta. And of course, it was fun spending time with Jarvis. The little bistro in the village was wonderful. The food was delicious and the atmosphere was quite… romantic really, Gwen couldn't help thinking. So she'd been really careful to talk about Christine, to show an interest, be encouraging. She didn't want Jarvis to think that she was thinking anything… untoward. They stayed talking until the restaurant closed and asked them – politely – to leave.

When they returned to Acorns the next day, the door flew open to reveal a sparkling-eyed Greta, wearing a jaunty white scarf square with bright pink spots, her hair brushed smooth, and holding a capacious tapestry handbag. She looked as if she was off to teach an art class. 'I've something to tell you,' she promised as she climbed into the Fiat. 'Once we're all settled.'

With a bit of internet surfing, Jarvis had found a diner in a nearby village that was famous for brunch. They ordered pancakes with bacon and syrup and sat salivating while they waited. And Greta told them her news.

'I'm not going to the home; I'm moving to Hopley,' she announced. 'Turns out I have one more new beginning in me after all. Who knew? Maybe more. And I'm not done with happiness either.'

Apparently, when Jarvis and Gwen left, she'd phoned Effie. They'd laughed and cried catching up on the last five decades. Effie gave Greta the name and number of the assisted living complex where Mrs Dantry lived and warned that there was a waiting list. 'But you can stay with me,' she suggested. 'For as long as you like.'

'It was lots of things really,' Greta explained airily as their food arrived and she drizzled syrup over her pancakes. 'What you said about happiness, Gwen. Remembering St Dom's and dear old Hopley. And what you said about Hopley too – that it's gone a bit down in the mouth. It was never like that in my day. Sounds as if it could do with a bit of a boost, I thought to myself. And that's where I come in. I'm good at that.'

She'll be staying with Effie for another month and then her flat will be available. Apparently, since moving home, she's caught up with Mrs Dantry, introduced herself to Vicar Dave and badgered the library into letting her hold a book club there. The proceeds from the sale of her big old house have come through and, now that she doesn't have to pay for a home for the rest of her days, she's donated £4,500 to St Dom's. Gwen donated £500 out of her first pay cheque, which has left her completely skint, but the satisfaction of logging on to the JustGiving page as a donor was worth every penny. Jarvis has done the same, leaving them only £700 short of their target. And really, as they all agree, what's £700 when they've raised so much? They'll get it somehow.

After lunch, Gwen, Amma and Justine, and Effie and Greta, go to the community centre where the party's being held. It's an unlovely building, square, concrete and typical of its kind, but it was cheap to hire and they've been amazed by the number of people who've said they'll come. The centre will have room for them all.

They spend a couple of hours stringing coloured crepe-paper chains from the struts in the ceiling and blowing up clusters of balloons – no green ones – to add some colour to the grey interior. Meanwhile Bradley makes a couple of trips with the estate car full of clinking bottles, home-made brownies, mini quiches and countless multipacks of Mini Cheddars. Justine arranges the trestle tables, and soon they're groaning under copious displays of food, always a comforting sight.

Royston wanders in at one point with his laptop and his DJ deck and gets the music all set up in one corner. Then he wanders out again with a wave and a vague, 'Sayonara.'

Vicar Dave bobs back and forth with barely contained excitement. 'He's coming!' he announces gleefully. 'The archdeacon is coming. He didn't believe in my vision, but now he will.'

Gwen smiles. Vicar Dave's so happy to have his faith in St Dom's vindicated that he's just a whisker away from saying, 'Ya boo sucks.'

At 4 p.m., Gwen, Amma and Justine go home to change. Gwen notices a text from Jarvis.

Something's come up at work. I have to stay a bit. I've checked the trains, should be there by 6.15.

'Oh, what a shame,' exclaims Gwen, staring at the message. Jarvis shouldn't have to miss a single minute of this party when he's worked so hard and when it was all his idea after all, even if that *was* only so he could meet girls and see if any of them were Christine. She supposes Christine is coming tonight. Jarvis has been a bit vague about her lately. Maybe he's too loved up to communicate properly.

Gwen and Amma get dressed in Lalie's room, where Gwen is staying because George, apparently, is coming to the party. 'Lalie's really disappointed she can't make it,' Justine explained. 'But *George*! I think he feels invested in everything after we auctioned off his body. And he's donated £350 by the way…'

Amma has a stunning aquamarine dress – figure-hugging with a split up one side. The venue may be modest, but the dress code is Dress to Impress and she has. Gwen's brought two dresses, both new, one a smart black cocktail dress and the other a showier red one with a fluted hem and the skirt gathered in a rose on one side, with red net showing underneath. A proper party dress. She only brought it because Amma made her and now, while Amma's in the en suite, she slides into the black one and nods. Simple and elegant. Good.

Then Amma comes back into the room. 'Oh no you *don't*!' she shrieks and grabs the red dress. 'This is the dress for tonight, Gwen Stanley. Do you hear me?'

'I *hear* you, Ms Bossy Pants – you're shouting in my face. But it's a bit much, don't you think? It's only Hopley Community Centre.'

'Look at me!'

'Yes, but you're gorgeous. You can get away with it.'

'You're perfectly gorgeous yourself, especially now we can actually see your *face*.'

It's true that Gwen wears contacts sometimes now, and more often wears her lovely purply-blue eyeliner to accent her eyes. Her hair is still long and chestnutty, and she often clips it back or ties it up. Tonight it's in a high ponytail.

'The black dress is great,' continues Amma. 'It's great for after-work drinks. A business dinner. A *funeral*. Think of the *occasion*, my friend. The culmination of a project that has benefitted the whole town. A project that has revolutionised your personal life. A celebration of yourself and *lovely* Jarvis, and you want to dress like a *barrister*? Trust me, I know those people. You don't want to dress like them.'

'And yet you make such a brilliant one,' exclaims Gwen, wriggling out of the dress. 'OK, you win. I'll wear the red one.'

'That's better,' Amma exclaims, when Gwen has changed. 'My word, Jarvis's sultry eyes are going to pop out of his pretty head when he sees you.'

Gwen scowls. 'I thought this was about celebrating my achievements, not impressing a boy. Who has a *girlfriend*. Remember?'

Amma only rolls her shoulders enigmatically.

They're all back at the hall by 6 p.m. Vicar Dave, Annie and Wendy are already there. And people start pouring in. Gwen gasps – it's a little overwhelming.

A prompt arrival is George, and when the Croxleys see him, they greet him like their long-lost son. He comes over and shakes hands with Gwen in a formal, congratulatory manner, and she introduces him to Amma.

'He's related to Jarvis?' marvels Amma when he moves off. 'The miraculous diversity of genetics.'

'They're pretty different,' Gwen agrees.

Then there's a steady trickle of donors: Bryan and Miranda, Irene and Douglas from Whitstable (with lemon meringue pie), a plump woman who turns out to be Willa from Tonbridge, who's thrilled to meet Amma and talk about Ghana, and James. Gwen makes introductions and hugs them all. She no longer feels as though she's meeting characters from a book; she feels as if she's greeting old friends. There's no music, since there's no sign of Royston, but there's an excited buzz of conversation which fills the place and makes the atmosphere festive anyway. Speaking of absenteeism… it's 6.15 p.m. Gwen checks her phone.

Stuck on train. Delay outside Hopley. Been here 20 mins already. Hope to be there soon.

Aaaargh. Gwen swallows her despair. Jarvis *can't* miss the party, he can't. And what a lamentable lack of pronouns. No 'I', no 'we'. *Is* Christine with him? But why does it matter either way? She texts back:

Oh no. This is bad. I hope it moves soon. Btw pls can you check in Swan on way past? Royston not here.

Will do. Don't worry, GP, Royston can DJ drunk.

Very encouraging.

By the time she looks up, the hall has filled remarkably. She sees lots of familiar faces from Hopley – Jeannie again, bless her, the grumpy librarian, the owner of the café. There's a bunch of complete strangers who stand grouped together until she sees Vicar Dave go over and coax them in. They're the Baha'i group from Folkestone, she realises, and starts her way over to say hello when she hears her name being called. She turns to see a slender woman with long, glossy hair and lots of tiny silver bells on her wrists: Mahira.

'Mahira? Oh my God, what a surprise. It's so lovely to see you.' She can hardly believe that the woman who gave her some hope to cling to during her darkest days is standing here in front of her.

'Gwen. You look *wonderful*. Like a completely different girl from the one who came to my groups and looked as if her sadness would never end.'

'All this has helped. The fundraising, these wonderful people. I was so bereft when you closed up here. Your shop was the one bright spot in Hopley for me back then, you know. How's the new place in Yorkshire?'

Mahira wrinkles her delicate nose. 'Boring. When things got tough in Hopley, I thought going into partnership with my friend, in an established business, would be the answer. Secure. But it's not the same, Gwen. Not enough autonomy. I miss the thrill of making all the decisions. I realised I gave up too soon…'

'Oh Mahira. Are you thinking of coming back?'

'I've taken over the hardware shop that's just closed down. I'm giving it a facelift and reopening in time for Christmas. You'll have to come down from London and check it out. I'll give you a discount.'

'I will, I promise. Oh, Mahira, that's amazing news. Hopley needs you.'

'Where's Jarvis anyway? I thought he'd be up front and centre.'

Gwen sighs. 'Stuck on a train.'

By the time she's greeted the Baha'i group and then the Muslims, it's 6.45 p.m. Still no Jarvis and no further update. '*Boys*,' she fumes, throwing her phone back in her bag.

'I know, darling, they're bastards, all of them, and my husband's the worst,' says a smooth voice behind her. 'The dear little vicar pointed you out. My name's Patricia Lansdowne.'

Gwen stares, trying to place the name, then it comes to her. 'One of our very first donors!' she exclaims. 'Thank you so much for your help, Patricia, and thanks for coming.'

The woman in front of her is immaculate. Forty or so, quite beautiful, except for a hardness in the eyes and around the mouth. Shoulder-length honey-blond hair and a fabulous emerald-green dress. Gwen remembers Jarvis recounting the conversation he had with her all those months ago and feels her lips twitch. *Oh why isn't bloody Jarvis here to share this?*

She explains how successful their efforts have been, but Patricia doesn't seem too interested in the church. 'Nice to get away from Chorleywood for the day,' she confides, sipping steadily at her Prosecco. 'I told the husband it's an all-day affair and went shopping. Seven bags. Serves him right, the tight bastard. I nearly divorced him last year, you know. It just became unbearable. I used to be a *model*. He doesn't appreciate me at all. But then I lost my nerve I suppose. Better the devil you know and all that. Even though he is a complete and utter shit. This is very, er... sweet, I must say. Not my usual sort of function. He'd *hate* it if he knew I was here. Hasn't got a giving bone in his body...'

Gwen looks around desperately, wondering if she'll be stuck here all night. Suddenly Amma appears and pulls her away. 'So sorry, church emergency,' she says to Patricia and drags Gwen to a far corner.

'Thank you,' gasps Gwen. 'This is why you're my best friend. What on earth can we do with her? Who would she want to talk to?'

'You don't need to worry,' says Amma, pointing. 'Look.' Patricia has honed in on Jarvis's father, and from the slightly startled expression on his face, her monologue appears to be running uninterrupted.

Gwen laughs. 'Poor Bradley.'

'Poor Bradley,' echoes Amma. 'Who's that, Gwen? By the door?'

Gwen looks up to see a burly man looking ill at ease in a white shirt and stiff jeans in the doorway. He has black-and-white stubble, and elaborate tattoos cover every visible body part: hands, throat – there's even one on his face. A younger woman as thin as string stands behind him. 'I wonder…' Gwen murmurs. She goes over to them.

'Are you by any chance Jase Norris?' she asks. He looks relieved as he nods. 'I'm Gwen. Thank you so much for your donation and for coming. Come in. Would you like a drink?'

'No beer,' says Jase at once. *Of course, he said he was a 'bastud on the drink'*. Gwen notices a bronze AA sobriety chip on a cord around his neck. *Well done, Jase.*

'No problem. We've got orange juice, water, Coke… Come in. Hi, Lisa, thank you too.' She draws them in and introduces Vicar Dave, knowing he'll *love* their story. At first Jase is quiet, but David asks about his tattoos and that draws him out. He rolls up a sleeve to show them a panther but advises Gwen against getting any. 'Backs of the knees especially painful.'

Gwen feels deeply happy. The evening is wonderful. Everyone is here – almost. Now if only Jarvis would… *there* he is. Finally.

A red-faced, panting Jarvis appears in the doorway, and Gwen runs towards him, pulling Amma with her. 'Jarvis! You made it. Thank heavens. I thought you were going to miss it all.'

'Hi,' he puffs, shucking off his rucksack and jacket, reaching for a hug. He pulls back with a grimace. 'Sorry, I'm all sweaty. Ran from the station.'

'Who cares?' demands Gwen, standing back to look at him. He's wearing a vintage-style shirt like the one Lalie gave him, she notices, but this one is red with tiny black flowers. It's a little bit flamboyant. They match.

'Gwendoline Poppy, you look stunning. Wow. So do you, Amma. How are you?' He kisses Amma then sags theatrically against the door frame. 'I'm exhausted. The stress of just sitting on a train, not moving, when you have somewhere to be. I want to stash my things somewhere and cool off for two minutes before I join the fray. Royston's right behind me, by the way. You were right, he was in the pub. Lost track of time.'

'Fantastic. Come to the little room out the back. I'll grab you a drink. Where's Christine?'

His dark eyes flicker. 'She's not coming.'

Gwen feels Amma elbow her unsubtly in the ribs. *Why? Why isn't she here? A simple scheduling glitch or trouble in paradise?* 'That's a shame. Did she have something on tonight?'

'Um, well actually—'

'Oh my *God*. Is that Jarvis Millwood?' shrieks a voice that could cut wood. A raspy, throaty, smoky voice as resonant as a tuba and loud as a motorbike. Everyone stares as a statuesque woman in her mid-sixties, with a huge stack of bottle-blond hair and layers of black eyeliner, bears down on them. 'Well, all my days! I thought you sounded like *such* a nice young man, but I never guessed you'd be such a handsome one too. Just as well I'm old enough to be your grandma, lovely boy. Oh, look at your poor little frightened angel face, bless you now. Do you know who I am, lovely?'

'Um, Alice?' he says in a small voice.

'That's right. Come all the way from Wales, I have. And my Bronwen is here with me, and her little one, and I want to hear all about this church campaign and how it's going. Now come and fetch your Auntie Alice a stiff drink, lovely boy.'

She drags Jarvis off, arm in arm, leaving Amma and Gwen staring after. 'Wow,' says Amma. 'I want to be like her when I grow up.'

CHAPTER THIRTY-EIGHT

Jarvis

What was that expression that he saw on Gwen's face when he said that Christine wasn't coming? It was completely unfamiliar to him, and he can usually read Gwen like a book. He's been nervous all the way here about telling her the news – because of the questions that are sure to follow. She's been so pro-Christine the whole way through, so supportive, so happy for him. She *found* Christine for him, for goodness' sake. So he hopes she won't be *too* curious about his reasons for what he's done. Though she almost certainly will.

'Well, well. Fancy you've raised all the money you need then. Well done, lovely boy. Well done. Not many young men nowadays would take the bother. All drugged up, the ones round by my way, or on the booze they are. Either that or attached to the Game Boys 24/7.' Alice pauses to down her wine and hold out her glass for a refill. In practically the same breath she begins again.

'I rang my Bronwen, I did, and I says to her, "Bron, love, listen now," and she says to me, "What is it now, Mam? I'm in the middle of feeding Ellie," and I says to her, "You'll never believe the phone call I just had, like," and I told her all about you, and she's been meaning to come to the church to say hello, but she's been so busy with the little one, and all these months have flown, like, so I says to her, "Come to the party with me, love, and then you can see for yourself what this young man has done…"'

Jarvis is touched – and entirely unsure of whether he deserves such attention. Even while he listens and smiles, he can't help looking around. His things have vanished, so he supposes Gwen's put them away. They won't have been nicked; who would take them? Mrs Dantry? The imam? He sniggers quietly. He sees Royston stagger in, not entirely steady on his feet, but he's seen him worse. A few minutes later music starts up and a few of the oldies start jigging a bit. He can see Vicar Dave throwing his head back in laughter and wonders what joke he's missing. He wants to excuse himself, but Alice literally doesn't draw breath.

'And my boys, they says to me, "*Mam*, you can't go all the way to Kent *just* for a party. Stay a few days. The pub can run itself, like – have a little holiday," so I says to myself, "You know what? I've been working since I was seventeen. Seventeen. I think I do deserve a little holiday and all…"'

Who can he find to take his place as passive listener? He wants to talk to their other donors. He can see Bryan and James chatting away over there and Mahira in a gorgeous purple-and-silver sari. He wants to say hello. Then a young couple – pretty black girl, rugged-looking blond guy – edge towards them and hover nearby.

'Hi, are you OK there?' asks Jarvis at last. 'Sorry to interrupt, Alice, but I think these people might need something.'

'No, no. You do what you need to do, lovely boy.'

'We wanted to say hello,' says the young woman. 'The vicar pointed you out. I'm Hattie Walsh, and this is my husband Ben. I gave you the tiniest of donations, but you and Gwen sent such a lovely note of thanks, as if I'd given a thousand pounds.'

'I remember you!' exclaims Jarvis. 'Citizen of the World. You'd just got married.'

'Wow, you've got a good memory.'

'Thanks for coming tonight. We're so pleased to have you. Gwen would love to meet you too, but I'm not sure where she is. Can I introduce Alice, another of our wonderful donors? Our very first, in fact.'

He feels a bit bad leaving them together, but he's already missed an hour of the party. He greets his parents and George, Greta and Effie and Vicar Dave, and then he feels more as though he's arrived. He's starving so he gets stuck into the mini quiches as he works his way around the room, accepting congratulations and gradually relaxing. What a wonderful thing they've done. Where's Gwen?

He sees her at last, deep in conversation with James, and hurries over to join them. James gives him a hearty handshake and Gwen grins. 'You escaped. Guess what? James has got amazing news.'

'I'm moving to Hopley,' says James with a smile. His formal demeanour seems a little more relaxed than when they met him, and the heartache in his eyes is mixed with something else, something more hopeful.

'You serious, man?'

'Absolutely. It's too sad to be there in the old life I shared with Harry. And the costs are astronomical: after losing him, I'd like to go easier on myself. So I've put the flat on the market. Property in Hampstead doesn't hang around so I'm hoping to be here by Christmas. I'm thinking of opening a small antiques store if I can find the right place. I'm tired of the TV business, and I learned so much from Harry. I'm sure I can make a go of it.'

'Isn't that a *wonderful* idea,' Gwen says, beaming.

'It's great, but won't you miss the city? And what about your love life? Hopley's not exactly filled with sophisticated men. Case in point…' He gestures to where Royston is making himself cross-eyed juggling peanuts while his trousers slide ever downwards.

'I like it here; I like the people I've met. The city won't be far away; I'll be able to hop on a train whenever I need a fix. And my love life isn't really going to be a concern for a long time. Cross that bridge when I come to it.'

'Then it's fantastic news. Well done, man.'

'Jarvis, can you believe it? That's *three* people moving back to Hopley because of the visitors' book. Greta, James and Mahira too. Have you heard? It's like the whole town's coming back to life. There's Mahira's shop and Greta's book group, and can't you just *tell* that James will do wonderful things…?'

Gwen's eyes are shining. It's good to see her so happy – this whole thing has meant so much to her, from the very beginning. She's not wearing her glasses, he notices. He likes her glasses, but she looks pretty without too. She wouldn't mind him noticing that, would she? That's not sleazy. He swallows.

'We've resurrected it,' he jokes. 'Nice. It can do with a bit of life.'

'Well done, you two,' says James. 'You know, you really do make the loveliest pair. I know, I know. You're just good friends.'

Jarvis frowns. *Is he making mischief?* Then Amma comes over with a grey-haired lady in tow.

'Guys, another donor for you to meet. This is Ann Wilson.'

For a moment Jarvis can't place the name, but Gwen immediately clicks.

'Ann from Aylesford,' she exclaims. 'The retired teacher from Morehouse Primary. How lovely to meet you, Ann. Thanks for coming.'

'I'm impressed. So many people must have helped out I'm amazed you can remember.'

'They're a special pair,' says James, shaking her hand. 'They care about everyone. I'm James Varden, another donor. Good to meet you.'

They chat for a while and then, when it seems obvious that Ann and James have settled into a cosy conversation about antiques, Gwen looks at Jarvis. 'Shall we go outside for ten minutes?' she suggests. 'I'm feeling a little overwhelmed, and it would be nice to take a breath, catch up a bit.'

Jarvis swallows. But he reckons the more he puts it off, the more of a big deal he'll make it seem. Play it casual, that's the way to go. 'Sure,' he says with a shrug.

Outside, a velvety violet sky smiles down on the party, but that's the extent of the magic that Hopley has to offer. A gang of drunken youths staggers by, and one stops to throw up just along the road. A motorbike revs up and shoots past, doing a couple of laps around the block before vanishing, the sound receding gradually into the distance.

'Ah, sweet poetry,' says Jarvis. 'I hope James and the others don't live to regret coming here.'

'They won't,' says Gwen stoutly. 'They're pioneers. Eventually they'll tip the balance, and Hopley will be all lovely and charming again.'

'You dream big.'

'Maybe a bit. Thanks to you. So, Jarvis, where's Christine? Tell me before Alice turns up again, or Patricia comes to tell you how awful her husband is and eat you for breakfast.'

'*Patricia's* here? Oh God. OK, well, the thing is, Gwendoline Poppy, we're not together anymore.'

'Whaaaat? *Why*?'

'It just wasn't right. She's a lovely girl – well, you met her – and as beautiful as I'd remembered, but she was just a dream, a memory. In real life, we got on fine, but there was no real spark, you know?'

'Really? Well, as long as you're OK… who ended it?'

'Me, but it was mutual really. It didn't come as any big surprise to her, put it that way. She's fine, Gwendoline Poppy, honest.'

'I'm glad. I had no idea. I thought you seemed so perfect together. When did this happen?'

'A couple of weeks ago.' *Like, as soon as I got back from Devon.* 'And we really weren't perfect together. It wasn't… *real*. Or vibrant. Anyway, I hope you're not mad at me. Or disappointed?'

'Why would I be?'

'Because you cared so much and went to so much trouble to find her. I didn't mess up, honestly. I just wasn't feeling it, and I said so. That's right, isn't it?'

'Oh yes, absolutely right. No, I'm only… pensive, I suppose. I did care, but only because I wanted you to have your happy ending. If Christine isn't it, then of course you shouldn't stay with her.'

They fall quiet. Inside the volume cranks up as Beyoncé comes on with 'Crazy in Love'. Jarvis peers through the window. Mrs Dantry's going wild to the music. Vicar Dave is doing a dad dance with his arms in the air.

Jarvis turns back to Gwen. Although the spot is not Hopley's most picturesque, at least the summer evening air is soft and warm, and a gentle breeze plays with her ponytail. He badly wants to touch her hair, even kiss her, but they're just friends and you don't paw your friends. He sighs heavily. He really wants to tell her the rest of it, but is now the right time? Will there ever *be* one?

'Thanks for wanting me to be happy, Gwendoline Poppy. You're… well, you're wonderful.'

She looks at him, her pansy-coloured eyes startling in the summer light. 'Jarvis, I want to tell you something. I'm not sure this is the time, but I'm worried that if I don't just say it, I'll lose my nerve.'

He nods. 'OK.' *Oh God, she's met someone.*

'Um, I don't want you to worry about this because you and I will always be friends, OK?'

'OK.' *Super. Just what I wanted to hear.*

'And I don't want to be jumping into dead men's shoes or anything, but I also kind of like you. As in… you know. And I know you don't see me that way, and my goodness, if Christine wasn't right for you then obviously I'm not going to be—'

'Wait,' Jarvis cuts in because once Gwen starts rambling it can take a while, and he wants to be sure he's got this right. 'Let me just check. You mean you *like* me? As in, boyfriend-girlfriend like? As in, romantically?'

Gwen goes as red as her dress and drops her eyes. 'Mmhmmm,' she mumbles.

'Thank God.' Jarvis gives the air a victorious punch, and then another two or three for good measure. Gwen looks startled. Fair enough, not the most romantic of moves.

'Thank God?' she queries. 'Why?'

'Because I like you too of course. God, Gwen, Christine's *great*. She's pretty, kind, sweet… But you're all those things and more. Clever as hell. Quirky. Funny. And you have this enormous belief in me. The whole time I was with her, I kept remembering our summer together. I kept looking forward to when I'd see you next – my trip to London, our time in Devon, the party tonight. Those were the things that kept me going. I didn't think for a minute you felt the same, so I kept telling myself it was just nostalgia, because the visitors' book was special to us. But it wasn't that. When we left Devon, I knew I wouldn't see you for a while and that felt terrible. I tried comforting myself by thinking, "Well, I will see Christine – my girlfriend," but it didn't help. Not for a minute. And that's when I knew.'

She gazes at him, looking slightly stunned. '*Really?*'

'Yes.'

'Seriously?'

'*Yes!* It's not like I'd wind you up about something like that, is it?'

'No, I just… well, I never thought. Amma was going on about it after she met you, you know? She thought she saw something between us… But I couldn't let myself think… You said, remember that first day we went to the pub, that it was safe to say we'd never fancy each other?'

He rolls his eyes. 'I remember. What can I say? I fancy you now.'

'So do you want… Do you want us to… y'know? Go out together?'

He nods. 'I don't want our time together to be over, just because the project is. I want to keep hanging out with you, not because we have a job to do, but because you're my girl. What do you reckon?'

She gives the shyest smile. 'That would be nice.'

'Um, Gwendoline Poppy, can I…?'

'Yes,' she breathes, leaning forward, and Jarvis winds an arm around her waist to pull her close, then bends his head for the sweetest kiss of his life.

CHAPTER THIRTY-NINE

Vicar Dave

David looks around the hall. Gwen and Jarvis have done this, brought his vision to life in exact detail, before his very eyes. Parishioners, townspeople, newcomers, returners, out-of-towners, people of completely different faiths, all gathered together to celebrate the saving of St Dom's. He feels a great, embracing love for each and every one. People are dancing, talking, laughing; it's exactly like the dream he had back in the spring.

He glances over at Annie, who's chatting with Justine Millwood and that new lady, Greta. Her face is lit up with happiness. He searches the crowd for Wendy, who's shrinking away from a rather strident-looking woman in an emerald-green dress. He hastens over to rescue her and explains her colour aversion to the woman so she doesn't take offence. Wendy won't have to move schools. She can stay where she is, with all her friends, and keep making excellent progress.

Thank you, he thinks, casting his eyes upwards. He'll say a proper prayer at the end of the night, when it's all over, but for now he's just brimming with gratitude.

The archdeacon said it couldn't be done. The archdeacon told him to face the fact that no one cared, that St Dom's had had its day. But isn't resurrecting the dead a bit of a theme in their religion? William scoffed at his vision and now here it is, unfolding all around. It's not Christian to say 'I told you so'. At least, it's not very mature. But David can't help but feel smug. *Ha, you were wrong and I was right. You were very disdainful at the idea that God told me to have a party. But He did, and here it is and plenty of people care about St Dom's as it happens, thank you very much, Archdeacon.* That's what he'll say to him if he ever shows up.

'David?'

The serious tone of the deep voice beside him is all too familiar from countless dispiriting finance meetings.

'Archdeacon. You made it. Welcome, I'm pleased you came.' Oh alright, perhaps he'll be mature after all.

'Thank you, David. Well, well – this is quite a scene.'

'These are all our donors and supporters, Archdeacon. We just needed to spread our net a little wider. I'll introduce you to some of them but first, a drink? Something to eat?'

'Nothing to eat, thank you. And just a still water, if you have it.'

'Of course – come with me.'

But the archdeacon is tempted by the sausage rolls after all. And then Justine's home-made brownies. And then he accepts a small bottle of the local ale, which David hastily pours into a glass because the sight of William swigging from a bottle would be just too much.

'Very fine refreshments. So, David, are you really telling me that you've raised *all* the money you need for the roof? That in the last five months, you've acquired the extra £38,000, without robbing a bank.'

'We have. No mugging of old ladies needed either. Come into the back room for a moment and I'll show you.'

In the little room at the back of the hall, David has stowed Jarvis's church tower chart, the laptop and the visitors' book. There's also a copy of *Magic Moments*, open to the article about the church. He explains how all these things played a part. He shows William the gradual progress monitored in the spreadsheet and the coloured-in bricks on the church tower. 'We were just seven hundred pounds short as of this morning, but two final donations came in today, to bring us to total. Jarvis Millwood's brother and sister contributed £350 each. In fact, I need to tell him that.'

'Millwood? That's the fellow who's been helping you?'

'Yes. And Gwen Stanley too. In fact, they've done more than help – they've run this project. Two rather lost young people, at the outset, yet their efforts seem to have done as much for them as they have done for the church. It's been a pleasure to see.'

'I'll meet them tonight, I suppose?'

'Oh certainly. Yes. Well, Archdeacon, I think it's time I made my speech or some of our older guests will be heading home. Will you help me carry these things out to the hall?'

When he's all ready to thank the guests, with every atom of sincerity in his heart, he looks around for Gwen and Jarvis. No sign of them. He threads his way through the throng, asking here and there if anyone's seen them. James thinks he saw them go outside. That's understandable – the hall is really quite stuffy now after all the dancing. He steps outside, into a soft summer evening, and sees a young couple kissing passionately on the pavement. It takes him a moment to realise who it is. Good Lord. He hadn't realised.

'Ahem.' He clears his throat, somewhat stagily, and they spring apart, pink-faced. 'So sorry to disturb. I'm about to start my speech and I thought you'd want to be there. In fact, I *need* you to be there.' Everyone will want to see them of course, and Vicar Dave has bought them presents to say thank you. A bottle of champagne each, a huge box of Hotel Chocolat chocolates each and vouchers for afternoon tea at the Wolseley in London. Presumably they'll be taking that together.

They give each other a long, loving look then come towards him, hand in hand. 'So this happened,' says Jarvis.

'As I see! I'm very happy for you both. You make quite a team. And I have news for you. We've hit the target.'

'*Really?*' Gwen squeals, her eyes like saucers. 'But really? Every penny? We've really done it?'

'Every penny,' David confirms. 'The final donation came in this evening, Jarvis, while you were talking to the deep-voiced blond lady. Did Gwen tell you that your brother gave £350? Well, so did your sister. They agreed to split it between them.'

'They're not so bad, those two,' murmurs Jarvis, looking stunned. Then he lets out a loud whoop, startling David and Gwen, and picks up Gwen by the waist. He swings her round, and her red skirts fly up. 'We did it, woman – we did it!'

Gwen is laughing and crying. 'I can't believe it. Vicar Dave, does that mean St Dom's is safe? That you can stay?'

He nods and smiles. 'Thank you both for caring. Thank you for all you've done.'

'You didn't colour in the last bit on the chart, did you?' asks Jarvis.

'No. Why?'

'That's Gwen's job.'

'Oh, Vicar Dave can do the last bit if he likes.'

David wouldn't dream of it. As he leads them inside, he remembers the pair of them when all this started – unlikely, uninspiring, *gormless*, he'd thought, may God forgive him. Hard to equate with the radiant young couple they are tonight. He shakes his head, marvelling. Gwen Stanley and Jarvis Millwood. Who'd have thought it?

A LETTER FROM TRACY

I wanted to say a huge thank you for choosing to read *Hidden Secrets at the Little Village Church*. If you enjoyed it and want to keep up to date with my latest releases, just sign up at the following link. Your email address will never be shared and you can unsubscribe at any time.

www.bookouture.com/tracy-rees

Hopley is a fictional town, but typical of many, and made me think about all the things that give charm and soul to a place. I wanted St Domneva's to be its beating heart, even when on its last legs! I wrote this book, a story about connection, during 2020, a year when connection became so very difficult. It lifted my spirits to write, and I hope it lifted yours when you read it.

It wasn't written as a reaction to external circumstances though; I'd had the idea for several years. I don't really know where it came from but one day the idea of a visitors' book dropped into my brain. Like Gwen, I loved the idea of all the snatches of different lives that a book like that would contain. I also love stories about quests of any sort so that aspect of it – finding the people who could help save St Dom's – was very enticing. My dad, a keen artist, gave me the idea of a young man painting outside a church, which contributed to Jarvis's story, so when I finally got the chance to write it, I only needed the characters!

Gwen and Jarvis quickly came to life for me, and although they were an unlikely-seeming pair of heroes, I immediately became massively fond of them. I loved seeing how they both gradually realised their potential as their quest unfolded.

I do hope that you'll join me for my next book set in Hopley, which will be out in October of this year. Meanwhile, if you enjoyed reading *Hidden Secrets at the Little Village Church*, I would be very grateful if you could write a review. I'd love to hear what you think, and it makes such a difference to new readers discovering my books for the first time.

If you have any questions or comments please do get in touch with me via Twitter, as I love chatting to my readers.

All best wishes,
Tracy

@AuthorTracyRees

ACKNOWLEDGEMENTS

First and foremost, I want to say an enormous thank you to my partner, Philip, for being so wonderful during the past oh-so-difficult year. Without your love and connection, 2020 would have been a very different experience for me. Also, thank you for our fabulous research day in Dungeness and Rye – including your patience in the bookshop – which were fantastic inspiration for two chapters in *Hidden Secrets at the Little Village Church*.

Thank you, Mum and Dad, as always, for your love and support through good times and hard ones. You are the very best of parents. Treasures!

Thank you to *all* my dear friends – you know who you are – and especially Beverley and Paul Rodgers for walks and laughs and planning all kinds of adventures for 'one day when…'; these things lit a beacon in a murky time and have really kept me going.

Thank you, Mum and Bev, for being my first readers of this book and being so enthusiastic about it. Your excitement and positivity made me so happy and kept me moving forward, especially as I was trying something new with this one. And thanks, Dad, for the image of a young man painting outside a church.

Huge appreciation to Rev. Canon Chris Darvill for taking the time to advise me about church finances and repairs and for being so enthusiastic and encouraging. I hope you like Vicar Dave!

Enormous thank yous to my editor and friend Kathryn Taussig, who has believed in me from the very beginning and offered me unwavering support throughout my career. It's such a treat to be working with you again. You are a truly brilliant editor and nothing gets past you, not even 585 exclamation marks!!!

Thank you to Peta Nightingale for answering so many questions, Kim Nash for her enthusiastic welcome, Sarah Hardy for her publicity brilliance and everyone else at Bookouture. I'm looking forward to getting to know you all and I'm so happy to be part of the Bookouture family. Also, a special thank you to Debbie Clement for designing the beautiful cover. I love it.

Thank you to Pan Macmillan for being my other wonderful publishing home and for your support, especially to the divine Caroline Hogg.

Thank you to the book community at large – reviewers, publishers, illustrators, designers... and most of all thank you to my author friends. Your fellowship is like a safety net and a magical sky-ship rolled into one. Special mention to Gill Paul for organising authorly chats and cocktails on Zoom throughout the past year and keeping us connected. It was a gift.

And finally, a massive heartfelt thank you to my readers, old and new. You are what it's all for.

Made in the USA
Middletown, DE
16 December 2023

45773576R00156